DIRTY LAUNDRY

With a flourish and a smug smile, Lacker turned his cards over. "Read them and cringe, friend. Four aces." He extended his hands to rake in the pot.

"Not so fast," Owen said. "There is one hand that beats four of a kind."

"There are two hands." The drummer knew his poker. "A straight flush and a royal flush. But since I have all the aces, you can't possibly have a royal flush. That leaves a straight flush, and the odds against that—"

"Are pretty high, I know." Owen smiled. "But there is a third hand that beats four of a kind."

"There's no such thing."

"Sure there is. I have it right here." Owen drew his Colt and placed it on the table. "The next time you need your laundry done, you should do it yourself."

"What are you talking about?"

"I ran into Mrs. Harker. The lady you're boardin' with. She told me she did all the laundry you gave her, then went to your room to ask if there was more."

"So?" Lacker angrily snapped. "What does that have to do with you stealing this pot from me?"

"Your door was open. She saw you practicin' with that rig you have up your right sleeve."

Lacker heaved up out of his chair. In his left hand gleamed a nickel-plated derringer, which he trained on Owen. . . .

Ralph Compton

By the Horns

A Ralph Compton Novel
by David Robbins

A SIGNET BOOK

SIGNET
Published by New American Library, a division of
Penguin Group (USA) Inc., 375 Hudson Street,
New York, New York 10014, USA
Penguin Group (Canada), 90 Eglinton Avenue East, Suite 700, Toronto,
Ontario M4P 2Y3, Canada (a division of Pearson Penguin Canada Inc.)
Penguin Books Ltd., 80 Strand, London WC2R 0RL, England
Penguin Ireland, 25 St. Stephen's Green, Dublin 2,
Ireland (a division of Penguin Books Ltd.)
Penguin Group (Australia), 250 Camberwell Road, Camberwell, Victoria 3124,
Australia (a division of Pearson Australia Group Pty. Ltd.)
Penguin Books India Pvt. Ltd., 11 Community Centre, Panchsheel Park,
New Delhi - 110 017, India
Penguin Group (NZ), cnr Airborne and Rosedale Roads, Albany,
Auckland 1310, New Zealand (a division of Pearson New Zealand Ltd.)
Penguin Books (South Africa) (Pty.) Ltd., 24 Sturdee Avenue,
Rosebank, Johannesburg 2196, South Africa

Penguin Books Ltd., Registered Offices:
80 Strand, London WC2R 0RL, England

First published by Signet, an imprint of New American Library,
a division of Penguin Group (USA) Inc.

First Printing, April 2006
10 9 8 7 6 5 4 3 2 1

THE IMMORTAL COWBOY

This is respectfully dedicated to the "American Cowboy." His was the saga sparked by the turmoil that followed the Civil War, and the passing of more than a century has by no means diminished the flame.

True, the old days and the old ways are but treasured memories, and the old trails have grown dim with the ravages of time, but the spirit of the cowboy lives on.

In my travels—to Texas, Oklahoma, Kansas, Nebraska, Colorado, Wyoming, New Mexico, and Arizona—I always find something that reminds me of the Old West. While I am walking these plains and mountains for the first time, there is this feeling that a part of me is eternal, that I have known these old trails before. I believe it is the undying spirit of the frontier calling, allowing me, through the mind's eye, to step back into time. What is the appeal of the Old West of the American frontier?

It has been epitomized by some as the dark and bloody period in American history. Its heroes—Crockett, Bowie, Hickok, Earp—have been reviled and criticized. Yet the Old West lives on, larger than life.

It has become a symbol of freedom, when there was always another mountain to climb and another river to cross; when a dispute between two men was settled not with expensive lawyers, but with fists, knives, or guns. Barbaric? Maybe. But some things never change. When the cowboy rode into the pages of American history, he left behind a legacy that lives within the hearts of us all.

—*Ralph Compton*

1

Land of the Six-Shooter

The stage was two hours late. It came to a stop in a cloud of dust and woke up the old man dozing in a rocking chair. The bearded driver and the tall shotgun messenger jumped down. The driver stepped to the stagecoach door and opened it. "Whiskey Flats," he announced.

Like the head of a small bird poking from a birdhouse, the head of a passenger poked out. Coughing and swiping at the dust, he regarded the driver with annoyance. "I say, was it really necessary to drive the team so hard? I had to hold on for dear life."

The driver raised his seamed face and regarded the passenger as he might a new kind of bug. Spitting a wad of tobacco into the street, he asked, "Any bones broken, mister?"

"None that I am aware of, no. But I will be frightfully sore for a week or more." The passenger scrunched his thin face in distaste. "This whole experience has been a test of my fortitude."

"You don't say."

"I certainly do. The irony is that I paid to be bounced around in a box for days on end. Had I known what I was letting myself in for, I would have rethought the entire idea."

"I could tell you have a delicate backside"—the driver smirked—"from all the squawkin' you did when we hit a few bumps."

At that the shotgun messenger snickered.

"A few?" The passenger bristled. "If I did not know better, I would swear you hit every rut in the road on purpose."

"Now why would I do that, pilgrim?" the driver said, and winked at the shotgun messenger. Both laughed and went into the stage office.

The passenger blinked. "I have half a mind to file a formal complaint." He pushed the door wide and stiffly climbed down. Placing one hand at the small of his back, he stretched, then grimaced. "I daresay I am black and blue." He walked to the rear of the stagecoach and stared at the boot, then at the office doorway. "What about my trunk?" he called out.

"Are you helpless, sonny?"

Only then did the passenger notice the old man in the rocking chair. "I beg your pardon?"

"If your fingers ain't broke, you can get your own bag. Folks hereabouts don't cotton much to waitin' on others hand and foot." The old man grinned, showing a gap where most of his upper front teeth had been. He wore a broad-brimmed hat well past its prime and faded clothes as dusty as the street. "Besides, Bud never has much liked swivel dudes."

"How is that, my good fellow?" the passenger asked. "I am afraid I don't quite follow you. It's the vernacular."

"The who?"

"Vernacular. Surely you have heard the word before? It is part of the King's English, I assure you."

"Is it now?" The old man tittered. "In case you

haven't heard, sonny, we don't have kings in this country. We talk how we want."

The passenger flicked dust from a tailored sleeve. He was dressed in the height of sartorial splendor, in a navy coat, striped pants, and a double-breasted tartan vest. Perched on his neatly cropped head was a derby tilted at a rakish angle. "Exactly my point," he said. " 'Vernacular' refers to how people speak."

"You sure do it funny," the old man said.

"Me?" The passenger became a trifle indignant. "I will have you know, sir, I am a graduate of Eton. I speak English impeccably. It is you and most every other American I have met who mangle the language atrociously."

"Keep talkin' like that, sonny, and you might find it's not the only thing we mangle." The old man looked the newcomer up and down. "Land sakes, but you sure are the prettiest fella I ever set eyes on." He sniffed a few times. "And damn me if you don't smell like the girl over to the Nose Paint Saloon."

The passenger drew himself up to his full height and squared his bony shoulders. "I will thank you to address me with respect. I am here on official business at the behest of the Bristol-London Consortium."

"Never heard of it."

"The BLC," the dapper man said. "An association of British businessmen who have purchased extensive landholdings in Wyoming."

"Wyoming, huh? Now that I've heard of. Fine puncher country." The old man nodded his approval.

"Permit me to introduce myself." The passenger stepped onto the boardwalk and offered his hand. "Alfred Pitney, solicitor, among other things."

"Pleased to meet you, Mr. Solicitor," the old man

said, shaking. "My handle is Floyd Carter but everyone calls me Toothless." He stopped shaking and bent to examine the Britisher's hand. "Land sakes, but you have awful pink fingers. And not a callus anywhere." He arched a salt-and-pepper eyebrow. "What is it you do for a livin', anyhow? Fold towels?"

"I have already told you. I am a solicitor." When there was no hint of comprehension on the oldster's face, Pitney said, "An attorney."

"Ah. A law wrangler. That explains a lot. But I won't hold it against you like some will."

"What is wrong with being a solicitor?" Pitney asked in confusion. "It is a perfectly respectable profession."

"Maybe where you hail from," Toothless said. "But in our neck of the woods your kind are only a notch or two above rustlers." He gave an exaggerated yawn. "Now if you will excuse me, young fella, at my age I need all the shut-eye I can get. I have a nap to finish."

"One moment, if you please, Mr., ah, Toothless," Alfred Pitney said. "Perhaps you can be of assistance. I am looking for a ranch."

"Then you came to the right place. Texas has plenty. Are you lookin' to buy one? You might want to learn a little about cows first."

"No. You don't understand. I need to find the Bar 40 ranch, owned by a Mr. James Bartholomew. Have you perchance heard of it?"

Toothless snorted. "Hellfire, sonny, who hasn't? It's about the saltiest outfit this side of the Rio Grande. Bart is as straight as a wagon tongue, and all his hands are loyal to the brand."

"There you go again with the vernacular," Pitney complained. "Be that as it may, there was supposed to be someone here from the Bar 40 to meet me but obviously they are late. Do you suppose I could hire a horse? Or hire someone to ride out there for me if a steed is not available?"

"Another thing we're not shy of is horses. The only thing we have more of is lizards and you can't ride them."

Pitney tilted his head to one side. "Who would want to ride a lizard?" He snickered, then asked, "Would I have time for a repast or a drink, do you think, before my messenger and someone from the Bar 40 arrive?"

"You could drink a lake dry," Toothless said. "It'll take three days for a rider to get there and three days back."

"My word. I was under the impression the ranch was close to town."

"By Texas standards it is."

For the first time since he had stepped from the stage, Alfred Pitney gazed up and down the street. Whiskey Flats consisted of not quite a score of buildings, most of them plank affairs with false fronts. At several hitch rails weary horses dozed in the midday heat. A pig rooted in the dirt, watched by a scruffy dog lazing in the shade of an overhang. "My word. This isn't a town. It's a flyspeck."

"That pretty much sums Whiskey Flats up. Yes, sir," Toothless agreed. "But give us ten or twenty years and we'll be bustin' at the seams."

Pitney shook his head in mild dismay. "This won't do. This won't do at all. However am I to discharge my responsibilities?"

Before the old man could answer, harsh yells intruded from across the street. The next moment the door to the Nose Paint Saloon was flung violently open. As if hurled from within, out flew a man in seedy homespun who tottered on his heels for five or six feet and then fell.

"Sam Webber!" Toothless blurted.

"Who?"

"A harmless cuss who does odd jobs around town and spends all his earnin's on coffin varnish. Who would pick on a puny nobody like him?"

Out of the saloon strode a stocky man whose hawkish features bore the stamp of innate cruelty. He wore a black, flat-crowned hat, a gray shirt and pants, and boots with large spurs. They jangled noisily as he walked up to Sam Webber, his thumbs hooked in a black leather belt adorned with silver studs. In a holster on the man's right hip was nestled a Remington revolver with black grips.

"Uh-oh," Toothless breathed. "Poor Sam is in for it now. That there is Luke Deal, and he's bad medicine."

"You say the name as if he is someone important."

"Deal is the curliest lobo on the border. He's always on the peck. All you have to do is sneeze in his direction and he will pistol-whip you for the fun of it. Oh my, oh my. Sam, what did you do?"

Luke Deal walked up to Webber, who had sat up, and without warning, without so much as a word or a gesture, viciously kicked him in the chest. Webber cried out and writhed in agony. "What was that?" Deal asked, putting a hand to his ear. "I didn't quite hear you."

Pitney glanced at Toothless. "Shouldn't we intervene on your friend's behalf?"

"And be shot full of holes? Mister, there are some things you don't do, and one is stick your head in a bear trap."

"That statement is patently absurd." Smoothing his coat, Alfred Pitney marched into the street, declaring, "I say, my good fellow, that will be quite enough."

Astonishment rendered Luke Deal as still as a tree.

"Where I hail from, civilized men do not behave like animals. I daresay you should apologize for your atrocious behavior." Pitney reached down and slid his hands under Sam Webber, boosting him to his feet. "There, there. Do you need a physician? That was beastly, wasn't it?"

Webber was as stupefied as his attacker.

"What did you just say to me?" Luke Deal found his voice. Inner fires flared in his slate gray eyes.

"You are hard of hearing, I take it?" Alfred Pitney said, brushing dust from Sam Webber's back. "It is a good thing I was on hand to keep you from doing something you would always regret."

Luke Deal intently studied the Englishman as if he could not quite believe the apparition was real. Then a smile curled his slit of a mouth. But not a warm, friendly smile. It was the smile of a cat about to devour a canary, or an Apache about to slit a prospector's throat. A smile that would chill the blood of anyone who knew him. "What do you reckon we have here, boys?"

Unnoticed, two others had filed out of the saloon. One was short, almost as wide as he was tall, a slab of muscle with a thick neck and bulging shoulders. He wore a brown hat with a high crown and boots with heels twice as high as most other boots. His spurs looked more like spikes. The other man was middle-aged, with a face that would give women and small children nightmares; his chin was splotched with gristly stubble, his cheeks were badly pockmarked, his brows were thick and beetling, his lips were perpetually upturned in a sneer. Both men wore revolvers, and from the top of the second man's left boot jutted the hilt of a knife.

"We have us a walkin', talkin' mail-order catalog," declared the short one.

Luke Deal nodded. "I haven't seen one this fancy, Grutt, since the time we were in Dallas."

The pockmarked man licked his thick lips. "Just when we was hankerin' for some fun, too. We need to do him slow to draw it out."

"We sure don't want to end it too soon, Bronk," Luke Deal agreed, and abruptly spoke sharply to Sam Webber. "Light a shuck, you miserable wretch, before we change our minds and include you, too."

"Yes, sir, Mr. Deal, sir," Sam Webber bleated, and with an apologetic glance at Alfred Pitney, he scampered off.

Deal sauntered up to the Englishman. "Now then. Where to begin?"

"I am not looking for trouble," Pitney informed them. "I am here on business for the BLC, and I must admonish you gentlemen that they will not take kindly to having their representative interfered with."

Luke Deal snorted. "Did you hear this greener, boys?"

"He throws out fancy words like they were money," Grutt said. "A walkin' dictionary is what he is."

"What I want to know," Bronk said, his hand resting on the butt of his revolver, "is why he's wearin' his bandanna so strange?" Bronk's own bandanna was red and in dire need of a washing.

Pitney touched a hand to his throat. "This is called a cravat, gentlemen. In civilized society they are quite common."

"There you go again," Luke Deal said. "Callin' us gentlemen. If you were a horse you would be weedy." He sniffed several times. "What in hell? Maybe we were wrong, boys. This ain't no greenhorn. It's a wood pussy."

Bronk and Grutt laughed. Laughter as cold and as hard as they were.

"Dang me if he doesn't make me want to put windows in his skull," Bronk declared.

"No," Luke Deal said severely. "No spoilin' it, you hear? I won't take it kindly if you do, and you wouldn't want that."

"I sure wouldn't," Bronk said, with the barest trace of unease. "I would never do anything you didn't want me to, Luke."

Pitney looked from one to the other. "What is it you want of me, specifically? To make me dance, as I hear you cowboys sometimes do when indulging in hijinks?"

"Now there's a notion," Deal said. "But we should come up with somethin' special for a fancy hombre like you." He paused, then suddenly poked Pitney in the chest. "Call us cowboys again and you'll make me mad. You wouldn't catch us nursemaidin' a bunch of smelly cows for no measly forty dollars a month."

A new voice spoke, a voice as quiet as the whisper of the breeze, yet a voice of tempered steel. "Then it's mutual. The cows wouldn't want you there, neither. They have their standards."

Luke Deal spun, his hand hovering over his six-shooter. His companions likewise turned and visibly tensed, as if they had beheld a dangerous animal.

The creature that confronted them was a tall, broad-shouldered man in typical Western garb. His hat, his shirt, his chaps, his boots were as ordinary as mesquite, but there was nothing ordinary about his face. He was uncommonly appealing, with eyes bluer than the sky and a jaw like an anvil. It was those eyes that marked him as above the ordinary. They mirrored a quality of character of a high order. That, and something else. His hair was as black as ink.

"Owen!" Luke Deal exclaimed, and his whole body seemed to quiver like that of a hound straining at a leash.

"This isn't none of your business," said Bronk, with more than a little rancor.

"But it is," Owen responded in that quiet way of his. "I'm here to fetch that gent for the Bar 40. That makes his welfare my concern."

Grutt was coiled like a spring. "What if we don't want to hand him over?"

"Then we have it to do," Owen said, and lowered his right hand so it brushed the holster in which his Colt was sheathed.

"Took the words right out of my mouth, cowpoke," Grutt declared. "I've been waitin' for an excuse to throw down on you since who flung the chunk." He bared his teeth as if they were fangs.

"No," Luke Deal said.

Grutt did not take his hateful gaze off Owen. "What do you mean, no? This is our chance, Luke. You hate him as much as we do! Him and his airs. Just because he's Bartholomew's foreman doesn't give him the right to stick his nose where it shouldn't be stuck."

"No," Luke Deal said again, more harshly.

"But why? He's been a thorn in our side once too often. Remember that time he stopped us from beatin' on that drummer? And when he wouldn't let us burn that drunk Injun?"

"It's still no."

Grutt appealed to Bronk. "You're with me, right? Just the other day you were sayin' as how it's do-good jackasses like him who spoil it for those of us who ride the high lines. You want him dead as much as me."

"I wouldn't lose any sleep over buckin' him out in gore," Bronk said, "but we do what Luke wants. That's how it is. That's how it has always been."

Clenching his fists, Grutt hissed in anger. "You'll regret it. Both of you. See if you don't."

Luke Deal smiled at Owen. "You have more luck than an Irishman. One of these days, though, your string will play out, and then what will you do?"

"Cross that bridge when I get to it, I reckon," the handsome cowboy answered.

Deal nudged Bronk and Grutt and the three went back into the saloon, Grutt bringing up the rear and glowering at Owen as if daring him to do or say anything that would justify his quenching his thirst to spill Owen's blood.

Only after the door closed behind them did Owen walk to the middle of the street. Up close his blue eyes were even more piercing. "Are you all right, sir?"

Although his chest stung where Deal had poked him, Alfred Pitney replied, "Never better. Those bounders liked to hear themselves talk. I daresay they are perfectly harmless."

"As harmless as rabid wolves," Owen said in his quiet way. "Between them they have planted upwards of ten men. Not countin' Indians and such."

"By 'planted' you mean killed?" Pitney asked, and when the cowboy nodded, he said, "My word. How can that be? Why haven't they been arrested? Why aren't they behind bars?"

"They cover their tracks real well," Owen said. He

had shifted so he could keep one eye on the saloon. "Without proof there is not much the law can do."

"Yet you know for an indisputable fact they have murdered others in cold blood?"

"We can talk about them later," Owen said. "Right now we should talk to Harry Anderson about puttin' you up for the night. That is, I take it you aim to get a good night's sleep and head for the ranch at daybreak?"

"I have been told it will take three days to get there."

Owen smiled. "God willin' and the creek don't rise. I have a buckboard and a team over to the livery. It will only be the two of us, but don't fret. This time of year the Comanches stay pretty much to the north, and there have been no reports of bandidos lately."

Alfred Pitney was more interested in something else. "How did you know it was me?"

"Sir?"

"How did you know I was the one you were to meet? I never sent your employer a description."

"Your letter said you would arrive today, and you were the only one who got off the stage," Owen said. "That, and bein' from England, you can't help but talk peculiar."

"Me?" Pitney said, and chuckled. "My dear man, were you to visit Bristol, they would think the same of you."

"I suppose they would." Owen looked about them. "Where is your baggage?"

Pitney explained about his trunk still in the rear boot of the Concord. "Most is clothes. I also have several tins of fine British tea I can't do without. I can't buy the brand your side of the pond."

Owen made for the stage. "I'm not much of a tea swiller, myself. Give me coffee thick enough to float a horseshoe and I'm happy."

"Do you have a last name?" Pitney inquired.

"Not one I use much." Owen nodded at the old man in the rocking chair. "How's the gout today, Toothless?"

"It comes and it goes." Toothless smacked his lips. "Say, you wouldn't happen to care to treat a friend to a bottle, would you? I'm not fussy. The cheap stuff kills the pain as good as anything else."

"I might maybe consider half a bottle," Owen said. "Provided you get a note from the doc sayin' I can."

Toothless's bottom jaw drooped. "That was plumb cruel. It's my body. I can poison it howsoever I like."

Alfred Pitney surveyed the street from end to end. All he saw was the pig, the dog, and several chickens pecking at the ground in front of the general store. "Where are all the people?"

"It's siesta. This close to the border, folks tend to do like the Mexicans do and take it easy durin' the hottest part of the day." Owen squinted from under his hat brim at the blazing orb in the sky. "The saloon is nice and cool. We can pay it a visit after we get you situated."

"But the saloon is where those killers went," Pitney noted. "Is it wise for us to go there?"

"They're not likely to gun us in broad daylight."

"If you say so." But Pitney was not nearly so sure.

Owen produced a large new trunk from out of the boot. "Is this yours?" Pitney eagerly reached for it, but the cowhand, with remarkable ease, hefted the heavy trunk to his broad shoulder. "Follow me, sir."

Studying the individual buildings, Pitney commented,

"How is it I don't see a marshal's office anywhere? They had one in Cheyenne."

"Whiskey Flats doesn't have a tin star."

"Then how do you keep uncouth louts like Luke Deal and his fellow cads in line?"

"The same way we do the rest of the badmen. There's only one thing polecats like them understand." Owen patted the butt of his Colt.

"There are moments," Alfred Pitney said, "when I dearly miss Bristol."

2
A Knuckle Affair

Harry Anderson turned out to be the owner of the general store. A mousy man with big ears, he had a ready smile and a warm nature. He pumped Alfred Pitney's hand as if they were long-lost relatives. "Sure I'll put you up, and since you are here to visit the Bar 40, I won't charge you. Jim Bartholomew is a good friend of mine."

"You have extra beds in the back?" Pitney asked. The store was crammed with goods until it was near bursting at the corners. Everything from kerosene to clothes to tools to foodstuffs like flour, Saratoga chips, and more.

"Beds?" Anderson said, then laid a hand on the counter. "Here is where you will sleep, and be as snug and comfortable as a mouse in its hidey-hole."

Pitney eyed the countertop dubiously. It was long enough to accommodate him but rather narrow. It had one other flaw. "I'm not accustomed to sleeping on such a hard surface."

Anderson pointed at a pile of blankets on a shelf. "You can make it as soft as a feather bed if you want."

"Whiskey Flats doesn't have a hotel," Owen remarked. "Mrs. Harker puts up boarders but she only has one room and a drummer has it at the moment."

"Pushiest drummer I ever did see," Anderson said. "He doesn't know the meaning of the word 'no.' I told him over and over I do not need ladies' corsets but he kept pushing and pushing. Finally I bought one to shut him up." Anderson shrugged. "Maybe I can sell it to my wife's sister. She's coming to visit in a month, and she could easily pass for a buffalo."

"I thank you for your kindness," Pitney said.

"This is the best place to bed down short of the hayloft in the livery," Owen assured him while sliding the trunk to one end of the counter where no one would trip over it. "Now that you are fixed for the night, let's visit the saloon."

"I still don't think that is wise. Those bounders will be there."

"Who?" Harry Anderson asked.

"Luke and his pards," Owen said.

Anderson's features clouded. "I'll be glad when those curly wolves move on. They were in here yesterday and that Grutt thought he could help himself to a pickle without paying." Anderson nodded at the pickle barrel. "Tried to sneak one when I was busy with a customer. The nerve."

"Badmen are baddest when your back is turned," Owen commented, and unconsciously hitched at his gun belt.

"I close at seven," the store owner told Pitney. "Give me half an hour to shoo out those who always drag their heels, and you will be set for bedtime."

"I thank you for your kindness," Alfred Pitney said, "and for watching over my trunk until I return."

Anderson smiled. "Your belongings are perfectly

safe. The only ones liable to steal it would be Deal's bunch, and they'll be busy liquoring themselves up the rest of the afternoon. As they do pretty near every day."

A tiny bell over the front door tinkled and in came a striking young woman whose hair shone like burnished gold and whose dress, although as prim and proper as a dress could be, nevertheless did little to conceal a figure as shapely as an hourglass. She glanced down the aisle and seemed to give a slight start, then adjusted her bonnet and came toward them, displaying teeth as white as snow. "Good afternoon, Mr. Anderson. Would that be Owen I see with you? It has been so long since I saw him last, I about forgot what he looks like."

The broad-shouldered cowboy colored and suddenly showed an interest in a display of silverware.

"Miss Langstrom!" Anderson declared. "It has been a while since you graced my establishment with your lovely presence."

"Pshaw," the beauty said. "I have half a mind to tell Mrs. Anderson you have been flirting with me."

Now it was Anderson who reddened and quickly said, "Cynthia, you know I would never do any such thing. Edith knows it, too."

Cynthia Langstrom had a marvelous laugh. "Are we still on for supper Friday evening? Edith wanted me to bring one of my pies."

"Apple, I hope," Anderson said. "If you ever give up teaching, you could open a pie store and make a fortune."

"A pie store? Who ever heard of such a thing?" Cynthia flashed her dazzling smile at Owen but he was bent over the silverware.

Anderson turned to the Britisher. "Where are my manners? Mr. Pitney, I would like you meet Miss Langstrom, our schoolmarm. Miss Langstrom, Mr. Pitney here hails from England, and has come to conduct business at the Bar 40."

"You don't say?" Cynthia Langstrom said, offering Alfred her hand.

Pitney accepted her fingertips and dipped his chin. "My utmost pleasure, madam. Did I understand him correctly? You teach school?"

"You sound surprised, sir."

"It is just that I would not think Whiskey Flats big enough to have enough children," Pitney observed.

"There are six from town," the schoolmarm said, "and another eleven from the outlying ranches and homesteads. Believe me when I say they are more than a handful."

Owen gave a slight cough. "Ridin' herd on seventeen head of younguns takes a lot of sand."

Cynthia Langstrom put a hand to her throat. "Why, Owen, I had forgotten you were there. Did you say something?"

"I was just complimentin' you," the cowboy said sheepishly.

"You need to speak up more," Cynthia said. "I get enough mumbling from my students, usually when they do not know an answer and are trying to hide their ignorance."

Owen shifted his weight from one foot to the other. "I can't blame them. You can be a frightenin' critter when your dander is up."

As sweet as sugar, the schoolmarm said, "Oh, I am a critter now, am I? Comparable to cows and such?" She fluttered her green eyes. "What a wonderful compliment."

"I didn't call you a cow, dang it."

"I should hope not," Cynthia said. "Not when just last week you compared me to a star in the night sky. Or don't you remember that occasion?"

"I recollect it just fine, thank you very much. Of course, as stars go, it was a mite puny."

The schoolmarm's eyes became emerald sabers. "Is that so? I seem to recall you called it the brightest in the heavens. But then, we do tend to remember our *previous* associations in the most flattering light, don't we? Now if you will excuse me, I bid you good day." With a swirl of her dress she swept down the aisle and the tiny bell over the door tinkled once more.

Harry Anderson chuckled. "Ever notice how women always have to get in the last word? She hit you dead center."

Owen grinned. "Her aim has always been good. But she'll be plumb flustered when she realizes she forgot to buy whatever she came in for."

"If that was her intent," Anderson said.

"How's that?" the cowboy said. "Oh. You reckon she saw me come in and followed just to stick me with knives because she thinks I have been neglectin' her?"

Alfred Pitney cleared his throat. "Forgive my curiosity, gentlemen, but am I missing something?"

"It's a private matter," Owen said.

"Semi-private," the storekeeper amended. "Everyone in town has been counting on attending a wedding but a certain cowpoke who shall go nameless has turned out to be gun-shy."

"Does Ethel know you have such a leaky mouth?"

"Don't go off mad," Harry Anderson said.

But the cowboy was already halfway to the door, his long legs allowing strides that forced Pitney to hurry to catch up. A cloud of dust from a passing wagon billowed about them as Owen pulled his hat brim low and muttered, "Busybodies everywhere you go these days."

"I don't think he meant any insult," Pitney said.

Just then they both heard, clear and sharp, a female voice raised in anger. "Unhand me this instant!"

Two buildings down was a feed store. Between it and the saloon ran an alley. In the alley mouth stood Grutt, one hand on Cynthia Langstrom's wrist. Evidently he had come out of the alley as the schoolmarm was happening by.

"Didn't you hear me?" she demanded. "I will not stand for being accosted like a common tart. And next time be so good as to do your business out back, not here where anyone might see you."

"Now hold on, missy," Grutt said. "All I want to do is treat you to a drink. Where's the harm?"

"You do not want to do this," Cynthia informed him.

If Grutt heard the jingling of spurs, he did not look around. The first inkling he had that he had made a mistake he would regret came when a heavy hand fell on his shoulder and he was roughly spun into the street. "What the hell—?" he blurted.

Owen punched him, a hard right jab to the mouth that rocked Grutt on his high boot heels. "Don't ever lay a hand on her again."

"Owen, no!" Cynthia Langstrom cried.

Grutt touched a hand to his lips and stared in disbelief at the blood on his fingers. "You hit me, you son of a bitch!"

So mad he could not speak, Owen stood with both big fists clenched and his jaw muscles twitching.

"I should pistol-whip you, cowboy!" Grutt growled.

Suiting action to his wish, he clawed for the six-shooter at his hip, a new-model Smith and Wesson that was the only article on his person he kept clean.

Owen punched him again, a solid left to the gut that would have doubled most men over, but Grutt was solid muscle. All it did was back him up a step and elicit a grunt. Owen followed with a right cross to the jaw but Grutt brought both arms up to ward the blow off, then planted himself and smirked.

"No gunplay? That's fine by me. I've busted more than a few heads with my fists and my feet."

Cynthia placed a hand on Owen's arm. "Let it be. No real harm was done. I don't want you to fight on my account."

Owen took her hand and gently removed it. "I would be a sorry excuse for a man if I let this pass. Some insults can't be abided." He glared at Grutt. "And those without manners need to learn some."

"Reckon you can teach me?" Grutt taunted.

"Let's find out."

The cowboy tore into the other like a tornado into a wheat field. Grutt tried to block the swings but he was driven back several feet by a hail of powerful blows. Then Grutt set himself and would not be moved.

Pitney became aware of upraised voices, of shouts of "Fight! Fight!" and people running from all directions. Harry Anderson materialized at his elbow. Toothless vacated his rocking chair and excitedly crossed the street.

Out of the saloon rushed its patrons, Luke Deal and Bronk foremost among them. Bronk swore and made as if to go to Grutt's aid, but Luke Deal grabbed him and shook his head.

Owen and Grutt were circling, flicking punches, countering, Owen ablaze with wrath, Grutt sneering in contempt. There was nothing refined or chivalrous about their fistic exchange; it was violence for violence's sake, brutal, fierce, and savage.

Onlookers began to yell and whoop, urging the cowboy on. No one cheered for Grutt except Bronk.

The cowboy slipped an uppercut and retaliated with a jab to Grutt's cheek that split it like overripe fruit.

Alfred Pitney cried, "Bloody good show!" and blinked in surprise at his own vulgarity.

Blood smeared Grutt's lower lip and chin. Scarlet drops were trickling down his cheek. His hat had been knocked off and his right eyebrow was swelling. But judging by the set of his features, the blood and the pain meant little to him. He was focused on Owen like a bull on a rival, a portrait of hatred.

The cowboy moved with a fluid ease that spoke of whipcord sinews and razor reflexes. He was always in motion, throwing a punch, avoiding a punch, dodging, ducking. Grutt drove a straight left at Owen's throat, which Owen narrowly avoided. A second later Grutt arched a foot at Owen's groin, sparking insults from the watchers.

Then Owen feinted right and went left, and his fist, aimed at Grutt's chin, smashed into Grutt's ear instead when Grutt tried to duck. At the *crunch*, Grutt staggered, quickly recovered, and stepped back, shaking his head.

"Learned your manners yet?" Owen asked.

"Go to hell."

The fight might have continued had Luke Deal not unexpectedly stepped between them. "Enough," he told Grutt. "Come and have a drink."

"I don't want redeye. I want his skull split and his brains oozing out," Grutt snarled.

"It's not the time nor the place," Luke Deal responded with a meaningful gesture.

The ring of onlookers had escaped Grutt's notice. Straightening, he slowly lowered his arms. "What are all of you gawking at?" he demanded. "Don't you have better things to do?"

"Not me," Toothless said. "Watchin' the dog lick itself ain't near as much fun as seein' you have your ears boxed."

"It's over," Luke Deal said.

Something in his tone caused Grutt to blink. He uncoiled and said sullenly to Owen, "You hear me, cowpoke? We'll settle this another time."

"Just say the word."

"And count us in," said a newcomer, "so we can watch my pard's back."

Three riders sat their mounts in the middle of the street. Their dusty clothes and boots marked them as cowhands. The spokesman had sandy hair, tufts of which poked from under his hat like fingers. On his right was a broomstick whose homespun shirt and Levi's were a couple of sizes too large. On his left sat a puncher whose nose resembled a baling hook and whose ears were wide enough for a prairie dog to hide behind.

Owen beamed and went to greet them. He did not have a drop of blood on him from the fight, nor was he breathing heavily. "Lon! What in blazes are you shiftless varmints doin' in town? If the big sugar hears you snuck away from the herd, he'll have you skinned alive."

"Who you do reckon sent us?" the cowboy called

Lon responded. "Mr. Bartholomew figured you'd need someone to hold your hand."

"It's a good thing we came along when we did," grinned the toothpick, "or you'd have folks thinkin' Bar 40 hands are a pack of good-for-nothin' rowdies."

"That's right," the last cowboy declared. "When Mr. B hears about you brawling in the street, you'll be the one he skins and brands."

Owen introduced Alfred Pitney.

The broomstick, whose nickname, appropriately enough, proved to be Slim, nodded. "Right pleased to make your acquaintance, mister. It isn't every day we get to meet a foreigner."

"I wouldn't exactly call England a foreign country," Pitney protested. "America was a colony of ours once."

"You have to forgive Slim," said the cowhand with the hook nose and big ears, whom Owen introduced as Cleveland. "He's a fourth-generation Texican. To him, anyone who isn't from Texas might as well be from the moon."

"Says the brush thumper from Ohio," Slim retorted, and grinned at Pitney. "Which is why we named him after the town where he was born. As a reminder he's not a real cowhand."

Cleveland took the gibe good-naturedly. "What galls Slim is that a galoot from back East can ride and rope as good as he can."

"You must need spectacles."

The onlookers were dispersing except for Toothless, who was regarding the new arrivals as a miner might the mother lode. "Say, if you boys are stickin' around a spell, how about buyin' an old man a drink?"

"What's the occasion?" Lon asked.

"At my age," Toothless replied, "breathin' counts as occasion enough. But if you need a better one, how about you made Deal and his shadows turn tail."

"Luke is no coward," Owen said. "There were too many witnesses, is all. Luke will bide his time and get even when the mood strikes him." He rubbed his palms together. "Now then. Who is for some conversation fluid and a game or three of stud poker?"

"Just so the fluid is first," Slim said. "I swear, I'm dry enough to be mistook for a desert."

"You're always dry," Owen said. "A bottomless well in britches is what you are."

The three hands gigged their mounts to a hitch rail and dismounted. Lon arched his back and pressed a hand to it. Slim noticed his reflection in the saloon window and adjusted his hat and bandanna. Cleveland produced a pipe and tobacco pouch from his saddlebags and filled the pipe bowl, carefully tamping the tobacco down so as not to lose any.

Pitney politely stood to one side. When Owen led them in, after whispering a few words to Cynthia, he brought up the rear. The transition from the bright glare of the afternoon sun to the dim interior was striking. It took a few seconds for his eyes to adjust.

The cowboys wound among the tables to a far corner. They claimed an empty one that had only four chairs. Owen helped himself to an extra from an adjoining table and placed it to his left. "Here you go, Al."

"Barkeep!" Lon hollered. "A bottle of coffin varnish and five glasses and a deck of cards!"

"I really don't want a drink," Alfred Pitney said, but soon found a full glass in front of him anyway. By then he had noticed the three men at a table across the room. "I say, Mr. Owen, aren't those the three weasels you had words with?"

"Just call me Owen," the broad-shouldered cowboy said. "And yes, that's them. They have as much right to be here as we do."

"The looks they are giving you do not bode well," Pitney remarked. "You told me earlier they are murderers many times over. What is to stop them from doing the same to you?"

"Grutt and Bronk would like to," Owen said. "But like most coyotes, they won't jump me unless they have an edge. I don't aim to give it to them."

"Enough about those lunkheads," Lon said, refilling his glass. He had already quaffed his first in a single gulp. "Let's have us some fun."

Slim picked up the deck and shuffled the cards. He had talent. He would riffle them and flip them between and around and over and under his fingers with the most remarkable dexterity.

"Show-off," Cleveland said.

Pitney took too large a sip and promptly regretted it. Liquid fire burned a path from his mouth to the pit of his stomach. He had the illusion he was being fried alive from the inside out. Choking back a cough, he commented, "Potent liquor, this so-called whiskey of yours."

"You think this is somethin', you should try tequila," Lon suggested. "A couple of glasses and you're seein' twins everywhere you look."

"I can drink a whole bottle of that Mex snake poison and not bat an eye," Slim boasted while offering the deck to Cleveland to cut.

"Only because you can't hold it in," Lon said. "You're the only hombre I know who has to wet the mesquite between swallows."

Owen and Cleveland chuckled.

"I can't help it I was born with a bladder the size of a chicken's," Slim said in defense of his manhood.

"Chicken, hell," Lon scoffed. "A flea can hold more water than you."

Alfred Pitney laughed when the cowboys did, and in the relaxed silence that ensued, he said, "Pardon me, gentlemen, but I don't believe any of you have mentioned your last names. What would they be?"

The genial atmosphere evaporated under four less than friendly stares. "Why in hell did you go and ask a thing like that?" Lon demanded.

"Easy now," Owen said. "He's not from our neck of the woods. Where he comes from, folks wear their last names on their sleeves."

"I don't understand," Pitney admitted. "It's merely proper manners to fully introduce oneself."

"Not in Texas," Lon said. "Here a man's name is as personal as his war bag. Those who aren't on the cuidado usually have some other reason for not shoutin' it from the rooftops."

"I have nothing to hide," Cleveland said. "My last name is Hearns."

"I've plumb forgot mine," Slim joked.

Lon refilled his glass again. "I wish I could. But all it takes is to use a smoke wagon reckless and you're dodgin' tin stars until the cows come home."

Owen said, "There aren't any lookin' for you after all this time. Besides, you never shot anyone in the back."

"There are two things I don't ever take lightly," Lon intoned. "One is the Almighty. The other is Texas Rangers. Those boys shoot first and cuff you after, and I never have been partial to bracelets."

"The Rangers," Slim said, in the same reverent tone he might say "earthquake" or "flood."

Lon was about to add more but suddenly he grinned and declared, "Enough about me. Look at who just came through the door. Storm clouds are brewin' for our foreman, I reckon."

"Oh hell," Owen said.

3

Of Doves and Drummers

Into the Nose Paint Saloon had sashayed a raven-haired woman in a red dress. The dress was so tight, it was a wonder she could move her legs. Cut low at the top, it displayed ample cleavage. Her hair was done up in curls that jiggled as she walked. Her lips, like her fingernails, were as red as cherries. A face that once had been beautiful was now marred by the early signs of dissipation—lines around the eyes and mouth, bags under the eyes, and that slight sagging of the cheeks that was a sure sign of someone on the cusp of the long slide into old age.

Several of the men whistled and grinned. The woman smiled but the smile did not touch her eyes. She had a great weariness about her and she moved with a certain wooden quality, as if she were going through the motions of life instead of living.

There was a yell of "Welcome to work, Carmody!" that brought another of those listless smiles.

Then the woman's gaze fell on the corner table and she broke stride. Placing her hands on her hips, she came over, saying, "Well, look at this. They let the inmates out of the sanitarium early today."

"How do, Carmody," Lon greeted her. "You are lookin' as fine as ever."

"That's not sayin' a lot," was the dove's retort. She came to a halt between Owen's chair and Pitney's. Nodding at each of the cowboys, she studied the addition to their group. "Who is the new lunatic?"

The Britisher rose and bent in a slight bow. "Alfred Lloyd Pitney, at your humble service, madam. It is a genuine pleasure to meet a lady such as yourself."

"Lady?" Carmody scoffed, and laughed. "Brother, I don't know about where you come from, but hereabouts I am anything but."

Pitney noted that once again her eyes did not light with her humor. He had the impression she had seen it all and done it all and found it wanting. "I beg to differ. Even a barmaid may be a lady at heart."

"What a nice thing to say." Genuine warmth briefly lit her features. "What an awful nice thing to say."

Pitney sat back down.

Carmody placed a hand on his shoulder and declared, "Gents, take a good gander at my new favorite customer."

"I am honored," Pitney said.

She looked at Owen and her icy reserve returned. "How is my former favorite customer doin' today?"

"Don't start," the cowboy said.

"Why, whatever do you mean?" Carmody asked sarcastically. "Can't a gal say howdy to the man who used to be her beau?"

Owen was staring intently at the table. "I was never any such thing and you blessed well know it."

"That is the first lie I have ever heard you tell." Carmody motioned at Lon. "Tell him how it was."

"Leave me out of this," the sandy-haired cowboy said. Then, to Slim, a trifle gruffly, "Quit playin' with the damn cards and deal them."

"I should have known," Carmody said. "All you cow lovers stick together. Fine, Owen. Treat me as if I was never more than a rut in the road. But I know better and you know better." Her voice took on a tone of reproach. "Don't worry. I won't make a scene. It doesn't hardly matter anymore now that I've taken up with someone else."

Owen glanced up. "You didn't."

"Why in hell not? Ever since that schoolmarm showed up, you can't be bothered to give me the time of day. Well, a girl can't wait forever. Now I'm with someone who appreciates what a gal like me has to offer. Someone who doesn't think he's above the common herd."

"I think no such thing."

"That's the second lie," Carmody said. "You used to be one of us. Then an angel came to earth and now you walk on the clouds."

"Careful," Owen said.

"Or what? You'll slap me? A great respecter of womanhood like yourself?" Carmody's laugh was vicious. "I don't have blinders on anymore. I see you for what you are."

"We shouldn't talk about it here," Owen said, with a gesture at the Nose Paint's other patrons.

"I disagree. If you can't talk freely in front of your best friends and the woman you were fixin' to marry but jilted, who can you talk freely in front of?"

Owen started to come up out of his chair but sat back down. "I never mentioned marriage. That was your notion."

"You didn't exactly balk at the idea."

"I didn't exactly leap at the chance either."

Carmody's lips pinched together. "But you never

flat out said no, did you? It's wrong to give a girl like me hope. Doves tend to clutch at straws."

"The only thing wrong with you is the low opinion you have of yourself," Owen said.

"Now why would that be? Could it be because in the scheme of things, doves fall somewhere between whores and patent medicine salesmen?"

"Don't talk like that."

"Like how? Oh. That's right. I'm supposed to be as pure as the driven snow. Like your schoolmarm."

The look Owen fixed on her was a mix of hurt and an apology. "You are not helpin' your case any."

"Don't flatter yourself. I gave up on you. My new beau doesn't require nearly as much stoking." Carmody paused. "Wouldn't you like to know who it is?"

"I already know."

"And it sticks in your craw, doesn't it?" Carmody taunted. "It eats at your innards to where you want to throw down on him."

"Not over you," Owen said.

Carmody recoiled as if he had slapped her, then made straight for the table in the opposite corner. She moved around it and stopped beside Luke Deal and bent and kissed him on the cheek.

Lon swore. "She didn't."

"She did," Owen said sadly. "I heard about it this mornin'. He's been stayin' at her shack nights."

"Oh hell," Lon said. "Why doesn't she do it quick and just shoot you?"

"In her eyes I spurned her," Owen said, "and on all of God's green earth there is no more fearsome critter than a woman who has been spurned."

"That's why I have nothin' to do with them," Slim said as he dealt. "Females are more of a headache than they are worth."

"I wouldn't go that far," Cleveland said. "They come in pretty handy on cold winter nights."

The cowboys laughed but their hearts were not in it.

Pitney accepted his five cards and, doing as the others did, he looked at them without letting anyone else see what they were. "What is this game we are playing called?"

"Poker," Lon said. "Don't tell me you have never heard of it."

"I am afraid not, no," Pitney said. He raised his head from his cards to find all eyes were now on him. "What?"

"You're serious?" Lon asked. "Don't they have cards wherever it is you come from?"

"Bristol, England," Pitney said. "Do you honestly expect, Mr., um, Lon, that our two countries share the same conventions?"

"The same what?"

"That we eat the same foods and drink the same drinks and play the same games? I would wager a substantial percentage of my annual salary that you have never heard of cricket, yet it is as common in my country as this poker appears to be in yours."

"I see your point," Lon said. "Want me to tell you how it's played?"

"If you would be so kind."

Interrupted by comments from the others now and then, Lon proceeded to explain the ranking of the cards from a royal flush on down to one pair, and how a player could ask for three cards after the initial deal, except for the dealer, who was allowed to take four, and how each round of betting was done, and what it meant to call and raise.

"It sounds like marvelous fun," Pitney said dubiously.

"The only better ways to relax are with whiskey and a woman," Cleveland mentioned. "And women only half the time because they're not in the mood."

Lon refilled his glass. "So are you ready to commence?"

"If I am to be permitted," Pitney said. "I am afraid my whiskey has gone right through me. Where might the lavatory be?"

"The what?"

"The loo. You know, where I can heed nature's call, as it were?"

"Oh. The outhouse is out back. You can't miss it. It smells like a mountain of manure, only worse."

Pitney excused himself and made for a door past the bar but the bartender informed him that no one was allowed through there and he must go out the front and all the way round.

The experience was one Pitney would have preferred to forget. He held his breath but the reek was still terrible. As he finished and quickly shut the outhouse door behind him, he was taken aback to find Luke Deal leaning against the rear of the saloon, smoking a cigarette. Pitney nodded and started to walk by him.

"Hold on there, hoss."

"If you are looking for trouble—" Pitney began.

"I'm just waitin' my turn," Deal said, tilting his cigarette at the outhouse. "No hard feelin's about earlier, are there, pilgrim?"

"You haze all new arrivals, do you?"

"Only fancy-pants fellas like you." Luke grinned, and patted his revolver. "Nothin' like a lead chucker to make a tenderfoot dance."

"If you won't take offense at my saying so, you seem to possess a mean streak, Mr. Deal."

"No seems about it," was the reply. "I have snake blood, and I'd as soon as buck a man out in gore as look at him."

The fact that Deal was still grinning encouraged Pitney to ask, "How can you brag about being so despicable? In England murder is frowned upon."

"You're in Texas now. Killin' is as common as grass. I couldn't count the number of people I've seen killed or heard about bein' killed."

"How horrible," Pitney said. "I have never seen anyone murdered, and I truly don't care to."

"Then you'd best make yourself scarce," Luke Deal advised. "Those Bar 40 boys you're with are high on my list."

"What do you have against them?" Pitney made bold to inquire. "What harm have they ever done you?"

Deal's face clouded. "It's personal. There's a reckonin' to be had between Owen and me, and when it comes, blood will be shed. Make no mistake."

"He strikes me as a decent fellow," Pitney said.

"He'd do to ride the river with."

"Is that a compliment?"

"The highest."

"Then I am confused, Mr. Deal. How is it you can praise him so highly yet want him dead? It makes no sense."

"A lot of things in life make no sense. We're born just to die. We go from cradle to grave not knowin' why we're here or what it's all about. Life is a puzzlement with a nasty surprise at the end."

Alfred Pitney shook his head in wonder. "That was quite profound, Mr. Deal. There is more to you than you let on."

"Just because I'm not a fancy-pants like you doesn't

mean I'm stupid," Luke Deal said. "I think about things, the same as everybody."

"Yet your disposition is hardly admirable. You act as if you enjoy hurting others."

"I do."

"That can't be," Pitney asserted. "No one likes to see others suffer. It is inhumane. Surely a thinking man like you realizes that."

"You take a lot for granted," Luke said. He raised the cigarette to his mouth and blew a smoke ring in the air. "It shows you are city bred."

"I am afraid I don't quite follow you," Pitney admitted.

"City folks tend to think highly of themselves. They also think everyone should think the same way they do. But that's not how things are. I don't think like you and you don't think like me and neither of us thinks like a Comanche and a Comanche doesn't think like an Apache, and on and on it goes." Deal dropped the cigarette and ground it into the dirt with the heel of a boot. "You have a lot to learn about life, mister."

"I admit I have a lot to learn about you."

Luke Deal glanced up sharply. Amazingly fast, he drew his revolver and pressed the muzzle to Pitney's forehead. "Want me to show you how a pistol can splatter a man's brains all over creation?"

Alfred Pitney froze.

"The only reason I don't put a window in your skull is that Bartholomew would likely figure out it was me and have every hand at the Bar 40 out to treat me to a hemp social."

"You can't kill me in cold blood." Pitney found his voice.

Incredibly, Luke Deal laughed, then twirled the Remington into its holster. "You must have solid pine between your ears. You still don't savvy, pilgrim."

Pitney had to know. "Would you really have shot me? I mean, if you believed you could get away with it?"

"Just like that." Luke Deal grinned and snapped his fingers. "Now scoot back to your nursemaid before I change my mind."

Terribly confused, Alfred Pitney reclaimed his seat at the poker table. The cowboys had played a few hands while he was gone and Owen had just won a pot.

"Ready to lose all your money?" Lon asked.

"I'd rather not lose any, thank you very much."

Cleveland was the dealer. He gave each of them a card in turn until they had their five, then reminded them, "Jacks or better to open."

Pitney eventually won the hand with three queens. He went on to win five of the next six hands. The more he played, the more he enjoyed the nuances to the game—the need to keep what the cowboys called a poker face, the art of the bluff, the art of reading a bluff in an opponent's expression. "There is much more to this poker of yours than I would ever have imagined," he mentioned at one point.

The cowboys joked and laughed a lot. Pitney found himself liking their company more and more. He envied their easygoing natures. Emptying his first glass of whiskey, he asked for another.

"Be careful, hoss," Owen cautioned. "Tarantula juice will sneak up on you if you let it."

"I am perfectly sober, I assure you."

It was Owen's turn to deal. As he was sliding their

cards across, he said so only they could hear, "Don't look now, but we're bein' sized up for a fleecin'."

A portly man approached, smiling broadly. He wore store-bought clothes that did not quite fit him. The shirt was too small, the pants too short. A double chin bulged over his collar. "Mind if I join you?"

"This is a friendly game," Lon said.

"Then I will fit right in," the man said, and doffed his bowler. "William Lacker is my name, and I am as sociable a person as you will ever meet."

"You must be the drummer stayin' over to Mrs. Harker's place," Owen said.

"That I am," Lacker confirmed. "And may I say the old woman is as fine a human being as ever drew breath. Her rooms are immaculate, and she practically stuffs her boarders full of food."

"Much more of that stuffin' and you'll need bigger clothes," Slim commented.

"How long are you fixin' to stay in Whiskey Flats?" This from Owen.

"I should have left today but I decided to treat myself to a few pleasant diversions." Lacker slid a billfold from an inner pocket. "What do you say? May I pull up a chair and join you?"

"We would be plumb tickled to have you," Owen said, and was treated to the puzzled expressions of his friends. He moved his chair to make room for the chair the drummer pulled over, and when Lacker sank down, he shook the man's pudgy hand as warmly as if Lacker were long-lost kin.

"Yes, sir," the drummer said, "I've never been to a friendlier town anywhere." He opened his billfold. "I have mainly bank notes, state and national. Will they do?"

"So long as the state is Texas," Slim said.

"I played some cards here yesterday and won a little money. I hope to do even better today."

"I wouldn't be surprised," Owen said.

Alfred Pitney sensed there was more to what was going on than seemed apparent, but he could not begin to fathom what it was. He saw that the other cowboys were not happy about having Lacker join their game, Lon least of all. The sandy-haired puncher hardly uttered ten words over the next half hour.

Lacker had an astonishing run of luck. He beat Cleveland's two pair with a straight. He beat Slim's flush with a full house. After that, the drummer won about every fifth or sixth pot. About as it should be, given the number of players, but Alfred Pitney noticed that the pots the drummer won were always the bigger pots, always the ones with the most money piled in the center of the table.

"I seem to be holding my own today," Lacker commented along about six in the evening.

"You're doin' right fine," Owen complimented him. "If we're not careful, by midnight you'll have all our money."

"I doubt that."

But the drummer continued to win the larger pots. Pleading a weak bladder, he repaired to the outhouse at least once an hour.

Pitney and the cowboys had lost well over two hundred dollars when yet another hand was dealt. Luck favored Pitney, and he received a pair of kings among his five cards. He discarded three and was delighted to get another king and a pair of twos. A full house. The best hand he'd had all evening. Adopting a stone face, he counted what was left of the money he had set aside to play with and announced, "It will cost you seventy-seven dollars to see these cards, gentlemen."

Lon and Slim folded. Cleveland pondered a bit, then did the same. Owen, smiling, called. Then it was Lacker's turn and he not only met the seventy-seven, he added another fifty.

"But I don't have that much," Pitney said. He was fibbing. He had several hundred more on him but it was company funds and his personal code of honor prohibited him from venturing it.

Owen appealed to the drummer. "Are you willin' to take an IOU for the difference?"

"I don't know," Lacker said uncertainly.

"On my word of honor as a gentleman, you will be paid should I lose." Pitney said, adding his own appeal.

"Can you get the money to me before I leave on the stage?" the drummer wanted to know.

Pitney's hopes were dashed. "No. But I can send it wherever you want. Let me have your forwarding address."

"No offense," Lacker said, "but given how the mail is, even if you send it, there's no guarantee I will get it. I am afraid, sir, I must respectfully decline."

Owen sat up straighter. "I reckon that leaves you and me. Let's take a gander at those cards of yours."

With a flourish and a smug smile, the drummer turned them over. "Read them and cringe, friend. Four aces." He extended his hands to rake in the pot.

"Not so fast," Owen said.

"Why not?" Lacker was confused, and he was not

the only one. Lon and Slim and Cleveland looked at one another with furrowed brows.

"There is one hand that beats four of a kind."

"There are two hands." The drummer knew his poker. "A straight flush and a royal flush. But since I have all four aces, you can't possibly have a royal flush. That leaves a straight flush, and the odds against that—"

"Are pretty high, I know." Owen smiled. "But there is a third hand that beats four of a kind."

"If there is I never heard of it," Lacker said suspiciously. "Show me what it is."

"Five sixes," Owen said.

"There's no such thing."

"Sure there is. I have them right here." So saying, Owen drew his Colt and placed it on the table.

"You're joking." Lacker laughed nervously and glanced at the other cowboys but it was plain they were as mystified as he was.

Slowly, almost delicately, Owen scooped the pot toward him with his free arm. "The next time you need your laundry done, you should do it yourself."

"What are you talking about?"

"I ran into Mrs. Harker earlier today. The lady you're boardin' with. She told me how you asked her to do your laundry. How she did all you gave her, then went to your room to ask if there was more."

"So?" Lacker angrily snapped. "What does that have to do with you stealing this pot from me?"

"So Mrs. Harker said your door was open. She saw you sittin' on the edge of your bed, practicin' with that rig you have up your right sleeve."

For a few moments no one spoke or moved. Then,

swearing luridly, William Lacker heaved up out of his chair. In his left hand gleamed a nickel-plated derringer, which he trained on Owen. "No one calls me a cheat! Apologize, or so help me, I will shoot you."

4

A Strangulation Jig

The entire saloon was suddenly quiet. The bartender stopped wiping the counter, the cardplayers stopped playing, chips stopped tinkling, and the gruff laughter ceased. Every head swiveled and fixed on the portly man holding the nickel-plated derringer on the Bar 40's foreman.

Beads of sweat broke out on William Lacker's brow and a wild gleam animated his eyes—the gleam of fear, the fear of being caught in the act of doing something he should not have been doing. "I don't know what you are talking about!" he bluffed in a high-pitched whine that served only to confirm he knew exactly what the foreman was talking about.

For his part, Owen was surprisingly calm. "You don't want to do this," he said quietly.

"I'm taking my winnings and walking out that door and no one is going to stop me."

"How far do you reckon you'll get?" Owen asked in the same quiet manner.

"Use your head," Lon threw in. "So far all you've done is cheat. Don't make it worse."

"You have no proof," the drummer said.

Lon replied, "All we have to do is pull up your right sleeve."

Lacker pointed the derringer at him. "But who is to do it? You, cowboy? I think not. I want you to take off your hat and fill it with my winnings, and be quick about it."

"Take off my hat?" Lon repeated in a disbelieving tone.

"Just do it!" Lacker commanded, then suddenly shifted when the bartender started to lower his hand under the bar. "Don't even think it! I assure you I am rather handy with this."

Slim snickered and declared, "Says you, mister. I never yet met a drummer who could shoot straight."

"Hard to do with a derringer," Cleveland said. "They tend to fire wild unless you know exactly how to use them."

"I do!" Lacker boasted. He motioned at Lon. "What are you waiting for, damn you? Take off your hat."

Lon shook his head. "It will be a cold day in hell before I kowtow to the likes of you."

Bewilderment was added to Lacker's fear. "It's just your hat, for God's sake! Take the damn thing off and fill it with my money!"

Owen placed his hands flat on the table to show he would not make any abrupt moves. "The money isn't yours. You didn't win it fair and square."

"It's your word against mine, and I hold the trump." The drummer wagged his derringer.

Someone in the saloon moved and coughed. Instantly Lacker turned and barked, "Stay right where you are! All of you! I mean it!"

"This is gettin' ridiculous," Lon said, and pushed back his chair. "Mister, listen to me, and listen good. Folks say I'm quick. Mighty quick. So quick, I can

draw and put a slug into you before you can blink.
Even if you tie me, you're dead. So be reasonable and
put down that weak sister excuse for a shootin' iron
before you make me mad.''

"No one is that quick," Lacker scoffed.

"He is." Carmody was coming toward them. She
took slow steps so as not to agitate the drummer any
more than he already was. Holding one hand out in
appeal, she said, "So far no one has been hurt, but if
you're not real careful this can turn real ugly. I've
seen it happen before."

"Didn't you hear me?" Lacker threatened.

Carmody took another slow step, her voice as calm
as Owen's had been. "Please, Mr. Lacker. I haven't
quite caught what is going on, other than you were
cheatin'—"

"He has a rig up his sleeve," Owen said.

Carmody sighed and took another step. "Put down
your derringer. The worst they'll do is run you out
of town."

"I wasn't cheating!" Lacker cried shrilly. "And I
will not let my reputation be tarnished! I make my
living by selling things, madam. Who will buy from
me if word gets around I am shiftless?" He gestured
angrily at the pile in the center of the table. "All I
want is what is rightfully mine, and I will leave this
dust-ridden speck of nothing to the flies and the
lizards."

A cold laugh came from the far corner of the room.
"I want to thank you, drummer," Luke Deal said.

"Thank me for what?" Lacker nervously licked his
thick lips and swiped a sleeve across his neck.

"Whiskey Flats has been mighty borin' of late. I've
been wonderin' what I could do to liven things up."

Luke leaned on his elbows and sneered. "Then you come along and provide all the entertainment I could want."

Owen straightened in his chair. "This doesn't concern you."

"No, it doesn't," Lon agreed. "We're the ones he cheated, not you."

Luke Deal paid them no mind. Addressing himself to everyone else present, he asked, "Are we goin' to let this drummer get away with makin' fools of us? Let him ride out so he can brag to everyone he meets how he pulled one over on the sheep in Whiskey Flats?"

"I would never," Lacker said.

"If we let him ride out," Luke Deal continued, "it won't be long before we're the laughingstock of Texas."

"We can't have that," said a man at another table.

"No, sir," chimed in one at the bar. "Whiskey Flats might be a flyspeck but it's our flyspeck."

"I say we hang him," Grutt gleefully suggested.

Another silence fell. An unsettling silence, nearly every face a mirror of a rising collective thirst for vengeance. Their expressions caused William Lacker to take a step back and blurt, "Now all of you just hold on. I haven't done anything worth being hung."

Carmody was only a few yards from the table, and took yet another slow step. "Not yet you haven't," she said. "Give your derringer to Owen and we'll see to it you get out of town alive."

Owen nodded. "It's me you've been wavin' it at so I have the right to decide what to do with you."

The drummer wavered. He looked at Owen and he looked at Carmody, then he glanced across the saloon at the three hard cases who were eyeing him as wolves might eye prey. He shook his head and said, "No. I don't trust any of you. I'll keep my derringer, take my money, and go."

Luke Deal stood up.

"Don't you try anything!" Lacker cried. "I'm warning you."

"You're a gamblin' man, I take it?" Luke asked. "What do you want to bet you'll miss and I won't?"

"Luke, don't," Owen said.

"What's the matter? No stomach for what needs doin'?" Luke Deal laughed. "The rest of us aren't as squeamish. Are we, boys?"

Lacker aimed the derringer at him. "Enough of that! You are not helping matters by inciting everyone."

"Please, Luke," Carmody said, "leave this to me and no one need be hurt."

"You miss the point, darlin'," Luke Deal responded. "You should know me well enough by now to know I *like* hurtin' things."

"Me, too," Grutt said, rising.

Panic brought a mew of terror from Lacker's throat. "Sit back down, both of you! Or so help me, I'll squeeze this trigger."

"I'm tremblin' in my boots," Luke Deal mocked him.

Carmody turned to the drummer. "For the last time. Before it's too late, hand me your gun and everything will be fine. You'll see."

For a few seconds it appeared Lacker would do as she wanted. He took a half step toward her and started to lower the derringer but then jerked it up again and pointed it at her. "No! You're trying to trick me! You're on their side. You want to disarm me so they can string me up!"

"Don't be silly."

"I saw you standing over at that table," Lacker said, motioning toward Deal, Grutt, and Bronk. "I saw you with your hand on that longhair's shoulder."

The very air seemed charged with tension. Alfred Pitney did not know what to do or say. He had never been in a situation like this. He had never imagined a situation like this. He sat still but his heart was hammering and his palms were damp.

By now Carmody was only a few feet from Lacker. She held out a hand, palm up. "Give it to me," she softly requested. "I won't let any harm come to you. I give you my word."

"The word of a saloon trollop?" Lacker laughed, a laugh tainted by creeping hysteria.

"Please." Carmody took another step.

"Stop where you are!" the drummer cried, backing away. "I mean it! I won't let you or anyone else disarm me!" He backed around the other side of the table and turned toward the front of the saloon. "On second thought," he said to Owen, "you can keep the money. All I want now is to leave unmolested."

Luke Deal overheard. "How far do you reckon you'll get?"

"For the last time, keep out of this!" Owen said.

Lacker edged toward the door. "I am leaving and I will shoot anyone who tries to stop me."

Owen spread his arms wide and smiled. "No one will. Walk out nice and easy and head for your room and stay there until the stage comes." He started to rise.

They all heard the *click* of the derringer's hammer being thumbed back. "Stay where you are! No one is to move until I am out that door!"

"You can't stop all of us," Grutt said. "You only have two shots in that hide-out of yours."

"Mr. Lacker doesn't want to shoot anyone," Carmody said. "Do you, Mr. Lacker?"

"Not if I can help it."

"Tell you what." Carmody came around the table. "Why don't I escort you to the door? No one will try to stop you with me by your side. They won't risk shootin' a woman."

"Stop!"

"It's all right." Carmody did not halt. "I don't want anyone harmed. That includes you."

"Please stop," Lacker begged.

"Take my arm, Mr. Lacker. You have nothin' to be afraid of. We will walk out together." As casually as if she were about to go on a Sunday stroll, Carmody offered her elbow while saying sweetly, "Here. Take it. I won't bite you."

The derringer went off.

Shock seized every man present.

Lacker, stunned, gaped in horror and bleated, "No! I didn't mean to do that! Honest I didn't!"

Looking down at her bosom, at the hole between the swell of her breasts, Carmody swayed. "Oh my. What have you done, Mr. Lacker? What have you done?" Blood began oozing from the hole and she clutched at the table for support. "Owen?"

The foreman came out of his chair as if launched from a catapult. He did not run around the table to her side; he scrambled over it, scattering chips and cards and coins and bills. Springing between Slim and

Cleveland, he caught her as she started to fall. "Carmody! Dear God! No!"

Others stirred, shaking off their shock to glare at the drummer, and four or five began to rise.

"Stay where you are!" William Lacker ordered. "I will shoot the first man who tries to stop me!" Frantic, he backpedaled, swinging the derringer from side to side to discourage anyone from being overbold. He reached the door and pushed it open without looking behind him. "Don't come after me! You hear?" Whirling, he bolted out of there like a buck bolting from a pack of wolves.

A mass rush ensued. With shouts of "After the bastard!" and "He has to pay!" and "String him up!" nearly every last person, from the bartender to the townsmen to Luke Deal and his leather slappers, raced out. The Bar 40 punchers remained, up out of their chairs, watching, aghast, as Owen gently lowered Carmody to the floor and cradled her head in his lap. "No," he said. "No, no, no."

Carmody's eyes were open, her face only inches from his bent form. Yet she said, "Owen? Dearest? Is that you?"

"Can't you see me?"

"Everything went dark all of a sudden. Where did the light go?" Carmody's right hand weakly rose.

Owen clutched it and pressed his lips to her fingers. "Oh God."

"I can't believe he shot me," Carmody said. "All I wanted to do was help." She coughed, and a drop of blood trickled over her bottom lip.

Pitney could scarcely credit what he was witnessing. "Shouldn't we send for a physician?"

"There isn't one," Lon said. "The nearest sawbones is over to Laredo. It would take a week to fetch him."

"But there must be something we can do!"

Owen's entire frame shook as he kissed Carmody on the cheek. "I'm sorry. So very sorry."

"For what?" Carmody's voice was faint. They had to strain to hear. She tried to sit up but could barely move. "I'm dyin', aren't I? That silly man has gone and killed me."

"Is there anything we can get you?" Lon asked.

"Why isn't there any pain? I don't feel a thing. It's like my body isn't here. How can that be?" Carmody coughed again and more blood welled from her mouth.

"Someone get a cloth and water," Owen urged, and Slim and Cleveland both ran past the bar. "We'll make you as comfortable as we can," he said in her ear.

"Is Luke here?"

"No," Owen replied. "He lit out after the drummer with most everybody else."

"I only hooked up with him to spite you."

"I know."

"It broke my heart, you takin' after the schoolmarm like you did, after all we shared." Carmody closed her eyes. Her breathing was shallow. "I always figured you would propose."

Owen did not say anything.

"Silly of me, huh? Thinkin' a decent man like you would want me for his wife? Me, the town tart."

"Don't talk like that," Owen begged. "You're as fine a woman as any other."

"As fine as your schoolmarm?" Carmody asked, but there was no spite in her tone, only a weary resignation. "She's a good woman. She'll make you a fine wife one day. Raise a passel of kids and have a ranch of your own, like you always wanted."

"Please," Owen said.

Carmody opened her eyes and gazed anxiously about. "Are you still here? Where did you get to?"

"I haven't gone anywhere." Owen squeezed her hand.

"Do you hear that?"

"What?" Owen asked, but she did not answer. "There's a lot of yellin' outside. Is that what you hear?" He lightly touched his lips to her temple. "I blame myself. I should never have tried to teach that drummer a lesson. It wasn't mine to do."

"Pard?" Lon said.

"I was foolin' about. But I forgot an important fact of life. Even rabbits will turn when they are at bay." Owen ran a finger across her hair. "I'm sorry, Carmody. So, so sorry."

Lon gripped his friend's shoulder. "Pard? You can stop beatin' yourself. She can't hear you."

Owen looked up, then down at the still figure of the woman in red. A groan escaped him, torn from the depths of his being. "She deserved better than this."

Cleveland and Slim came barreling out of the back, Cleveland with a couple of towels, Slim with a pan filled to the brim with water. They stopped as if they had slammed into an invisible wall.

"Aw, hell," Slim said.

Owen tenderly laid Carmody down, and beckoned. "Give me a hand. We can't leave her on the floor."

"Where, then?" Lon asked.

"The bar."

Pitney sprang to help. He slid his hands under the dove's left leg and lifted when the others did.

Owen arranged her dress and folded her hands on

her bosom. "One of you go see if the parson is at the church."

Before any of the cowboys could move, the front door opened and the bartender hollered, "The drummer has disappeared! We're going door-to-door but so far we can't find the bastard!"

"Thanks, Farrel," Lon said. "We'll be right out."

"Not me," Owen said. "I'm stayin'."

"Are you sure you don't want in on it? Seein' him dangle will ease some of the sorrow."

"I'm stayin'."

Lon crooked a finger at Slim and Cleveland and they made for the door. Midway Lon stopped and glanced back. "What are you waitin' for, English? Or don't folks have manners where you come from?"

"Oh." Alfred Pitney sheepishly hurried after them.

Twilight shrouded Whiskey Flats. A few stars sparkled high above. After the smoky, stuffy saloon, the brisk breeze from the northwest was welcome. The town had transformed into a beehive of activity. The men were scouring every building. Distraught women stood in small groups, discussing the calamity. A few mothers clasped small children to them as if afraid the drummer would shoot the children next.

"I never suspected there were so many," Pitney said.

"How can he have vanished?" Cleveland asked no one in particular. "He has to be hidin' somewhere unless he grabbed a horse and lit a shuck when no one was lookin'." Luke Deal and four other men came hastening by, and Cleveland called out, "Are any horses missin'?"

"Not that we know of," a townsman responded.

The next moment a commotion erupted at the livery. Shouts and curses mixed with the thud of blows, and someone bawled, "We found him! He was hidin' in the hayloft!"

All the inhabitants of Whiskey Flats—every last man, woman, and child—streamed to the wide double doors, then fell back to make room as four huskies brought William Lacker out. The drummer was nearly beside himself. He struggled mightily, twisting and kicking, but the four men held firm.

"Murderer!" a woman shrieked.

"Why did you do it?" From Toothless.

One of the men holding the drummer scanned the crowd. "What should we do with him? Hold him for the federal marshal?"

Luke Deal cupped a hand to his mouth. "To the cottonwoods! To the hangin' tree!"

The suggestion became a refrain as a score of throats echoed it: "To the hanging tree! To the hanging tree! To the hanging tree!"

"Noooooooooooooo!" William Lacker wailed as he was bodily propelled toward a strip of woodland fringing a creek that bordered Whiskey Flats to the south. "You can't do this!"

His plaintive plea was drowned out by the cacophony of incensed voices calling for him to pay the ultimate penalty for his misdeed. Raising a strident din to the brightening stars, the crowd flowed in a body to a high cottonwood that stood by itself in the center of a clearing. That the tree had seen use before was attested to by deep scrape marks on a thick limb about twenty feet off the ground.

Alfred Pitney plucked at Lon's sleeve. "They can't be doing what I think they are doing! They can't hang a man in cold blood! It's barbaric!"

Lon had to yell to be heard above the uproar. "We have no law so we make our own. He's only gettin' what he deserves."

"But it's wrong!" Pitney exclaimed, appalled. "Morally and ethically and legally wrong!"

"Towns and settlements do it all the time," Lon said. "Vigilante justice, the newspapers call it. The right of the people to protect themselves."

"But Lacker can't harm anyone else! He should be held for trial. His fate should be decided by a judge. My God, man! Hasn't anyone in Texas ever heard of the rule of law?"

A cheer rocked the clearing.

A buttermilk horse had been brought, and a rope produced. Lacker's wrists were bound behind his back and he was roughly thrown onto the saddle. He fought but they held him fast as a man on another horse slipped a noose over his head.

The man on the other horse was Luke Deal. "Try holdin' your breath. You might last a few seconds longer."

"For pity's sake, don't!" Alfred Pitney pleaded but he was the lone dissenter in a sea of retribution. He attempted to force his way through the press but there were too many.

"Any last words?" Luke Deal asked.

"As God is my witness—" Lacker started to speak.

"On second thought, you don't deserve any." Suddenly Luke Deal yipped and took off his hat and slapped it hard against the buttermilk, and the horse broke into a trot.

A cheer went up.

Lacker gurgled and whined and flailed his legs, his face reddening, his neck bent at an angle by the knot.

To the delight of the crowd, his frenzied thrashing soon ended and he hung as limp as an empty potato sack, his face purple, the tip of his tongue protruding from between his thick lips, his wide, lifeless eyes fixed on the heavens.

5
Longhorn Country

The Bar 40 was considered one of the most efficiently run ranches in all of Texas, which was saying a lot. As solicitor and financial manager for the Bristol-London Consortium, Alfred Pitney had acquired all the information he could on the ranch and its owner before the BLC committed to the purchase.

James Bartholomew was a man of impeccable honesty, and a tireless worker. He had started the ranch when he was forty, and for his brand combined the first three letters of his last name with his age.

Prior to that, Bartholomew had worked at several jobs, including a stint in the Union Army during the conflict that nearly tore the United States asunder. After his discharge, he hired on as a puncher on a ranch known as the Flying T. The Flying T's owner, a Miles Cavendish, took a liking to the forthright young man and was grooming Bartholomew to be his foreman when fate threw an even better opportunity in Bartholomew's lap.

His mother had died when he was young. His father had grown too attached to the bottle, and never amounted to much. But an uncle made a lot of money in shipping, and when the uncle died, he left part of that money for his favorite nephew. Enough to enable James Bartholomew to realize a dream he had long held of having a ranch of his own.

Bartholomew bought all the land he could. It being Texas, and land being cheap, his spread was roughly the size of Rhode Island. He had a ranch house built, and a stable and corral, and a bunkhouse for the punchers he soon hired, and all the outbuildings a typical ranch needed, and when he was done, he had very little money left to buy cattle. But that was all right, since he had no intention to buy any. Not when there were untold thousands of wild cattle available for the taking.

Several hundred years earlier, the great world powers—Spain, England, France, and Portugal—were exploring every square inch of the planet and claiming those inches as their own. Spain claimed what would later become Texas. One of her explorers, more interested in wealth than in square inches, penetrated deep into the Southwest seeking the fabled fabulously rich Seven Cities of Cibola. Coronado was his name, and to feed the men of his expedition, he took along thousands of hogs, goats, and sheep. He also took about five hundred head of cattle.

Exactly how many head wandered off or were left behind was not known, but a couple of decades later, another Spaniard discovered that thousands of upstart wild cattle had overrun the countryside.

Later, Spain established a network of missions and stocked them with cattle, some of which strayed off, adding to the mix that would become a legend in its own right—the Texas longhorn.

The Nueces River country was thick with them, and within two years the Bar 40 had laid claim to thousands. Its cowhands, commonly called the 40 Outfit, were fiercely loyal to the brand.

James Bartholomew possessed a business savvy that other ranchers envied. Under his wise management the Bar 40 prospered. Its reputation spread, until cowmen as far away as Wyoming and Montana, when ranching was discussed, mentioned it as the best of the best.

Alfred Pitney agreed. After the ghastly affair at Whiskey Flats, he half expected to find the Bar 40 to be a motley circus of wild cows and violent men, but the order and discipline that prevailed were a testament to Bartholomew's no-nonsense approach to ranching as a business, and to the high caliber of the men he employed.

The first day out from town, Owen did not say much. A pall of sorrow hung over him as he sat the buckboard seat, his broad shoulders slumped. Following behind, the other three cowboys, Lon, Slim, and Cleveland, rode in silence out of respect for their pard.

For Pitney the trip was a grand adventure. He had never been to Texas, and the land and its people were new and indelible.

The second day they came upon a group of smiling, friendly vaqueros wearing wide-brimmed sombreros, short jackets, and pants that flared at the bottom. The vaqueros had been on business to a ranch west of the Bar 40. Their leader knew Owen, and stopped and talked for a few minutes.

It was about noon on the second day that they came to the boundary of the Bar 40, and shortly thereafter Pitney saw his first longhorns. The buckboard was winding through heavy brush when he spotted several cattle watching their approach with wary regard.

Sensational beasts, they were multihued. One was black splotched with white, another a mulberry blue, yet a third a mouse gray. They had remarkably high front shoulders and were thin at the flanks. They were also longer than any cows Pitney had ever seen, with bony spines and flat ribs. His initial impression was that they were all bone and legs. He guessed aloud that they must weigh close to eight hundred pounds but Owen informed him the total was closer to a thousand.

And then there were their horns. Incredible, unbelievable horns, swept wide and curved outward, not up. Horns six feet across on the black longhorn, closer to seven on the mulberry blue, and, Pitney was willing to swear, horns eight feet across on the *grulla*, as Owen told him the mousy longhorn was known.

Right then and there Pitney developed a whole new respect for the men who rode herd on such animals. He had seen a few buffalo from the train on his way south, contentedly grazing on the prairie, and the buffalo seemed tame compared to these huge bony cattle with their array of wicked horns.

"Why would anyone want cattle like these when they could have Herefords?" Pitney wondered aloud.

Owen, who had been lost in remembrance, stirred and answered, "Herefords are fine grazin' cows, but they wouldn't last long in country like this. It takes cattle as raw as the land to survive."

Eager to keep the cowboy talking, Pitney racked his brain for some of the tidbits his research in England had revealed prior to his trip. "They say longhorns are the hardiest breed ever known."

"They say right," Owen said, with more than a smidgen of pride. "I've worked with all kinds of cows, and longhorns are the orneriest, most cussed, most contrary critters to ever breathe. But I wouldn't trade them for all the Herefords, Guernseys, or Highland cattle in creation."

"I find it interesting you mention Highlands," Pitney said, impressed by the foreman's depth of knowledge, "since these longhorns you are so fond of remind me of them in a way." Bred in Scotland, West Highland cattle were smaller and hairier than longhorns, but they shared a common trait: They thrived in country no other breed of cattle could.

"The Scotsman who owns the Triple S brought several over a few years ago," Owen said. "One strayed into quicksand, another fell prey to a cougar, and the third wandered off into the brush and was never seen again."

"How do longhorns handle cold?" Pitney asked the question that had been crucial to the BLC's decision to send him.

"Texas has brutal winters but there's never a shortage of longhorns," was Owen's astute reply.

As the buckboard drew near, the watching longhorns wheeled and melted into the tangle of vegetation with barely a ripple of greenery. One instant they were there, the next they were gone.

"Remarkable brutes," Pitney said.

"Wait until you see the one you came for," Owen remarked. "He's so beautiful, he will take your breath away."

Pitney had never heard an animal described in quite so passionate a manner. "My only hope is that he will prove worthy of his cost."

They talked cows a while more, until Owen lapsed into his sorrowful silence. That evening they made camp beside a stream, the earth around it torn by the countless heavy hooves of roving longhorns.

Seated by the crackling fire, sipping a cup of tea he brewed himself, Pitney listened to the distant yip of coyotes, and smiled. "I envy you blokes."

Slim looked up from the dice he and Lon were taking turns rolling. "How so, mister?"

"This land, the people, the wildlife." Pitney sighed. "I spend most of my days behind a desk, working with accounts and figures until I have them coming out of my ears."

"I'd be no use at a desk job," Lon said. "I couldn't sit still long enough to get the work done."

"I don't have your freedom. A business manager has to pay close attention to the books and attend a lot of meetings and arrange an endless array of financial details. Some nights I am at my desk until midnight."

"Better you than me," Cleveland said. "I was raised on a farm. The outdoors is in my blood."

Owen, holding a tin cup filled with black coffee in both calloused hands, looked up. "You have your desk, we have our saddles. We spend most of every day on horseback, and there have been nights when I've been so sore and stiff, I wished I was mindin' a desk instead."

"Why, that's blasphemy." Lon grinned. "You might as well wish to be a store clerk."

Slim said, "At least store clerks get to see a lot of pretty girls each and every day. We see the hind ends of a lot of cows."

"Clerks also see a heap of biddy hens," Lon pointed out, "and have to put up with gripes and grumbles and stack boxes and tin cans and fold blankets and clothes. I don't reckon I could stand the excitement."

"Yep, those dumb clerks," Slim said. "They don't work under the bakin' sun when it's one hundred and ten degrees in the shade. They don't have to ride through thorn brush where the thorns are so sharp they can shred a man's legs if he's not careful. They don't get bucked or stomped on or gored. I don't know how they can stand it."

Alfred Pitney laughed. "It seems to me every profession has its good and its not-so-good aspects. Frankly, being here with you fine fellows is one of the highlights of my life."

"Are you pokin' fun at us?" Lon asked.

"Not at all," Pitney said. "Can you imagine a boy raised on the bustling streets of Bristol, sitting here under the stars in the midst of the American wilderness? In case you aren't aware, Bristol is a seaport, and an industrial center. Its streets teem with people. There are buildings everywhere. It is as different from your Texas as night is from day." Pitney breathed deep of the crisp night air. "Your most marvelous Texas."

"Uh-oh," Cleveland said. "You're starting to talk as if you like it here. Next thing you know, you'll put down roots."

"It's not our fault the rest of the world can't hold a candle to Texas," Lon remarked.

"Surely you like it here?" Pitney asked Cleveland.

"I reckon so, or I'd have gone back to Ohio a coon's age ago. There's something about Texas that gets in a man's blood. Once he sets foot in it, he never wants to leave."

Slim made a show of scratching his chin. "I thought

it was that pretty senorita at the cantina in Nueva who got into your blood?"

Lon cackled, and Owen mustered his first smile since leaving Whiskey Flats.

"Then there are those," Cleveland went on, "who say Texas is for simpletons who can't count past ten without their boots off."

"I can count to fourteen," Slim said.

The genial mood was abruptly intruded on by a low, guttural cough from out of the darkness. Immediately, the four cowhands shot to their feet, their hands on their revolvers, as several of the horses stamped and whinnied.

"Why the alarm?" Pitney asked. "What was that? A bear?"

"A jaguar," Owen said.

Pitney sprang erect, nearly spilling his tea. "This far north?"

"From time to time," Lon said, peering intently in the direction the cough came from, "one will drift north of the border."

"When one is hungry enough, it will go after anything," Slim added, "includin' people."

Cleveland snickered. "I've always wanted me a jaguar rug. There was an old coot by the handle of Charlie Stubbs who had one, and it was the prettiest rug you ever did see."

"A rug to go with the home you don't have to impress the woman you don't have?" Slim said. "That makes a heap of sense."

Owen went to the buckboard and retrieved his Winchester. Levering a round into the chamber, he announced, "I'll go have a look-see. The rest of you keep your eyes skinned."

"I would like to go with you if someone will lend me a rifle," Pitney volunteered.

"I'd feel better if you stayed."

"I've hunted stag and ducks and geese," Pitney said to justify his request, "and I'm more than a middling shot, if I do say so myself." He clasped his slender hands together. "As a personal favor?"

Lon had an opinion. "Mr. Bartholomew will throw a fit if we let one of those big cats rip you to bits and pieces."

"Please," Pitney said to Owen. "I will never have an adventure like this again."

"You're loco," the foreman said, then reluctantly grinned. "But if Lon will lend you his Henry and you agree to do exactly as I say, you can come with me."

In an excess of enthusiasm, Pitney gushed, "Thank you, thank you, thank you! Wait until the chaps at the BLC hear about this." He accepted the rifle Lon handed him and admired the gleam of the brass receiver in the firelight. "What did you call this? A Henry?"

"It's .44-caliber," Lon said. "Holds fifteen shots. You can blast the cat to hell and back if you have to."

Pitney grinned like a schoolboy given his heart's desire. "I hope I have the chance."

Owen started toward the brush. "Be careful what you wish for," he whispered. "Sometimes the Almighty is payin' attention."

As the thickets closed around them, some of Alfred Pitney's enthusiasm waned. The darkness was near total. He could barely see his hand at arm's length. It would be ridiculously easy for the jaguar to sneak up on them. Consequently, he stayed so close to Owen that twice he nearly tripped over him.

The second time, the Bar 40 foreman stopped and turned. "Walk quieter if you can. You're makin' enough noise to wake the worms."

Pitney tried, he honestly tried, but he snagged his clothes and trod on twigs that snapped unnaturally loud, and then he failed to realize Owen had stopped and bumped into him again. "I'm dreadfully sorry," he whispered.

"You should go back."

That was the last thing Pitney wanted. He was set to argue but another bestial cough diverted Owen's attention.

"Did you hear that? It's close."

The hairs on the back of Pitney's neck prickled. He was certain the jaguar could see them. He practically felt its eyes on his skin. But though he probed high and low, there was no sign of the phantom predator. "Is it wise to stand still like this?" he wondered.

"It is if we want it to take the bait."

With a start, Pitney divined *they* were the bait Owen alluded to, that the cowboy was deliberately trying to lure the jaguar in, to have it attack them instead of the horses.

A soft rustling hinted the plan might be working.

His throat bobbing, Pitney strained to spot the source. The inky thicket appeared to be a solid wall of vegetation but it wasn't. Plenty of gaps and openings would allow the jaguar to stalk near enough to pounce.

Suddenly there was a loud snort. Not from one of the horses, but from deeper in the brush. It was followed by a few seconds of total silence. Then a racket such as Alfred Pitney had never heard fell on his ears. Caterwauling, roars, and hisses mixed with bellows, basso shrieks, and throaty *uh-uh-uh* sounds. Brush crackled and popped. A war was being waged, a savage clash that brought goose bumps to Alfred Pitney's flesh when the brush in front of him parted and the two principals materialized, shadowy shapes locked in deadly combat.

One shape was that of a large feline, a stocky cat with steel-spring legs and flashing claws. The other was that of a monster that stood as tall as Pitney and had wickedly curved horns and sharp hooves.

The jaguar was battling a longhorn.

Glued in dumbfounded fascination, Pitney did not think to run as the combatants swirled toward him. The jaguar leaped and slashed and bit. The bull tossed its great horns and kicked out with its heavy hooves.

"Move, you simpleton!"

Pitney felt arms encircle his waist, and he was shoved toward the fire. But Owen's effort came too late. The longhorn and the jaguar were on top of them. A heavy blow to his side lifted him off his feet and hurled him half a dozen yards. Thorns and branches tore at his clothes, his neck, his face.

On his hands and knees, bleeding from cuts and scratches, Pitney sought to clear his head by shaking it. He heard Owen shout his name, and looked up as a living mountain towered above him. He glimpsed the jaguar on top of the longhorn's back, ripping and clawing, and then a hoof caught him on the shoulder and he somersaulted like a French acrobat into a wall of vegetation.

The pain was excruciating. Pitney smothered a cry and pried at a branch caught fast in his clothes. He struggled to stand and felt as if a hundred small knives tore at him at once.

Suddenly Owen was beside him, pulling and tugging. "If you value your hide, get up!"

Pitney tried.

Then the forms of the furiously battling beasts appeared behind Owen. Cat and bovine were locked in the most elemental of duels. Neither would yield until its adversary was dead. The jaguar's teeth and claws took a fearsome toll but the longhorn was holding its own.

Owen hooked an arm around Pitney and wrenched him from the thicket's embrace. Pitney staggered and would have fallen if not for the cowboy's grasp. He willed his legs to move but they did not respond as they should.

"I need to catch my breath."

If Owen heard, he made no sign of it, but only lengthened his strides. "For God's sake, run!"

The crash of underbrush was loud in Pitney's ears. He glanced back, and there was the living mountain again, moving with amazing speed for something so huge. It slammed into him with the force of a battering ram. Pitney was conscious of becoming airborne. He had the illusion he sailed through the night sky as high as the clouds. The ground rushed up to meet him, and this time he did cry out as a piercing pain shot through him from head to toe and the world faded to black.

How long Pitney was unconscious he could not say. Perhaps a couple of minutes. Perhaps more. A groping hand found his shoulder and the contact restored him to the land of the living. "Owen?" he croaked.

"Hush!" the foreman whispered. "Listen."

Pitney did, but heard nothing, absolutely nothing at all. The significance seeped in, and he blurted, "It's over!"

"Maybe not," Owen whispered, adding, "The jaguar could be anywhere."

Dread filled Pitney's every pore. He broke out in a cold sweat. The Henry had been knocked from his grasp. He was defenseless. He consoled himself with the thought that Lon, Slim, and Cleveland would come to their aid, but when time went by and they did not appear, it dawned on him that the cowboys did not realize anything was amiss. In any event, they were too smart to blunder blindly into the brush. He opened his mouth to call to them, but Owen realized what he was about to do.

"Not a peep. We lie still until we know it's safe."

Pitney swallowed, and nodded. He could barely see Owen's face so it was doubtful Owen had seen his nod, and he was about to say that he would do whatever Owen wanted when Owen clamped a calloused hand over his mouth.

Pitney did not need to ask why. He heard it, too: stealthy movement, very close. Something took long, heavy breaths, punctuated by a strange sucking noise. Pitney held his own breath in anticipation of a hoof or a paw flashing out of the night, but nothing happened. Soon the movement, and the sucking noise, faded.

"You can stand," Owen said.

"Are you sure?" Pitney responded, and was hoisted erect as easily as he might hoist a child.

"Anything busted?" the foreman asked with real concern. "That was quite a tumble you took."

Pitney wriggled both arms and lifted his right leg and then his left. "I think I'm in one piece."

"Bring a torch!"

Spurs jangled, and a miniature sun blazed.

Pitney blinked in the bright light and absently smoothed his jacket. His clothes were a mess and he had dozens of small scratches, a few bleeding, but nothing serious. "A miracle," he said softly.

Lon had the torch in one hand, his cocked Colt in the other. "Take a gander," he said, holding the torch low.

A glistening trail of blood led into the brush. Owen and Lon followed it, and Pitney, not caring to be left alone, followed them. In a few yards the gleam of burnished metal drew Lon to the Henry, and the glance he bestowed on Pitney was not flattering.

They cautiously advanced.

"I'll be damned," Owen said.

The jaguar lay on its side, dead. A hole in its chest and another high on its neck showed where a horn had caught it between its front legs and penetrated clear through its stout body.

"So what do you think of longhorn country now?" Lon asked.

Every nerve tingling from his thrilling experience, Alfred Pitney answered honestly. "It's magnificent."

6

A Cobbler Interlude

James Bartholomew was not an imposing man. He was five feet one in his boots and had a surprisingly pale complexion and graying hair. But as soon as he spoke, he became imposing, for he had a voice that was a gift from God. A deep, rich baritone, so full and resonant that had he devoted his life to singing instead of cattle, aficionados would have flocked to hear him from all corners of the world. He also had a warm, strong, confident handshake that spoke volumes.

With Bartholomew was his wife, Proctor. In one of life's little coincidences, she was exactly the same height. Her brown hair was done up in a bun, and she wore a simple calico dress, the garb of American working women everywhere, and not an elegant gown, as might be expected of someone as well-to-do as the couple were.

Their house, like the rest of the buildings on the ranch, was immaculate. The interior had been done in wood paneling and reminded their British guest of a manor house he had once visited. Tastefully furnished, including rugs and tapestries and paintings, it might have been the home of a British lord.

Bartholomew himself had opened the door at their knock. No servants were in evidence, another reflection of the man's character. After greetings were tendered, Owen, the only one of the four cowboys to escort Alfred Pitney to the house from the stable, excused himself.

"I have a lot of work to catch up on. The north herd tally is due, and the blacksmith needs to see me."

"He and the tally can wait," Bartholomew said. "As my foreman, I want you in on my talks with Mr. Pitney."

Bartholomew guided them down a long hall to a spacious sitting room, and once the Brit was comfortable on a settee, Mrs. Bartholomew, who insisted on being called by her first name, left to bring refreshments.

"So how was your trip out from town?" Bartholomew began.

Excitedly, Pitney told about the incident with the jaguar. "I can't wait to tell my friends in England. They will be green with envy."

"They could just as well be sad with remorse," Bartholomew said, his eyes silently accusing his foreman. "What were you thinkin', Owen? It's not like you. This man could have been killed."

Owen looked down at the floor and said contritely, "It was bad judgment on my part. I make no excuses, and I promise you nothin' like it will ever happen again."

"Don't blame him." Pitney came to Owen's defense. "I insisted on accompanying him. He was merely being polite."

"He was merely being a dunderhead," Bartholomew said, not unkindly. He leaned forward, his elbows on his knees. "Texas isn't England, Mr. Pitney. A mistake out here can cost a man his life. Owen rarely makes them. He is the best ramrod in the whole blamed state. Which is why I had no qualms about sendin' him to fetch you instead of comin' myself."

"I am sorry, sir," Owen said.

"Really, it was nothing." Pitney tried again. "No harm was done, other than a few bruises and scratches." He added as an afterthought, "The incident in town, to my way of thinking, was vastly worse."

Bartholomew quizzically arched his eyebrows at Owen.

"There was a killin', and a hangin'."

"Anyone I know?"

"The girl at the Nose Paint was shot." Owen's knuckles, where they gripped the chair, were white.

"Carmody Jones? But you and she were—" Bartholomew caught himself, and his face softened. "Please accept my condolences." He glanced at the doorway as if to make sure his wife would not overhear. "I take it they hung the bastard who murdered her?"

"That they did," Owen confirmed. "A corset drummer. He was playin' cards with us. Had a gambler's rig up his sleeve. When he was called on it, the fool drew on us."

"Drummers," Bartholomew said in disgust. "I have yet to meet one who doesn't irritate me to the marrow. Either they talk you to death, or have the manners of a goat, or both."

"There was no trial," Pitney mentioned. "The people just rose up and threw a rope over his neck, and that was that."

"Who did the throwin'?" Bartholomew asked.

"Luke," Owen said.

"Ah. He and those no-account pards of his are still hangin' around then, I take it? Too bad," Bartholomew said.

"You know Luke Deal?" Pitney inquired.

"All too well. He roams all along the border country, makin' life miserable for everyone he meets. But he always comes back to Whiskey Flats. He's shiftless and worthless and bad to the bone." Bartholomew smiled at Owen. "Not like you."

Proctor returned, bearing a tray laden with a pitcher of cobbler and four glasses, along with Saratoga chips and small plates. She placed the tray on a table next to the settee, then poured the cobbler herself and brought each of them a glass and some chips.

"You are a gracious hostess, if I may be permitted to say so." Pitney offered a compliment as she roosted next to her husband. He sipped the iced tea. "This is quite delicious after that long hot ride in the buckboard today."

"It will tide you over until supper in an hour," Proctor said. "I trust you won't mind beef? We tend to dine on simple fare."

"I am sure I will like whatever your cook prepares."

"Oh, I do the cooking myself, Mr. Pitney. Same as I do my own housework and laundry."

Pitney raised his glass to her. "I admire your work ethic, madam. In my country the life of leisure is all the rage, and as soon as a woman acquires any substance, she hires servants to do everything for her except clean her teeth."

Proctor laughed. "I have always been a hard worker. It's one of the things that attracted my husband to me, I suspect."

James Bartholomew cleared his throat. "Let's talk

business, shall we? I gathered from your letters that your consortium has business interests around the world?"

"The BLC is hardly mine," Pitney said. "I merely manage some of its affairs. I serve under a board of directors. It is they who believe the BLC's acquisitions in Wyoming can prove a lucrative investment. Especially with your help."

"A bold step, given they've never ranched a day in their lives," Bartholomew said.

"Money begets money. They are constantly seeking new business ventures. Several other British firms operate ranches in America and turn a nice profit. The BLC intends to do the same."

"And you are the one they have entrusted with the job? You are either very brave, or shy a few marbles."

Pitney laughed at the friendly joke. "I have been their business manager for going on seven years, and I have yet to let them down. I believe in hiring only the best. I believe in buying only the best. Quality will out, as they say, in all walks of life, and that includes ranching."

"I commend your foresight," Bartholomew said. "And I am naturally curious. How is it you came to choose the Bar 40 out of all the ranches in the Lone Star State?"

"I did not choose the ranch so much as I chose you. When I asked around of those most knowledgeable about the cattle trade, I soon learned of your reputation, Mr. Bartholomew."

"I'm flattered."

Owen, who had been silent since the mention of Carmody Jones, now sat up. "I hear tell you are hopin' to prevent another die-up."

"Such is my prayer, yes," Pitney admitted. "As you are aware, the BLC owns approximately six hundred thousand acres. Within a few years we hope to increase that amount to close to one million."

Owen whistled softly. "That's a big ranch even by Texas standards."

"To be perfectly honest, there are days when I think it is too big. The BLC employs over a hundred cowhands, yet it takes them the better part of a month to make an accurate count of our cattle each year. Before the die-up, our books showed us having close to eighty-five thousand head."

"That's more than we run," Bartholomew mentioned.

"We *had* that many," Pitney stressed. "We lost some to rustlers and some to wolves and some to fires and poisonous weeds, but those losses were negligible, and more than replaced by the number of new calves. Then we had two consecutive years of drought. The grass withered. We lost a few thousand more than we normally would but we were able to keep the rest healthy by rotating them between water holes, rivers, and streams."

"That must have taken some doin'."

"Indeed. Neighboring ranches lost even more than we did. We were proud of ourselves and, as our hands might say, thought we had it licked. But nature is a harsh mistress. The droughts were only a prelude. She was softening our herds up for an even worse blow."

"The blizzard?" Owen said.

Pitney sadly nodded. "The worst in Wyoming's history. Snow six feet deep, with drifts of ten to fifteen or better. Winds that snapped trees like they were twigs. And the cold! I was in Britain at the time, but my American foreman recorded mornings where the temperature was in excess of fifty below zero."

Proctor set down her drink, saying, "Your poor cattle."

"We lost a third of our herd. I was on the next ship over as soon as word reached me, and I arrived as the last of the snow was melting." Pitney shuddered slightly. "It was terrible, simply terrible. The foreman took me out to see for myself. Acre after acre, mile after mile, of dead animals. Frozen to death, or dead of starvation because they couldn't break through the snow to reach the grass."

"I'm sorry for your loss," Bartholomew said sincerely.

"It will take the BLC years to recover. We have taken steps to make sure the disaster does not repeat itself by setting up feed stations throughout our range. Sheds where we store hay to be used in the event of heavy snow."

"I'd say that is darned prudent."

Pitney sat back and sighed. "But it is not enough. Our hands have to reach the hay to distribute it, and in a blizzard, that will take some doing. Then there are those periodic droughts I mentioned, about which we can do precious little."

Bartholomew shrugged. "We have droughts in Texas but we get by."

"You have something else in Texas, something we don't have in Wyoming, something which might be the answer to our direst needs."

"I can't make any guarantees," Bartholomew said.

"I know, and I would not presume to ask for any. But my idea seems logical enough."

"What idea?" Proctor asked.

"The BLC has lost so many head due to one factor and one factor alone," Pitney told her. "Under normal conditions, our cattle thrive. They fatten nicely, and return a nice profit. But only so long as they are fed and watered regularly and the weather cooperates. The least little hardship and they weaken and die."

Owen remarked, "I wouldn't call droughts and blizzards little hardships."

"True. But you see my point? Our cattle are not all that hardy. They are certainly not as hardy as, say, your Texas longhorns, which thrive under conditions that would kill our cows outright."

"Longhorns are tough critters," James Bartholomew conceded. "They have to be to survive. Texas summers are scorchin' hot, Texas winters can be cold. The brush country has little water and not much grass, so they have learned to do without."

"All of which makes them ideal for what I have in mind," Pitney said enthusiastically. "Namely, to infuse the BLC's Wyoming cattle with Texas longhorn blood."

"Why not take a herd of our cows north?" Owen asked. "You wouldn't need a large herd to start. Eventually you could replace all your cattle with longhorns."

"Eventually, yes. But in the meantime our expenses would increase. And then there is the very important consideration that pound for pound, our Wyoming cattle yield more beef for the money invested than we could ever get from longhorns." Pitney shook his head. "No, when I say I want to infuse our Wyoming cattle with longhorn blood, I mean exactly that. I want to breed the two together. I want to make our cattle hardier while at the same time maintaining our high yield."

"Others have tried similar notions," Bartholomew commented. "Charlie Goodnight bred longhorns and a buffalo once. Sort of by accident. He had a pet buffalo he called Old Spike, and it took a fancy to his longhorn cows. Ended up with a critter folks called a cattalo. Some thought it would give a boost to the cattle industry, since buffalo are even hardier than longhorns. But a lot of cattalo were stillborn. Most of the males that lived were sterile. The final blow was that cattalo didn't have much meat on them."

"And those awful sounds they made," Proctor said.

"I beg your pardon?"

"Buffalo don't make the same sounds cattle do," Proctor explained. "They don't moo or low. They grunt. Cattalo grunt, too, only they sound more like pigs. I couldn't stand to hear them. They gave me the shivers."

"There is something else," Bartholomew said. "It might sour the sale, but I have to be honest with you, Mr. Pitney. You are not the first person to think of crossbreedin' longhorns with ordinary cows. Others, right here in Texas, have done the same. The longhorn traits don't always stick. Sometimes the opposite happens. Sometimes they are bred out of the stock."

"Breeding is an inexact science, yes," Pitney said. "I have researched it heavily, and I feel that, all things being equal, my grand scheme has a fifty-fifty chance of achieving success." He gazed out the window at longhorns grazing on a nearby hill. "In my estimation, the potential reward justifies the experiment."

"An expensive experiment," Owen spoke up.

"Like I said, I always go with the best. The Bar 40 herd, by all accounts, qualifies."

Bartholomew placed his hands on his knees. "But to do as you propose, to buy a bull and have it taken all the way to Wyoming." He cocked his head. "Do you have any notion what you are lettin' yourself in for?"

"The burden is not entirely mine," Pitney said. "Part of our agreement was that you would see to the delivery."

"And I am a man of my word. I have already spoken to three of my top hands, the same three who escorted you here—Lon Chalmers, Slim Vrains, and Cleveland Hearns. They will take the bull north."

"I will accompany them," Alfred Pitney said.

Bartholomew did not hide his surprise. "You never mentioned wantin' to go along."

"Why wouldn't I? As you pointed out, it is an expensive investment. Since this whole arrangement was my idea, its success or failure rides on my shoulders. Should it fail, it will do so through no lack of effort on my part. My employers must be satisfied I have done my utmost on their behalf or I could find myself unemployed."

"But it's such a long way," Proctor said.

"And there are dangers," Bartholomew said. "Not the least of which is the bull itself. Longhorn bulls admit to no master. They do as they want, when they want." He frowned. "To be honest, I almost declined your offer. I am convinced you will regret this."

"Give me more credit than that," Pitney said. "And be advised that nothing you can say will persuade me not to go. The BLC has too much as stake. *I* have too much at stake."

"In that case," Owen addressed his employer, "maybe I should go with them and uphold the Bar 40's end."

"That isn't necessary," Pitney said.

Bartholomew's brow was puckered in thought. "My foreman has a point. I have a stake in this, too, seein' as how it's my bull you're buyin', and my word that we will get it to your ranch."

"I would rather not impose," Pitney said. "I'm confident your three cowboys and I are up to the challenge."

"Can you spare me for a few months?" Owen asked.

"Oh, I think I can hobble by." Bartholomew grinned.

Alfred Pitney chuckled. "You Yanks are pulling my leg. Isn't that the expression? It won't take that long to reach Wyoming. We will have the bull there within two weeks, possibly less."

"It can't sprout wings and fly," his host responded.

"Who needs wings when we can avail ourselves of the railroad?" Pitney rejoined. "We will take the bull to the nearest station, load him on board, and off we go." Pitney beamed. "The railroad has special stock cars, you know."

"For horses and cattle, yes," Bartholomew replied. "Normal livestock, normal cattle. Longhorns aren't normal. And a longhorn bull will no more stand for bein' confined than, say, a grizzly would."

"Aren't you exaggerating? Railroad cars are sturdily constructed. I daresay that once we have the bull inside, it can act up to its heart's content and we can laugh it to scorn."

"Never laugh at a bull."

"Why on earth not? Surely you are not suggesting

the animal will take exception? Honestly, Mr. Bartholomew, I hope you won't take this in the wrong vein, but you seem to regard longhorns in general, and longhorn bulls in particular, as if they are more extraordinary than they are."

"Think so, do you?"

Pitney grinned and indicated the cattle visible out the window. "They are animals. Simple beasts. Dullwitted beasts, at that. No different than the many other creatures man has domesticated."

"I am beginnin' to regret my decision to sell it," Bartholomew said.

"Why? Because I regard cows as a commodity? As a means to an end and nothing more? My dear sir, I am a businessman. Cows just happen to be part of the business in which I am currently engaged. If I am to be truthful, I hold them in no more esteem than I do horses. Indeed, I hold them in less, because their sole purpose is to be fattened and slaughtered, whereas horses have a variety of uses."

"I should have expected this."

"Expected what? That I refuse to place longhorns on a pedestal? If you ask me, you are overreacting."

Bartholomew looked at his foreman. "Pack your war bag. You're goin' to Wyoming."

"I hear it is right pretty country," Owen said, "although it suffers from the handicap of not bein' Texas."

Pitney gestured sharply. "Have either of you listened to a word I've said? I do not need Owen to come along. The three cowboys you have already mentioned are more than sufficient."

"Whether you want the help or not, you have it," Bartholomew said. "In fact, I'm puttin' Owen in charge until the bull reaches the BLC."

"Once I pay you, the bull is mine to do with as I deem fit," Pitney said in annoyance. "I will be in charge. Please ask your three hands to do as I tell them, and we will all get along quite fine."

"We haven't signed the agreement yet," Bartholomew noted. "And I am not goin' to sign until you accept the following conditions. First, Big Blue does not legally change hands until he gets to the BLC. Second, Owen is big sugar the whole way."

"I do not believe this."

"If payin' in advance makes you uncomfortable, I am willin' to accept half now and the other half upon delivery. That's more than fair, don't you think?"

"Need I remind you that I have come a long distance to make this purchase? Need I also remind you that we agreed on the terms before I left Wyoming? But most importantly, it is improper to change the terms halfway through a transaction."

"It's proper when it is in my best interests, and yours, as well, whether you know it or not."

Anger brought Pitney to his feet. "I have half a mind to walk out and forget the whole arrangement."

"Go right ahead," Bartholomew said. "But I won't sell to a man unless I respect him, and I don't have much respect for those who can't accept good advice."

"Are you saying I am an imbecile?"

"All I am sayin' is that I don't want your death on my conscience. Is that too much to ask?"

"Now you have me dying? This is becoming more ridiculous by the moment. Be reasonable, will you?"

Bartholomew had a ready response but his wife held up her hand and said, "We should discuss this later, after everyone has a chance to simmer down. Right

now why don't my husband and Owen show you
around while I fix supper?''

"I would like to see the bull," Pitney said. "This
Big Blue of yours. He is here, correct? Not off in the
brush somewhere?"

"I had some of the hands bring him in a week ago,"
Bartholomew said. "He is out in back of the stable."
Bartholomew rose. "I am more than happy to show
him to you. It will give you a better idea of what you
are in for."

Proctor stood and pecked her husband on the
cheek. "Don't be too long. We will eat in half an hour,
and I don't want your meal getting cold."

The men trailed her from the sitting room. She went
left and they turned right, down the hall to the front
porch. The sun was poised on the western rim of the
world, its blazing radiance contrasted by vivid splashes
of red, orange, and pink.

"There is nothin' like a Texas sunset," Owen
declared.

"Oh, I have seen a few in Bristol that rival any you
have here. And Wyoming is noted for its spectacular
sunrises and sunsets." Pitney sniffed a few times. "My
goodness. Where is that tantalizing aroma coming
from?'

Bartholomew pointed at a building halfway between
the stable and the bunkhouse. "The cookhouse. I believe in treatin' my men right, so I hired the best feed
and trough man I could afford. A gent who once
worked at one of the fanciest restaurants in St. Louis.''

The corral was partly in shadow as they came
around the stable. It appeared to be empty, prompting
Pitney to ask, "So where is this holy terror of yours?
I'm eager to set eyes on the brute."

"Then open them," Owen said, and nodded toward the darkest part of the shadow.

Alfred Pitney turned. His mouth fell open and he took a step back. "It can't be!"

7

Big Blue

The size of the monster was beyond belief. Longer than a horse, taller than a man, the bull was no lean-flanked scarecrow of the brush. It was massive, an enormous slab of muscle, with a hump on its front shoulders reminiscent of a buffalo. A redwood neck supported a great triangular head that sported the most amazing horns, nine feet long from tip to tip, with the trademark wicked curl. Its hooves were as big as buckets. Here was a living, breathing engine of destruction, the undisputed lord of the brush country.

Indeed, as Alfred Pitney gaped in wonderment, the thought crossed his mind that here was the lord of all the longhorns, the most magnificent bull ever—and it would soon be his, or, rather, the BLC's.

Its size was enhanced by its color, an extremely striking brindle blue. Blue was fairly common among longhorns. Pitney had already seen half a dozen or so. But the blue of this bull was twice the blue of any other. It was the blue of the sky or the blue of a lake, and it lent the creature a certain inherent majesty that no mere black or brown could rival.

"You do realize, I trust, that I could not sell you my biggest bull," James Bartholomew commented.

"This gargantuan isn't your largest?" Pitney marveled, trying to comprehend an animal that eclipsed this one.

"Big Blue is third, behind bulls I've named Bowie and King. I breed them exclusively with my own stock."

"Big Blue," Pitney repeated softly, as he might the name of a secret lover. "How fitting."

"Now that you've seen him, can you understand why takin' him north in a cattle car is out of the question?" Bartholomew asked.

"He would bust the car to kindlin'," Owen said.

Pitney stepped to the rails and extended a hand, thinking the bull might come to him to be petted. "How tame is he?"

"Not very," Bartholomew answered. "A tame bull wouldn't last long in the brush. Oh, he will let us lead him by a rope when he is in the mood to let us, but generally he does what he wants when he wants and there isn't a whole hell of a lot we can do about it."

"Then how in the world do I get him from here"—Pitney pointed at the ground—"to the BLC in Wyoming?"

"With a lot of care," was Bartholomew's reply, and he was not being glib.

"We have a few tricks," Owen said. "There are ways of makin' a bull do what you want."

"In season?" Pitney bent slightly to stare under Big Blue. "Will that work, though? I mean, how long do longhorns stay in season? And won't the cows be intractable as well?"

"Some of our cows are as tame as any you have at the BLC," Bartholomew informed him. "Not as a result of any effort on our part. They're friendlier to people, and don't spook as easily." He paused. "The cows I've picked for you are as tame as longhorns ever get. I think you will be happy with them."

"I'm happy with this brute." Pitney grinned at Big Blue. "He is everything I had hoped for, and more besides."

"So you think you have made a wise purchase?"

"Mr. Bartholomew, I could not be more pleased if he were made of solid gold. The infusion of his blood into the BLC's herd will work wonders. We will have the hardiest cattle in all of Wyoming."

"You hope," Bartholomew said. "Remember what I told you, though. There is no guarantee."

"I understand. But you must excuse me if I brim with confidence. Just *look* at him! I only wish the directors of the BLC were here so I could see the looks on their faces." Pitney laughed.

Owen came to the rails, reached into a shirt pocket, and held his hand toward Big Blue. The behemoth lumbered over and out flicked a tongue nearly as thick around as the cowboy's wrist.

Pitney arched both eyebrows.

"Sugar," Owen explained. "Big Blue has a sweet tooth. Another trick that might come in handy on the trail."

"I can't wait to start. How soon can we leave?"

"The cook was due yesterday," Bartholomew said. "I have the wagon all set to go but he will probably want to add a few provisions."

"What's this?" Pitney turned. "No one said anything about a wagon. It will slow us down."

Bartholomew grinned. "Big Blue doesn't walk all that fast unless he's so inclined. Don't worry. The wagon can keep up."

"Surely you don't expect us to eat our own cookin' the whole way?" Owen asked. "Why, that would be plumb inhuman."

"On long drives to market, and when my hands are out on the range brandin', a cook wagon always goes along. It's how we do things," Bartholomew said.

"It's a necessity," Owen amended.

"Wouldn't a string of packhorses suffice?" the Brit hopefully inquired.

"Horses can't carry all the grub and supplies a wagon can. And they sure as blazes can't whip up a hot meal as good as Pedro Chavez's brother."

"Who?"

It was Bartholomew who explained. "Pedro Chavez is my cook. He's from a village just over the border, and he can cook anything under the sun. Mexican dishes, American dishes, you name it. I can't spare him for as long as it will take you to reach Wyoming, so I've hired his older brother, Benedito, to cook for you. Pedro swears Benedito is a wizard with a fryin' pan."

"He better be," Owen said ominously.

"I had no idea cowboys attached so much importance to their stomachs," Pitney commented.

"You don't sound very pleased with the arrangements I've made," his host observed.

"Forgive me if I seem upset. It is just that there is a lot more to this enterprise than I envisioned, and I am not entirely convinced, as Owen would have it, of the necessity. However, I bow to your superior judgment in these matters. If you say a train is out of the question, then a train is out of the question. If you say we must have a cook and a wagon, then we will have a cook and a wagon." Pitney smiled. "Just so you don't tell me I must carry Big Blue piggyback, as you Yanks sometimes say."

The rancher chuckled, then moved toward the gate. "I suppose we might as well get it over with, then."

Pitney followed him. "Get what over with?"

"The introductions. Big Blue doesn't take to everyone, and if he doesn't take to you, you might want to rethink buyin' him or one day he's liable to put a hole in you where there shouldn't be a hole."

"He has gored others?" Pitney was horrified.

"Only two or three that I know of," Bartholomew said. "Two were rustlers whose rustlin' days are over. The third was a hand of mine by the name of Whiffy. He wouldn't take a bath but once a year. Claimed it was bad for the constitution."

"Bad for the nose, too," Owen said.

"Whiffy came close to Big Blue one day, and Big Blue took one sniff and lit out after him like a riled bear," Bartholomew related. "Luckily for Whiffy a horse was handy and Big Blue lost interest after a while. Scared Whiffy so bad, he up and quit on me."

"And good riddance." From Owen. "Whenever he was in breathin' distance, I about gagged."

Bartholomew opened the gate and beckoned to Pitney. Failing to hide his nervousness, the Britisher stepped into the corral and smiled thinly at Big Blue. "Nice bull," he said. "Be a nice bull and like the dickens out of me."

Owen hid a grin by tucking his chin to his chest, then looked up and said, "Don't worry. If he doesn't cotton to you, he'll snort and paw the ground before he charges, givin' you time to get out of there."

"How encouraging," Alfred Pitney said, but he did not sound encouraged. His throat bobbing, he stopped when Bartholomew halted some six feet from the longhorn. "What do I do?" he whispered.

"Just stand there."

Big Blue did not move, make a noise, or in any way acknowledge their presence. The seconds dragged into minutes.

Nervously wringing his fingers, his face slick with a sheen of sweat, Pitney made bold to ask, "What the deuce is it waiting for?"

"Stay still," Bartholomew cautioned.

Pitney tried. He repeatedly gnawed on his bottom lip and repeatedly clenched and unclenched his hands. Several more minutes went by, and he said in rising irritation, "I must be honest with you. I do not know how much more of this I can stand."

Suddenly Big Blue snorted and tossed his huge head, his horns dipping and rising as they would if he were to use them as weapons.

Startled, Pitney involuntarily backed up, straight into Owen, who had come up unnoticed behind him.

"Whatever you do," the foreman said, "don't run. He might come after you."

Pitney had to swallow to get his voice to work. "You don't say?" He raised an arm and wiped a sleeve across his face. "I'm not a coward," he said, defending himself. "It's just that—"

"No need to make excuses," Owen said. "We all feel jittery the first time. It's only natural."

Big Blue took a step toward them. His eyes were dark pools of bovine mystery; it was impossible to tell what the animal was thinking. Each wheezy breath was akin to the rasp of a bellows. His ears flicked and his nostrils flared, and he stamped a front hoof with a heavy *thud*.

"Oh Lord!" Pitney exclaimed, certain the sound had been the peal of his personal doom.

"Easy does it," Owen advised. "He's not fixin' to charge or he would lower his head. He's testin' you, is all."

"Bulls do that?"

"Longhorns do."

Big Blue ignored Bartholomew and Owen. Focused exclusively on Pitney, he came so close that Pitney saw a fly crawling about on the top of his head. Big Blue's warm breath fanned Pitney's face. Suddenly Pitney felt fingers touch his own, and something was pressed into his right palm. Something small and square.

"Give it to him," Owen whispered.

Pitney held the sugar on his palm below the bull's nose. "Let's make friends, shall we? That's a good chap. I promise all the sugar you can ever want and a harem that would turn a sultan green with envy."

Big Blue's tongue curled across Pitney's palm. Gobs of spit were left in its wake. The tongue was so slimy, Pitney was reminded of a giant snail. He could barely repress an unmanly shudder.

James Bartholomew smiled and clapped his guest on the back. "You did it. Big Blue has accepted you. So long as you abide by the rules, the two of you should get along just fine."

"What do you mean by rules?"

"There are things you shouldn't do when around a longhorn. Never startle one. Never shoot a gun too close to one, or shout unless you have to. Never walk directly in front of one. Never ride too close in front of one. Never walk or ride too close behind. Never put your hands anywhere near a longhorn's eyes or ears unless it's ailin', and then only if you absolutely have to."

Pitney studied his acquisition with rising dismay. "Is that all?"

"Don't ever get between a bull and water when it's thirsty. Don't ever get between a bull and a cow when romance is in the air. Don't ever smack this bull to get him to stand up or move. Don't ever wave a rope in his face. Or a blanket or a shirt. It goes without sayin' that you never hit or kick him. And for God's sake, whatever you do, don't ever try to ride him."

"You jest, of course?"

"We had a hand try it once," Owen said. "He was drunk, which is a poor excuse. Figured he would throw his saddle on Bowie and ride him." The cowboy sadly shook his head. "He learned the hard way a bull isn't a horse."

"That's preposterous," Pitney said. "I would never do anything so silly."

"I never reckoned Dexter would be so foolheaded, either," Owen said, "but that's what happens when you're so booze blind you can't count past three."

Bartholomew was holding the gate open for them. "I don't know about you two, but I'm famished."

"I'm invited to table?" Owen swatted dust from his shirt. "Why didn't you say so sooner? I should change."

"Proctor won't mind. She doesn't get fussy over a little dirt."

The sun was almost gone. The bright colors of a while ago had faded to gray except for a pink band that divided the horizon from the vault of sky. On the nearby hill several steers were starkly silhouetted in all their primitive majesty.

Pitney remembered the lean longhorns he had seen in the brush, and thought to ask, "How much does Big Blue weigh?"

"The last time we had him on the scale, close to fifteen hundred pounds. Mind you, weighing him is a challenge. He can be temperamental," Bartholomew said.

Owen remarked, "But he's nowhere near as bad as a bull we once had by the name of Lopsided. We called him that because one of his horns pointed up and the other pointed down. He wasn't near as big as Big Blue but he was snake mean. He liked nothin' better than to sneak up on a rider from the rear and bowl the horse and puncher over. Strange thing was, once they were down, he never gored them. He'd just stand there and look at them as if he thought it was funny."

"Forgive my presumption," Pitney said, "but you seem to attribute human characteristics to mere animals."

"There is nothin' mere about longhorns," Owen replied. "You'll learn on our way north to Wyoming. I only hope, after all the trouble we're goin' to, that Big Blue lets us take him there."

"Excuse me, but the bull doesn't have a say in the matter. I'm paying for him. He's going. It's that simple."

"Some bulls won't leave their home range," Owen said. "They go only so far and then stop and they won't go any farther. You can prod, you can cuss, you can rope them and pull on the rope until Armageddon, and they won't budge."

"That is my worry, too," Bartholomew said.

"A healthy swat on the rump should do the job, I

would think," Pitney said. "I have dealt with stubborn horses and mules."

Owen clucked like a disapproving hen. "Swat Big Blue on the backside and he will toss you on his horns until you look like a sieve."

"He's not a man-hater, though," Bartholomew said. "A few bulls hate people on general principle. About ten years ago there was a wild one called El Rojo. He had the nasty habit of attackin' every person he came across, whether mounted or on foot. Anyone passin' through El Rojo's range knew not to make a campfire at night because he was sure to come chargin' out of the dark at them. As I recollect, he killed five or six people. His last victim was a prospector. To give you some idea of how vicious that bull was, he not only gored the prospector to death, he also gored the old man's burro."

"Nothing was done about it?"

"Of course. Texans will only put up with so much contrariness, whether it's from Santa Anna or a longhorn. Punchers and hunters were always on the lookout for El Rojo. A settler named Nelson swore he put a slug into him. Four cowhands for the Slash H outfit chased El Rojo for over five miles, Winchesters blazing, but El Rojo got away."

"He was one tough bull," Owen said in admiration.

"It was a killer," Pitney declared. "It deserved to be exterminated without mercy." The next slipped out without him meaning to say it. "Or do Texans make distinctions between bulls that kill and, say, drummers who kill?"

"An eye for an eye," Owen said.

Bartholomew finished his account. "When the end came, El Rojo didn't go down fightin', as everyone thought he would. There was this old woman, Iris Mitchell. She and her husband built up a small spread, then the husband went and got himself killed by Comanches. So there she was, all by her lonesome one night, when she heard a ruckus outside. A brave soul, she took her husband's shotgun and went to check if the coyotes were tryin' to get at her chickens again. But it wasn't coyotes, it was El Rojo. Iris had left the barn door open and he had wandered in and was tearin' the place apart for the hell of it. When Proctor and I talked to her later, she told us she never suspected it was El Rojo. She thought it was a mangy wild longhorn. That old gal waited by the door, and when El Rojo poked his head out, she touched both barrels of her shotgun to his ear and squeezed both triggers. About knocked her on her backside, but she blew his brains clear out of his brainpan."

"Some of the ranchers took up a collection," Owen said. "Gave her a reward of five hundred dollars." Owen nodded at his employer. "Mr. Bartholomew put up the hog's share."

"It was only fittin'," Bartholomew said. "Iris wasn't well off, and she was too proud to ask for help. So in the end El Rojo did someone some good."

Proctor was waiting for them on the porch. "I was just comin' to fetch you. Supper is served, and I hope you have a healthy appetite."

"I could eat a longhorn," Pitney joked.

As it turned out, he did. The main course was beef. Specifically, thick, simmering longhorn steaks, dripping in their own juices, along with baked potatoes drowned in butter, crisp toast, and fresh-cut string beans. Prior to the main course Proctor took a page from a fine restaurant she once visited in St. Louis and offered steaming chicken soup sprinkled liberally with dumplings. Her side dishes consisted of bacon and collard greens, and corn pone, an indirect tribute to her grandmother, who hailed from Tennessee.

There were three desserts to choose from. Just out of the oven, a sweet potato pie proved popular with James and Owen. Pitney was more partial to what Proctor informed him was known as pandowdy, essentially sugar, spice, and apples mixed together, with a thick crust. A pudding with molasses as the main ingredient was also much to the Brit's liking.

Of all the differences between England and America, the most glaring, to Pitney, was their respective diets. The British loved their tea, while in America, ever since the Civil War, coffee had become the rage. Americans also had a fondness for butter that Pitney on occasion regarded as downright disgusting. Butter was lavishly used in pastries and puddings, lavishly applied to potatoes, lavishly added to every meat sauce, and layered thick on bread and biscuits.

Pitney was a firm believer in the adage that a little of anything went a long way, and that included butter. He also did not share the American passion for sweets. "The sweeter, the better" summed up that passion, as evinced not only by Proctor's three desserts, but by the many and sundry pies, pastries, and cakes offered at every eating establishment he had visited since crossing the pond, as he liked to think of the Atlantic Ocean.

Still, the pandowdy was delicious, and so unlike any of his customary fare back in Merry Olde that he treated himself to a second helping.

Proctor had heard the British were fond of tea, so

she had prepared a pot specifically for Pitney. Her husband would not touch tea with a ten-foot pole and she was not all that fond of it herself. Both the Bartholomews were addicted to washing their meals down with coffee. Lots and lots of coffee.

Afterward, James Bartholomew led the men into the sitting room and handed out cigars. Pitney preferred a pipe but to be polite he cut his cigar, lit it, and leaned back in his chair. "I could not have eaten another morsel," he commented, patting his stomach. "Please convey my highest esteem for your wife's culinary skills."

"Her food does make the mouth water," the rancher agreed. "I have to be careful or I'll pile on the pounds like a hog." He puffed on his cigar. "I don't suppose there is any chance you will reconsider goin' along?"

"We have been all through that."

"True, but folks have been known to change their minds." Bartholomew motioned at his foreman. "I've tried. Do the best you can. I won't hold it against you if he doesn't make it."

Alfred Pitney laughed. "Stop trying to scare me. It won't work. I didn't step off the boat yesterday." He inhaled too deeply on his cigar, and coughed. "I have lived in Wyoming Territory, off and on, for several years."

"Wyoming isn't Texas," Owen said.

"Oh, please. Texas has trouble with the Comanches, Wyoming has trouble with the Sioux and the Bannocks. Texas has longhorns and a jaguar or two, Wyoming has grizzlies and mountain lions. Texas has countless miles of wilderness, of plains and river country, Wyoming has countless miles of mountains and forest and prairie." Pitney smirked. "So you see, gentlemen, when you get down right to it, to quote you Yanks, there really is not that much difference between Wyoming Territory and Texas."

Owen erased the smirk by asking, "Have you ever shot anyone?"

"What a ridiculous question. I never have, I never will. What possible importance can that have?"

"I was just wonderin' how fond you are of livin'."

"There you go again." Pitney sighed in exasperation. "I thought you were a cowboy, not a gunsman. Your job is cows, not killing. Or would you have me believe the nonsense spouted by the penny dreadfuls? That all cowhands are deadly pistoleros? That is the right word, is it not? 'Pistoleros'?"

"You are entitled to believe what you want," James Bartholomew said. "We've done our part. We've warned you what's in store. Now whether you and the others make it to Wyoming Territory alive is in the hands of the Almighty."

"It can't be as bad as all that," Pitney said.

"It can be worse," Owen told him.

8

As Right As Right Can Be

The village of Carro seemed to be deserted. Nothing stirred except for a pair of pigs that were squabbling over a snake. One pig had the snake's head in its mouth, the other had the snake's tail, as, grunting and squealing, they engaged in a tug-of-war over which ate the spoils.

Four riders neared the adobe buildings. Peons were seated in the shade, backs to the walls, sombreros pulled low.

"It's siesta," James Bartholomew explained. "An hour each day when Mexicans take it easy."

"Odd habit," Alfred Pitney said. "But then, many say the same about us British and our teatime." He tilted his head to squint at the fiercely burning yellow disk in the center of the sky. "Can't say as I blame them for wanting to get out of this heat."

Lon Chalmers was in the lead, riding a claybank. His clothes, like theirs, were caked with dust from their three-day ride from the Bar 40. He rode with his right hand on his hip, close to his Colt, and alertly flicked his gaze from doorways to windows as they entered the narrow street. "Let's hope our comin' is the secret we hope it is."

Owen pushed his hat brim back and arched his

spine to relieve a kink. "The bandidos mostly stick to the hills." He repeated for emphasis, "Mostly."

Pitney took his handkerchief out and wiped his face and throat. "I still don't understand what this is all about, beyond the fact it has something to do with your cook's brother, the one you hired to go to Wyoming with me."

"You will understand soon enough," Bartholomew said, and did not elaborate. "I just wish you had stayed at the Bar 40 like I wanted. My wife was lookin' forward to showin' you off to her friends."

"I'm sorry, but I couldn't pass up the opportunity to see Mexico. I have never been here before."

"It's a great place for lizards to rear a family," Lon said.

They came to the plaza. In the center stood a fountain as dry as the surrounding desert. Across the square stood one of the few two-story buildings Carro boasted. Owen reined toward it and angled slightly to the right. Lon angled to the left. Their employer moved up between them and all three came to a halt just as a hatless man emerged.

Unlike the majority of the villagers, who wore plain white cotton shirts and pants, this man wore a baggy suit. He was balding. His moon of a face betrayed a worried expression, as did a nervous tic to his mouth.

"You are the alcalde?" James Bartholomew asked.

"Sí, señor."

"You know why we are here?"

The alcalde nodded. "Benedito told me you were coming." His English was flavored with a heavy accent. "I have been expecting you."

"And you have no objections? You did not notify the federales?"

"No, señor. Some of them are yours, and a man

must protect his own, no?" The alcalde offered a timid smile. "As for the soldados, we are a very small and very poor village, far from Mexico City. We do not want soldados to come. They always make us house and feed them, and some of them are very fat." Again he offered his timid smile.

"It is important no one interferes," Bartholomew said.

"Not to worry, señor," the alcalde said. "We do not—" He stopped. "How is it you Americanos say? Ah, yes. We do not stick our noses where they should not be. That is right?"

"I am obliged." Bartholomew lifted his reins. "About a mile past your village, and then a quarter of a mile to the hills?"

"Sí, señor. Be very careful. They are poison. They have killed many. They will not let you leave alive."

"That works both ways." Bartholomew touched his hat brim, then nodded at Owen and Lon Chalmers, who headed down a street that would take them out of Carro to the south. A few sombreros rose and dark eyes studied them without hostility.

Pitney goaded his sweaty sorrel up next to the rancher's bay. He thoughtfully regarded the bleak, arid landscape that stretched before them. "I see what Mr. Chalmers means about the lizards. He's quite the wit at times."

"Don't judge the whole country by one sleepy village. When I was younger I made it clear down to Chiapas once. Mexico is not all dry and dusty. There are spots as pretty as any you'll find north of the border."

"Isn't this the village where your cook, Pedro Chavez, is from? And his brother Benedito, who was supposed to be at your ranch a week ago?"

"It is," Bartholomew confirmed.

"Where is he? I want to give him a piece of my mind. He has unnecessarily delayed our departure."

"He has a good reason for not comin' sooner."

"What might that be?"

"He got word to us about an important matter that requires my immediate attention," the rancher said.

"I have a ranch in Wyoming to run. I can't spend the rest of the summer twiddling my thumbs in Texas."

"Well, if it's any comfort, your twiddlin' is about done. Benedito will ride back with us, and you can leave the next mornin'."

"I can hardly wait."

To the west, shimmering in the heat haze, rose a series of brown hills. Other than a lizard that skittered across the dirt track they were following, there wasn't a sign of life anywhere.

Owen and Lon drew their six-shooters. Each inserted a cartridge into an empty chamber under the hammer, then slid the revolver back into the holster.

"What was that all about?" Alfred Pitney inquired.

"As a precaution most gents only keep five pills in the wheel so if they drop their six-gun or it slips out of its holster, it won't go off by accident," Bartholomew explained. "A sixth pill is added only when it will be needed."

"Then my suspicion is correct. There is more to our being here than the cook," Pitney said. "You are up to something. You wanted me to stay behind because you are either afraid I will be a liability, or you are afraid I might be harmed."

"You've never shot anyone, remember? 'Never have, never will.' Weren't those your exact words?"

"Well, yes, but—" Pitney began.

"There is no law in these parts. No tin star to make arrests. The nearest garrison is over a hundred miles away. A man has to stand on his own two feet, which includes takin' the law into his hands if he has to, or the coyotes and the buzzards will pick him clean."

"Which is your quaint way of saying there might be violence?"

"No might about it," Bartholomew said. "You heard the mayor. The people we're after are the kind who would as soon slit your throat as look at you. That's why we soon part company for a spell."

"Like hell," Pitney declared. "You are not leaving me alone in this godforsaken wilderness."

The two cowboys reined up and leaned on their saddle horns. Bartholomew and the Brit followed suit. They were at a junction with another dirt track. This one, rutted by wagon wheels and pockmarked by hoofprints, led due west into the brown hills.

"This is it," Bartholomew said. "If we're not back in two hours, head for the border and don't stop until you're in Texas."

"Are you hard of hearing? I am going with you."

"It's too dangerous," Bartholomew insisted. "Be listenin', and when you hear shots, be on the lookout. If you spot riders wearin' sombreros instead of us, ride like the wind." He nodded at his foreman and Chalmers, and gigged his mount.

The Brit flicked his reins and within moments was once again at the rancher's side. "You are not losing me that easily."

"Please, Mr. Pitney. I ask you as a friend."

"I don't have the right to do as I want? I thought you Yanks were all about freedom. Isn't that why you fought to throw off Britain's yoke? Isn't that why the North fought the South? To free the slaves?"

James Bartholomew was quiet a while, his eyes hidden by his hat brim. Finally he said, with no enthusiasm, "All right. It's on your shoulders. I don't want any gripes after, if it wasn't to your liking."

"Gripes in what regard?" Pitney asked, but he did not receive an answer. The rare discourtesy rankled.

Save for the dull *clop* of hooves and the creak of saddle leather, the four of them rode in silence. Gradually the hills grew until they were as high as any along the front range of the Rockies. But where the foothills of Wyoming were often lushly timbered, on these vegetation was sparse. A few scrubs, a few dry blades of grass, and that was it.

As they came closer, Lon Chalmers moved ahead of Owen. Lon's hand was always on his Colt and he rode with the wary posture of a man who expected at any moment that a mountain lion would spring out at him.

The trail wound like a serpent in among the hills. A slash of green midway up the next slope was a remarkable exception to the general aridity. Not surprisingly, the track pointed directly toward it.

"That's where they'll be, boss," Lon said without turning his head. "A spring, most likely, to water the stock."

"Remember my instructions. Owen, are you sure about this?" Bartholomew stared at his foreman's broad back. "It's not why I hired you on."

"If Lon can do it, I can." Owen sounded offended.

"Maybe there will only be a few," Lon said. "Maybe I can take care of all of them, if it comes to that."

"It will," Owen predicted.

The oasis covered several acres. Grass grew thick, sprinkled with trees. A fence enclosed two of the acres, the workmanship shoddy, consisting of broken limbs lashed together with rawhide. Over thirty head of cattle were at ease near a large spring. Some were longhorns, some were not.

To the left were buildings, half a dozen, all as shabby as the fence, the largest a shack that looked fit to be blown away by the next strong wind. A barn stood halfway completed, and from the look of things, never would be. Scattered about were old saddles, rusted tools, and general litter.

"What a hovel," Pitney muttered.

Lon Chalmers reined to the left and came to a halt within a few yards of the shack. Owen drew rein in front of the stable. Bartholomew gestured at Pitney to stay well back, then came to a stop between the two cowboys. All three sat quietly, waiting. They did not wait long.

Leather hinges creaked and the shack door swung out. Through it came a burly Mexican in a brown sombrero and a brown leather vest decorated with silver studs. His huge spurs jingled loudly. Strapped around his thick waist was a pair of pearl-handled revolvers. Swarthy features curled in a cold smile. "What is this? Four gringos have come to visit Paco?"

"Then you are Paco Ramirez," Bartholomew said, stating it, not asking. "We have the right place."

Ramirez's bushy brows knit. "You have heard of Paco, gringo? From who, Paco wonders? Paco wonders, too, why you are here?"

Lon Chalmers slid his right boot from its stirrup, swung his leg over his saddle horn, and slid to the ground, his back to his horse and his hand on his Colt. Not once did he take his eyes off Ramirez. "Tell your pard at the window to step out where I can see him."

"You have eyes like a hawk, hombre." Paco Ramirez shifted and barked a command in Spanish. Not one but two more men came out of the shack, their clothes much like his, their dark faces similarly stamped with the imprint of the worst traits human nature offered. Both wore pistols. They stepped to the left, spreading out until they were six feet apart.

"I was told there are more," Bartholomew said.

Ramirez grinned wickedly. "There are, gringo. Plenty more, eh?" He hollered, again in Spanish, and four more Mexicans materialized out of the dry air, two from the stable and two from behind other buildings. Nearly all were grinning, as if at a great joke.

"Nice herd you have there."

"It is not very big," Ramirez said, "but it is big enough for Paco's needs."

Bartholomew kneed his mount over to the fence. One of the men who had come out of the house turned as Bartholomew's horse moved so Bartholomew was always in front of him. The rancher dismounted and studied the animals. "Strange, how many brands there are."

"I bought them from many different ranchos."

"You have bills of sale, do you? Signed by the former owners?" Bartholomew's face had hardened.

Ramirez laughed. "Who bothers with those little pieces of paper, eh, gringo? I use them to light my cigarros."

"That's not very wise. Without proof, there are some who will say you helped yourself to these animals without their owners' knowledge."

"Those who say so would be calling Paco a liar. That would upset Paco. It would upset Paco very much."

"Paco's inglés es muy excelente."

"Gracias, gringo. Your español, it is pretty good. But so there is no mistake, I say this next only in your language." Ramirez paused. "It is not healthy for you to be here."

"Why, Paco, was that a threat?" Bartholomew quietly asked.

"No, gringo. You know what it is. So please, por favor. Paco does not want trouble."

"Then Paco should keep proof that all his cows are his. Otherwise he is bound to have trouble whether he wants trouble or not."

"Can you count, gringo? There are seven of us and only four of you. So again, por favor, climb back on your caballo and go. Because I know how gringos think. If you and these others do not return to where you came from, more gringos will come, and more after them, until poor Paco has gringos up to his ears."

"Poor Paco should not help himself to gringo cattle if poor Paco does not want gringos knockin' at his door."

The amusement in Ramirez's eyes faded and was replaced by flinty resentment. "No more, gringo. Do as Paco has told you, and do it pronto."

Bartholomew stayed where he was. "Why, look there," he said. "As I live and breathe."

"Look where?" Ramirez glanced down the hill and then up the hill. "I do not see anyone."

"Yonder." Bartholomew pointed. "That longhorn with the Bar 40 brand. And there's another. And another. Why, there must be five or six. They have strayed a long way off their range."

"You know of this Bar 40, gringo?"

"I own the Bar 40, bandido. I would call you a rustler but I hear that when you are not busy stealin' cows, you steal money."

Paco Ramirez scowled. "So that is how it is. You have come all this way over a few cows?"

"I do not expect you to savvy. But to a cowman, his cows are his life, and when you take one, you insult him worse than if you called his mother a puta."

Ramirez digested that, then said confidently, "But there are still seven of us and only four of you. That one"—he jabbed a thumb at Alfred Pitney—"has not the cojones, eh? So maybe it is really seven to three, and the three are cowboys. Good with cows but maybe not so good with pistolas."

Slowly turning, Bartholomew came back and stood between Owen and Lon. He motioned at the latter. "I would like you to make the acquaintance of one of my hands. His name is Lon Chalmers. Maybe you have heard of him? Not quite four years ago, it would be."

"Chalmers?" Ramirez repeated, scratching his stubble. "I cannot say I have. It is importante?"

"Four years ago," Bartholomew reiterated. "In a cantina in Piedras Negras."

Ramirez jerked his head up, his eyes widening. "He is *that* one? Es verdad? You would not lie to Paco?"

Lon Chalmers finally spoke. "Es verdad." He hooked his thumbs in his belt in an attitude of casual indifference, but under his sandy hair his face was chiseled from marble.

"This Paco does not like." Ramirez looked at his companions and said something in Spanish, the words tripping swiftly from his tongue. To a man, they tensed and studied Chalmers with keen interest.

"We are taking the Bar 40 cows back with us," Bartholomew announced.

"Paco is feeling generous today, gringo. Paco thinks he will let you. With his blessings."

"That is not all," the rancher said. "We must make sure Paco does not help himself to any more Bar 40 cattle."

"So you want Paco to give his word, eh?" Ramirer's smile reeked of insincerity. "Very well. Paco swears by the Blessed Virgin that he will never again come near your Bar 40. How is that?"

"It's not enough."

"What else can Paco do? Or is it you want him to take his men and go south to Coahuila? Or west to Sonora?"

Bartholomew shook his head. "You still do not savvy."

Astonishment, and something more, caused Ramirez to scowl darkly. "It is a joke, gringo, yes? You tease poor Paco? You would not go so far, would you?"

It was Lon Chalmers who answered him. "Whenever you're ready to roll the dice."

"An hombre like you?" Ramirez said to him in mild surprise. "Over a bunch of stupid cows? How can this be?"

"I ride for the brand," Lon said proudly.

"Paco sees." Ramirez lowered his arms. "But maybe you are not the man you were, eh? Four years is a long time. You are maybe not so fast as then, Paco thinks."

"Paco thinks wrong." Without taking his eyes off the bandit leader, Lon raised his voice. "I'll take our friend, here, the one on my left, and the two on my right. Mr. Bartholomew, can you take the string bean nearest you? I'd be obliged. Owen, that leaves the last two."

"We will kill you, gringo," Paco Ramirez hissed. "You and these cow herders and the gringo with the small hat."

Lon said nothing.

"Paco knows how you gringos are. You think you are better than us, eh? More noble than us lowly greasers. So you will let us draw first, and you will die. Because Paco is quick, too. Paco would not have lived so long if Paco was not." Ramirez poised his hands over the pearl handles of his twin pistolas.

"Paco has it all worked out," Lon Chalmers said. "Except for his mistake. But it is the mistake that makes all the difference."

"What mistake?" Ramirez angrily demanded.

"Thinkin' I'm noble. Thinkin' I would do like a marshal or a sheriff and let you go for your hardware first. Lawdogs can't gun folks in cold blood. But I'm not wearin' a badge. I can shoot anyone, anywhere, anytime." And with that, Lon's right hand flashed down and up, moving so fast it was a blur. One instant the Colt was in its holster, the next it boomed like thunder. The slug tore through Paco Ramirez from sternum to shoulder blade and the bandit leader staggered back with a look of incredulity on his swarthy face.

Even as he fired, Lon Chalmers pivoted on a boot heel and instinctively centered his Colt on the chest of the bandido to his left. The man was much too slow in reacting; his fingers had not yet curled around his revolver when Lon's Colt banged a second time.

The two shots had been fired so swiftly there was

barely a whisker between them. Now Lon reversed direction, swinging to his right, the Colt low in front of him, his knees slightly tucked. The rest of the bandits were belatedly clawing for their revolvers. Lon fired, and the temple of a third Mexican burst in a shower of hair and skull bone.

Just like that, Lon fanned his Colt, slapping the edge of his left hand against the hammer while keeping the trigger pressed. His fourth shot in half as many seconds dissolved a dark eyeball and blew out the rear of the fourth bandit's skull.

The man Bartholomew faced had been looking at Ramirez and was so shocked at seeing Ramirez take a slug, he was sluggish in reaching for his pistol. Bartholomew had the precious twinkling of time he needed to take deliberate aim at the middle of the man's face and squeeze.

That left the Bar 40's foreman.

Owen was not as quick as Lon Chalmers but he was faster than his employer, and his first shot rang out before Bartholomew's. The throat of the bandit in front of Owen flew apart, spouting a scarlet fountain. Owen spun. He had not mastered the trick of fanning, as Chalmers had, but he could bang off several shots in succession more swiftly than most. He proved it now by putting three slugs into the last Mexican before the man could fire.

In the silence that ensued, the only sounds were Alfred Pitney's sharp intake of breath and the moo of a cow disturbed by the blasts.

"That's that," James Bartholomew said.

Lon Chalmers immediately began to reload. He did not look around when Pitney clucked to his sorrel and came over close to the body of Paco Ramirez.

"You killed them."

"That was the general notion, English."

"But how? I mean, I never saw anyone draw and fire a gun so fast in my life. You shot four men before a single one got off a shot."

"They were born with a bad case of the slows," Lon said.

"There is more to it than that."

"I wasn't always a cowboy," Lon said. "When I was younger I was wild and reckless. I lived by my wits and my Colt. I gambled. I spent my nights with doves. I was in more than a few shootin' scrapes." About to slide a cartridge into the cylinder, he stared at the body at his feet. "Once, down to Piedras Negras, I killed five men when they accused me of cheatin' at cards and went for their artillery. One of them winged me. I got blood poisonin' and about lost an arm. It made me think. When I ran into Mr. Bartholomew not long after that and he offered me a chance to start over, I jumped at it. I've been a cowboy ever since, and made some good friends, like Owen."

"Were they right, Mr. Chalmers?"

"Who?"

"The five men in Piedras Negras. The five men you killed. The five who accused you of cheating. Were they right?"

Lon Chalmers twirled his Colt into its holster. "As right as right can be."

9

Feathers and Frying Pans

Owen and Lon Chalmers were given charge of the cattle. Bartholomew told them to swing wide of Carro, in case Ramirez had friends there.

"Mr. Pitney and I will catch up with you by noon tomorrow at the latest. Once we're back at the ranch, we'll check the brands, and I'll send word to as many owners as we recognize."

They had mounted and were about to depart when a sound from inside the shack caused Lon Chalmers to whip around in the saddle and streak out his Colt, and Owen to yank his Winchester from its saddle scabbard.

The sound was a strangled gurgle ending in a high-pitched whine, and there could be no doubt it came from a human throat. Bartholomew swung down. Flanked by his punchers, he moved warily to within a few feet of the shadowed doorway. "Come on out, whoever you are," he commanded.

No one appeared. Lon gave the rancher a questioning look, and Bartholomew nodded. Instantly, the former gun hand darted inside. Owen had the Winchester to his shoulder, prepared for the worst. Tense seconds went by, and then Lon filled the doorway and beckoned for them to enter. Pitney brought up the rear.

The inside was filthy. Dirty dishes and cooking utensils were haphazardly piled beside a wooden bucket never used to bring in water to clean them. Clothes and other personal items were scattered about the floor. The place reeked of body odor and other unsavory odors. Cards lay on a table ringed by chairs. Blankets lay against each of the walls.

Lon led them across the room to a dark doorway. Instead of a door, it was covered by a tattered blanket. He pulled it aside and indicated they should precede him.

Bartholomew stepped through first, and grunted in surprise. Owen slid through with his Winchester still tucked to his shoulder, then lowered it and uttered an oath. Pitney, his face scrunched in disgust at the filth and the reek, merely poked his head in the room, and gasped.

All the room contained was a bed that had seen better times. Spread-eagle on it, her wrists and ankles bound to the wooden frame, was a woman from north of the border. A female of exceptionally obese proportions. Her face was a moon of pale skin, her neck hung in folds, her breasts were pendulous watermelons, her thighs a pair of alabaster pillars. She was so wide, the bed barely contained her.

"How hideous!" Pitney blurted.

A gag was over her mouth. Her pale blue eyes mirrored mute appeal as she tugged at the ropes binding her and mouthed words they could not understand.

Bartholomew moved to the head of the bed and hurriedly undid the gag. As he removed it, she coughed and spat, then barked angrily at him, "About damn time! I thought you were going to stand there all day ogling my lovelies."

"Ma'am?"

"The wrists, you idiot," the woman said, wriggling them. "The wrists and the ankles so I can get up and find something to wear. You don't expect to get so grand a view for free, do you?"

"Ma'am, I assure you—"

"Spare me your male lies. Hustle, damn it. If you knew how long I've been lyin' here, you wouldn't be standing there like a lump of wood."

Bartholomew took one side, Owen the other, and they soon had the woman free. They reached down to help her up but she pushed them away and came up off the bed in a rolling wave of pale flesh. Without any explanation, she waddled from the room, shoving Pitney from her path with a curt "Out of my way! The outhouse is calling!" She was out the front door with surprising swiftness.

"Land sakes!" Bartholomew breathed.

"What do we do with her?" Owen asked.

"We could add her to the herd," Lon said.

Pitney shuddered and followed them out, saying, "What would those men want with a woman like that?"

"What do you think they wanted?" Lon rejoined. "Or don't you Brits like a jab now and then?"

"Don't be vulgar," Pitney said. "Besides, you couldn't pay me to jab her, as you so quaintly phrase it." He shuddered again. "It would give me nightmares."

"She is a lady and will be treated as such," Bartholomew informed them.

"If she's a lady, I'm the ruddy queen."

"How do you reckon she got here?" Owen wondered.

Lon Chalmers replied, "The ocean dried up and she was stranded with the rest of the whales."

Bartholomew colored. "Enough of that kind of talk."

By then they were outside. The outhouse door slammed and the woman came around the rear corner of the shack. She made no attempt to cover herself, and was fussing with her tangle of light brown hair, which had not been washed in so long it was filthy.

"I must look a sight."

"No more than a buffalo with mange," Lon said, earning a stern glance from his employer.

"What is your name, ma'am?" Bartholomew inquired. "And how is it you came to be among these bandits?"

"First things first. You wouldn't want the sun to burn my delicate skin to a crisp, would you?" The woman waddled inside.

The four men looked at one another and after a bit Lon said, "I say we light a shuck while we can."

"Just run off and leave her?" Bartholomew shook his head. "It wouldn't be decent."

"Well, it's a cinch we can't keep her," Owen said. "Not unless you want Proctor to use you for target practice."

Pitney adjusted his derby, commenting, "What is the problem? We turn her over to the Mexican authorities and let them deal with her."

"That's the last thing we want to do," Bartholomew said, indicating the bodies that lay in postures of violent death.

They hushed as the woman reemerged. She had slit

a blanket in the middle and was wearing it as an over-sized poncho, a rope tied around her waist as a belt. "I don't know where my dress got to," she remarked. "That damn Paco probably burned it to spite me."

Bartholomew asked, "Do you have a name, ma'am?"

"Of course. Doesn't everyone? Folks call me Sweet Sally. My last name is Fitzsimmons but I don't hardly ever use it. I'm from Rhode Island originally. My husband took me west. He worked for the railroad. But there was an accident and he was run over by a train, leaving me a widow. I had twenty dollars to my name. It didn't last long. One thing led to another, and I ended up doing what most girls do when they need to eat and don't have any other means to earn their food."

"We understand."

"How could you? You're men." Sweet Sally glanced down and saw her former captor. "Well, lookee here. Mr. Come-with-me-and-we-will-pay-you-a-hundred-gringo-dollars-a-week. My ass." She raised her right foot and brought it smashing down onto the dead bandit's face. Ramirez's nose crunched and his mouth was pulp. "I wanted to kill him so bad I could taste it."

"They lured you with the promise of money?" Bartholomew said. "Then held you against your will? How despicable."

"Against my will? Mister, when were you hatched? I stayed because Paco promised to make good the money he owed me after he found a buyer for the cattle he stole."

"But the rope. The gag."

"That's how Paco liked to do it. He was working up to pleasuring me when you rode up."

"My word!" Pitney declared.

Sweet Sally bestowed a warm smile on him. "Foreigner, aren't you? Say, you sure do dress peculiar. But you must have money to afford those fancy duds." She winked slyly. "I like men with money."

"Thank God I'm broke," Lon said, and before she could retort, he asked his employer, "Do you want me to make a tally of the stolen cattle before we head out?"

"It can wait," Bartholomew said. "Now that I think about it, we have something else to do first. We can't ride off and leave these bodies to rot."

"Why not?" Lon asked. "Buzzards have to eat."

"We shot them, we should plant them. Owen, you two hunt for a shovel. If you can't find one, use sticks or rocks. Dig shallow graves. No need to wear yourselves out."

"Yes, sir," the foreman said, and with Lon Chalmers in tow, he headed for the barn.

Bartholomew faced Sweet Sally. "We will keep you company until they are done." He introduced himself and the man from Britain. "Sorry about your friend Paco, but he rustled some of my stock. I had to make an object lesson of him or pretty soon every rustler south of the border would think he had the God-given right to help himself to my cattle."

"No need to apologize, mister. Paco wasn't a friend or anything. We had a business arrangement, nothing more." Sally fiddled with her hair. "Pokes don't come free, although most men wish they did."

"How could you?" Pitney asked, horrified at the images his imagination conjured of her and the bandits.

"A gal doesn't have a whole lot of choices these

days, mister. Maybe it's different wherever you hail from, but over here there aren't a lot of good jobs for those of us in dresses. There's sewing, but my fingers are so big I can't hardly work a needle and thread. There's cooking, but I can't keep my hands off food as it is."

"Even so," Pitney said, "how could you permit men to touch you so intimately for money? Don't you find it reprehensible?"

"Hell, I don't even know what that means." Sweet Sally undid her rope belt and loosened it slightly, then retied it. "As for the other, back when I was married I used to think my body was special. I was skinny then, believe it or not, and no one ever touched me except my husband."

"Your personal life is your own," Bartholomew interrupted.

"I don't mind sharing the details," Sweet Sally said. "There's not much more. I was hired on at a high-priced bawdy house in Denver. That's where I learned the tricks of my trade. How to do it without really doing it. All the ways to hoodwink a man and get it over with sooner. Those sorts of things."

"We really don't need to hear this."

"I worked some of the best houses until I put on too much weight for the clients. None of the madams would hire me. I started working in saloons, drifting from place to place, half the time so drunk I didn't know where I was, and ended up in a dive just over the border. That's where Paco found me and offered the hundred a month he didn't have."

"How terrible," Pitney said.

Sweet Sally smiled and brazenly hooked her arm through his. "I like you, foreigner or no. Want to go for a stroll? I can stand the exercise. And I know a quiet spot where it's nice and shady."

"I would rather not, if you don't mind," Pitney said, prying at her hand. "Perhaps some other time."

"What's the matter? You shy, Pitley? Or is it that you've never done it with a red-blooded American girl and don't think you can keep up?"

"It's Pit*ney*, not Pitley." Pitney glanced to the right and the left as if contemplating fleeing. Instead he stammered, "I have never paid for—that is, I am not the—that is, it's all well and good—that is to say, this is hardly the time and the place."

"I suppose not." Sweet Sally ran a pudgy hand along his forearm. "Tell you what. While you boys are burying the bodies and whatnot, I'll go take a bath. I usually only do it once a month, but for you, Pitley, honey, I'll get extra clean." She flounced off toward the spring.

"Dear God," Alfred Pitney said.

"I reckon she's taken a shine to you," Bartholomew said. "It must be your dashin' foreign air."

"That's not even remotely humorous. The mere thought of bedding that creature makes me queasy. It's ludicrous."

"Not to her. Could be she'll move on you tonight," Bartholomew cautioned. "To a woman like her, you're quite a catch. She might already see herself as Mrs. Pitley."

"Preposterous," Pitney said in disgust. His gaze drifted toward the bulk in the blanket, and fear blossomed. "She wouldn't think that, would she? That I would take her as my wife?"

"There's no tellin' with females. My Proctor is as sensible as they come and she still does things that make me want to beat my head against a tree. Doves are even more fickle."

"But she just met me!"

"Ever hear of love at first sight?" Bartholomew grinned. "I'll do what I can to help but once a woman sets her sights on a man, he's as good as branded."

Within the hour the bodies were underground. Sweet Sally came back with her wet hair plastered to her head and beads of water dripping from her stout arms and legs. "Smell me now," she urged Pitney, tilting her neck in invitation. "I'm clean enough to eat off of."

Owen and Lon rounded up the bandits' horses. The largest was offered to Sally, who had to be boosted into the saddle. It required both cowboys; she was too heavy for just one.

Bartholomew rode point, Pitney hovering close. He visibly cringed when Sweet Sally brought her mount up next to theirs and beamed happily at him.

"Let's get acquainted. I want to learn all there is about you. Where you are from, why you talk so funny, whether you have any land and your own house, that sort of stuff."

"We have something else to talk over first," Bartholomew interrupted. "Where do you want us to leave you? This side of the border or north of it?"

Sweet Sally did not hide her disappointment. "I'd rather go wherever you're going. Pitley and me are just getting acquainted."

"We are bound for my ranch, and I am afraid my wife would take exception to your presence." Bartholomew winked at Pitney. "So where will it be? We pass near Laredo. Or I can have one of my hands take you as far as San Antonio."

"I've always wanted to go there. A friend of mine—we call her Gimpy on account of she was born with one leg shorter than the other—she told me that the men there like their womenfolk on the heavy side. I'd be in clover."

Alfred Pitney had a better idea. "Why don't we stop at the first town we come to and I will foot the bill for a new dress? I might even be persuaded to buy you a stage ticket to San Antonio."

"You would do that for me?" Sweet Sally's hand fluttered to the fleshy folds of her neck.

"It would be my distinct pleasure."

"Then that's what we'll do," Bartholomew said. "First, though, I have a cook to collect." He yelled to Owen and the foreman trotted up from the flank. "I'm goin' to fetch Benedito. Be lookin' for us about noon tomorrow."

Pitney quickly piped up, "I would like to go with you, if you don't mind. I am eager to meet Mr. Chavez."

"You are?" Owen said.

Sweet Sally put a hand on the Britisher's arm. "You're leaving? I was looking forward to spending the night together."

"Business before pleasure, I am afraid," Pitney intoned, and kneed his horse over next to his host's. "Ready when you are."

They left the herd raising dust in their wake and rode north until Carro's adobe dwellings sprouted from the baked plain. Bartholomew reined due east. Presently the character of the land changed. Spots of green appeared, small plots worked by farmers who barely eked enough bounty from the soil to feed their inevitably large families.

"I've never seen such poverty," Pitney commented.

Their garments were simple cotton, like those of the villagers, only plainer. Many went barefoot. Sandals were a luxury they could not afford. The women dressed in simple shifts or loose blouses and wide skirts as plain as the clothes of their men. The well-to-do among them owned a burro. Horses were another luxury, and only one farm in twenty had one.

Their meals, as Bartholomew related to his guest, consisted largely of frijoles, or beans, boiled and mashed and fried in lard, and cornmeal tortillas, a thin bread common to tacos, enchiladas, and tostadas. Rice was another staple.

"It sounds most unappetizing."

Bartholomew gave him a sharp glance. "Thank God you said that to me and not a Mexican. They're liable to stab you. And just so you know, I find Mexican food as tasty as any other." He rose in the stirrups to better view a farm ahead. "You'll change your mind before you reach Wyoming."

"I will believe it when that happens," Pitney said.

The farm they were approaching was no different from the others except that there was a certain neatness and order. The straw on the roof was fresh, the walls had been swept clean of dust, and the windowsill and jambs had been painted a bright yellow. In a small corral stood a burro. Nearby, on a hammock slung between two trees, lay a man with a big belly in a serape, a sombrero pulled low over his face.

Bartholomew alighted, handed the reins to Pitney, and ambled over to the hammock. "Buenos tardes. Would you be Señor Chavez? Benedito Chavez?"

"And if I am?" came a muffled reply from under the sombrero.

"Then you should be expectin' me. I'm James Bartholomew. Your brother, Pedro, is the cook at my ranch. You sent him word about a certain bandit who had cattle of mine. I'm in your debt."

"Paco Ramirez is a pig."

"Paco Ramirez *was* a pig," Bartholomew said. "But he is not the main reason I am here. Your brother told you, did he not, about the position I have open?"

"Sí, Señor Bartholomew. He sent word asking me to go with some of your cowboys to a place far to the north. A place with a strange name. Why-ome-ing. I sent word I was not interested."

"What?" Bartholomew blurted. "The way Pedro talked, I took it for granted you had agreed."

"Perhaps the man I sent did not reach him."

"I ask you to reconsider. I need a good cook, and Pedro says you are as good as he is."

"I am better, señor," Benedito stated.

"All the more reason for me to hire you. Why did you decline, if I may ask?"

The hammock moved to the shrug of the man's shoulders. "It is a long way, this Why-ome-ing. I will be gone from my home many weeks. You ask me to give up my casa for how much money?"

"Forty dollars a month," Bartholomew said. "The same as I pay most of my punchers."

"But these punchers, they do not cook, sí? They cannot make tostadas that would have your mouth water? Or enchiladas to make your stomach growl?" Benedito raised his hat brim a fraction. "It seems to me, señor, someone who can do all that is worth a little more than the same as most of your punchers."

"Fifty dollars a month, then, with three months

guaranteed whether it takes that long or not," Bartholomew offered.

"That is something to think about," Benedito said. "It is also good to think about the many rivers that must be crossed. Rivers in which a man can drown. And since it is summer, the days will be as hot as my oven. Most uncomfortable, sí?"

"What is it you want? Sixty a month?"

"I only want what is fair, señor," Benedito said. "How much would be fair to pay you to endure the rivers and the heat?"

Without hesitation Bartholomew said, "Sixty it is, then. Is that acceptable?"

"It helps me accept the rivers and the heat. But then there are the Indians. The Sioux, I hear, like to take hair that belongs to others. White hair, Mexican hair, is all the same to them."

"Sixty-five dollars."

"That is most generous, señor. But my hair is worth more than five dollars to me. Is your hair not worth more than five dollars to you?"

"Seventy dollars," Bartholomew said. "And that's as high as I can go."

"You surprise me, señor. You have a big ranch, one of the biggest in all of Texas. You have many cattle, one of the biggest herds north of the Rio Grande. Yet you can only pay seventy-five dollars to the man who will keep your punchers well fed?"

"Enough tomfoolery," Bartholomew said. "How much do you really want?"

"One hundred dollars a month. Plus expenses, of course."

Bartholomew stared at the sombrero. "I can't decide whether to laugh or leave. I've never paid a cook that much. Not even your brother."

"Would you pay eighty dollars for my services as a cook? Keeping always in mind the rivers and the heat and the Indians who like to take hair."

"I reckon I can go to eighty, yes." Bartholomew held out his hand. "If we have a deal, let's shake."

"In a moment, señor. First, how much would you pay for the services of a doctor? Fifty? Sixty? Perhaps another eighty?"

"You're proddin' too hard."

"Not at all, señor. Or hasn't my brother told you? I am not without some small skill as a healer. And because it is a small skill, I will not ask for more than twenty dollars more. One hundred dollars is fair to pay for the services of a cook *and* a healer, yes?"

"For both, yes." Bartholomew capitulated, but he was grinning. "Now how long will it take you to pack whatever you want to take along?"

Benedito Chavez pushed his sombrero back, revealing friendly brown eyes and a sincere smile. "I hope you will not think badly of me, señor, but I have been packed since my brother sent word you would like me to work for you."

"Damn," James Bartholomew said.

"One more thing, señor. Please do not tell Pedro how much you are paying me. He will be very mad."

"He's not the only one," the rancher grumbled.

The two men laughed.

10
Why-ome-ing or Bust

They left the Bar 40 at the crack of dawn. The night before, Benedito Chavez had checked and rechecked the chuck wagon and all it contained, ensuring that he had everything he would need for their arduous trek of eleven hundred miles. His brother, Pedro, helped.

It had been decided that Owen would take two extra horses for each hand. On a normal trail drive each puncher had a remuda of anywhere from six to ten, depending on the size of the herd. Since they were taking only Big Blue and five cows, two extra horses were considered more than enough. They tied the animals to the rear of the chuck wagon.

The punchers were excited. None of them had ever been to Wyoming Territory. Lon Chalmers had come close when he visited Denver back during the days of his wild and violent youth.

"I don't need to remind you," Bartholomew said to them the evening before, "how much is at stake." He had invited them all up to the house for supper. "Not only for the Bar 40 but for the BLC. Big Blue is an important investment for them. I have given my word you will get him to their ranch, and I trust you will carry it out as if I were with you."

"He wants to go," Proctor mentioned. "He wants to go so much. It's just not possible. He's needed here."

Owen cleared his throat. "You have my range word we'll get the job done, boss. The four of us are as loyal to the brand as they come."

"I know that," Bartholomew responded with deep emotion. "I would trust the four of you with my life."

The cowboys shifted uncomfortably in their chairs. Slim actually blushed. Cleveland developed an interest in the flowers in a vase.

Alfred Pitney picked that moment to say, "I won't hold it against any of you if something goes wrong. I have been most impressed with your meticulous preparations. You have anticipated everything that can happen."

"We have tried," the rancher said, "but on the trail there are a thousand and one things that can go wrong. Luck plays as much a part as plannin'. Maybe more."

"Don't forget Providence," Proctor said. "The Good Lord will watch over them and preserve them."

"That reminds me," Bartholomew said. "Have all of you packed extra ammunition?"

"We could hold off the whole Sioux nation," Owen said.

Their employer smiled. "Hopefully it won't come to that." Then he went around the table, from puncher to puncher, silently shaking their hands. He shook Owen's last. "Make it back alive. All of you. The bull is important but your lives matter more."

So there they were, the next morning, about to depart. A golden crown rimmed the world. The rooster crowed out by the coop. A male wren warbled from his perch on the birdhouse that hung from a tree near the ranch house. High atop the stable a flock of pigeons cooed.

Punchers filed from the bunkhouse to see them off. Most had been on trail drives and had experienced the many perils.

Slim opened the corral gate and rode in. A coiled rope in hand, he swung his arm and said, "Rise and shine! You're goin' for a walk."

Big Blue came out of the shadows. He was so immense he seemed to dwarf Slim's horse. Slowly, almost regally, he walked out the gate. Fortunately he was higher than the top rail and his horns could make it through. He allowed himself to be guided to a position ahead of the chuck wagon.

"Bring the others," Bartholomew commanded.

Lon and Cleveland rode around to the other side of the stable and returned herding five longhorns. All were cows. Some of the hands exchanged knowing looks. Steers could be more tractable but Alfred Pitney wanted cows. The Brit had hopes of not only breeding Big Blue with the BLC's own cattle, but also starting a herd of longhorns of his own. All the cows were young, and none had yet calved. If they had, they would not have been chosen. There was no separating a cow from her calf. She would die before she would let that happen.

The five selected were different hues. One was yellow, one was cream. There was a brown with bay points. There was a black with white splotches. And there was a red. Not the common pale red but a rare rich red much like that of Herefords.

Owen gestured, and Lon Chalmers took point. He always took point. He had the best eyes of anyone in the outfit, and a quick mind to go with his quick hands, traits essential for a point rider, who sometimes had to make spur-of-the moment decisions and who was usually the first to encounter danger, whether it be a war party of hostiles or the stinging fury of a dust storm.

On a typical trail drive there would be swing and flank riders who rode on either side of the strung-out herd and kept cattle from straying. With only a bull and five cows there was no need for swing and flank men; Slim and Cleveland served as both. Slim moved to the right of Big Blue and the cows, Cleveland gigged his buttermilk to the left.

The least desirable position on a drive was that of drag. Drag riders brought up the rear. Their job was to encourage lazier cattle to keep up. They ate a lot of dust in the process. Now Owen moved between the longhorns and the chuck wagon team. The longhorns would not raise much dust, but it was still typical of the foreman that he chose the position most hands disliked for himself.

Pitney reined his mount in next to Owen's. The Brit sat his saddle stiffly and held his arms higher than was customary. "I say, how do we drive that big brute, anyhow? With a whip?"

"That would be plumb cruel," Owen replied. "The trick is to have cattle drive themselves. You point them in the direction you want them to go and let them do the rest."

"That's all there is to it?" Pitney skeptically asked.

"It's not as easy as it sounds," Owen said. "Sometimes a critter will get it into its head it likes a different direction."

"This should prove to be highly illuminating. I don't mind telling you, I am as excited as a small boy on his first day of school."

"I never went," Owen said.

Pitney's jaw dropped. "You have never had any formal education? No schooling whatsoever?"

"You make it sound like a calamity. I can wrestle with the alphabet, and count past a hundred without takin' my boots off."

"I'm sorry," Pitney said. "I didn't mean to offend you. It's just that in my country, education is the cornerstone of our society. The better the school, the brighter one's prospects."

"Out here, it's the straighter you shoot, the longer you live. Book learnin' can't stop a Comanche arrow."

"Point conceded," Pitney said, grinning at his little pun.

Over in front of the stable, James Bartholomew cupped a hand to his mouth. "What's the holdup? Are you waitin' for Christmas?"

"No, sir," Owen said. Removing his hat, he waved it overhead and whooped, "Heeyah!"

It was the crucial moment. Lon Chalmers flicked his reins, and twisted in the saddle. Slim and Cleveland were also watching the longhorns to see what Big Blue would do. Would the bull cooperate? That was uppermost in all their minds.

Big Blue stood immobile, his great head held high, his formidable horns glinting in the morning sun. Then he gave a loud *uh-uh* and lumbered into motion. When he moved, so did the cows.

Slim yipped, Cleveland beamed, and there were shouts from the assembled punchers.

The first day they made eighteen miles. That night, seated around the campfire, Alfred Pitney remarked that at that rate, they would reach Wyoming well within two months.

"Every day won't be like this," Owen said. "We're still on our home range. There are no hostiles hereabouts. No rustlers to fret about. We'll have two more days as easy as this one, then the real work commences."

"I wonder if word got out?" Cleveland remarked.

Pitney waited for more and when it was not forthcoming, he asked, "What word would that be?"

Owen answered him. "Word of us takin' Big Blue north for you. He's a prize bull. Worth his weight in gold as breedin' stock."

"You're suggesting others might try to steal him from us?"

"It's not a matter of might," Owen said. "It's a matter of when. Owlhoots can't pass up an opportunity like this."

"It won't be the usual brand artists," Slim commented. "Big Blue is too famous for them."

"There's that vernacular of yours again," Pitney said. "I'm sorry, but what in the world is a brand artist?"

"A type of rustler," Owen explained. "He carries a brandin' iron with him everywhere he goes, and when he comes across cattle out in the brush, and no one is around, he helps himself and changes their brands so he can claim them as his own."

"And this wouldn't work on Big Blue?"

"No, sir. A brand artist could change the brand any way he wanted, but sooner or later someone would recognize Big Blue. Mr. Bartholomew has shown him off to a lot of people."

"Still," Pitney said thoughtfully, "if a rustler took him far enough, say, to another state, and kept anyone from seeing him, they could get away with it."

"Yet another reason we have to keep our eyes peeled."

The next two days were exactly as the foreman predicted. Once the Bar 40 was behind them, a new wariness was evident in the four punchers. At night they took turns keeping watch, walking around and around the camp, and often singing softly. When Pitney asked why they sang, he was told it soothed the longhorns.

"No one knows why it works, but it does," Owen elaborated. "Just like singin' to a baby will calm it down when it's bawlin', singin' to cows calms them down and helps them sleep."

"Fascinating," Pitney said.

"Don't Wyoming punchers sing?"

Pitney looked down at the ground. "I'm ashamed to admit it, but I've never been out with the herd at night."

"That's all right, sir. You push a pencil for a livin'. You don't push cows."

A routine was established. Each day they were up before dawn. They ate breakfast, then the cowboys saddled the horses they would use that morning, and the cook loaded the chuck wagon. As the sun peeked above the horizon, they were under way. They traveled until noon. After a brief rest, they were again on the move, pushing on until close to sunset. By then Lon invariably had found a likely spot to camp. The cook would set up his stove, the punchers would bed down Big Blue and the cows, and they would relax around the fire for a few hours. They seldom stayed up late. There was no drinking, no gambling. Their employer prohibited both when on the trail, and it was unthinkable to them to go against his wishes.

Within a week, Benedito Chavez had endeared himself to the punchers. They were aloof around him at first, until his brother's boasts about Benedito's skill were demonstrated to their satisfaction.

The chuck wagon contained everything Benedito needed, including a Dutch stove. He had an array of pots, pans, plates, and implements, and enough food-stuffs to feed a small army: flour, salt, pepper, bacon, cornmeal, beans, rice, raisins, lard, dried fruit, baking soda, coffee, and more.

Only Arbuckle's coffee would do. The Arbuckle brothers of Pennsylvania had come up with the brilliant brainstorm to pre-roast their beans and coat them with egg whites mixed with sugar to retain the flavor. The beans came in manila one-pound bags with the word "Arbuckle's" across the front and the image of an angel wearing a red scarf. Benedito had wisely stocked up enough bags to last the entire trip.

Most of the food, the condiments, and the cutlery were stored in the chuck box at the rear of the wagon. As was customary, the gate had been removed and in its place a cupboard constructed. As wide as the wagon, and about four feet high, the cupboard had drawers and shelves and compartments for everything the cook needed. Two large folding doors held it all in place when the wagon was on the move. Hinges ingeniously attached to the bottom permitted the cook to swing the whole cupboard down to make a table. The lid could also be let down to serve as a work-bench.

Benedito, and only Benedito, was allowed anywhere near the chuck box. It was his private domain, and he became surly with anyone who violated it.

Not that the cowboys gave him much cause. They soon came to treat him with a respect bordering on reverence, and when he called them to eat, they came eagerly, like ravenous wolves, and ate with un-feigned enthusiasm.

Even Pitney was impressed, and he had eaten at some of the best clubs and restaurants in England and on the Continent.

Benedito was a master at Mexican cuisine. His tacos were crisp and crunchy, his bean burritos so soft and delicious that they melted in the mouth. His cheese enchiladas became a favorite. His gringo food, as he called it, was just as superb. Their staple was stew, more commonly known as son-of-a-bitch stew, which the punchers downed by the gallon. Pitney once asked what went into it, and Benedito, eyes twinkling, replied that it was better for his digestion if he did not know.

Benedito's sourdough bread was another favorite. The cowboys liked biscuits, buttermilk especially, and they tolerated corn bread, but sourdough bread they could eat all day and all night. They positively loved it.

Benedito further endeared them by preparing what Slim referred to as fancy foods. Spotted pup, made of raisins and rice, was popular with all four. Owen and Slim liked a jelly dessert called Shiverin' Liz, but Lon refused to eat anything that moved when he poked it. Cleveland wasn't the last bit fussy; he would eat whatever was put in front of him, whether it was still moving or not.

Then there were Benedito's pies. The aroma they gave off had every mouth watering. The crusts were always fluffy and light and sweet. Each slice was savored as if it were a condemned man's last meal.

One evening Alfred Pitney remarked that he had never eaten so good, and for his courtesy Benedito gave him a stick of striped peppermint.

Ten days out, and things were going well. Supper was over with, Slim was on watch, and everyone else had turned in.

Pitney lay on his back, his head propped on his saddle, and gazed at the myriad stars sparkling in the vast firmament. "I never realized."

"Sir?" Owen said.

"Oh. Sorry. I was talking to myself. I didn't know you were still awake."

"I've been thinkin' of Cynthia." Melancholy tinged the foreman's voice. "Folks say that absence makes the heart grow fonder, and they're right." Owen paused. "What is it you never realized?"

"How grand your life is," Pitney said. "How glorious. All these years I have worked for the BLC, I never saw what was right in front of me. How deucedly strange."

"Our noses hide an awful lot, don't they?"

Pitney chuckled.

"Is there a Mrs. Pitney hid away somewhere?"

"Would that there were. I spend so much time working, the fairer gender does not loom large in my personal life. But I'm young yet. Only twenty-eight. Plenty of time for me to find a woman willing to tolerate my many quirks and accept me as her husband."

"You're not much older than me. I'm twenty-six, and I'd like to be hitched before I turn twenty-seven."

"Miss Langstrom?"

"The signs are favorable. We might have done it before now except I've been loop shy. Not on her account. I can't quite get it through my noggin that I won't make a mess of her life. Mr. Bartholomew says it's normal to be scared, and I just have to take the bull by the horns."

"I wish you much happiness," Alfred Pitney said.

Owen rolled onto his side and cradled his cheek in his hand. "The first time I set eyes on you, I took you for a swivel dude. But clothes are only feathers. You have some peculiar notions but you'll do to ride the river with."

"Thank you. I think."

The next day they had their first taste of trouble.

They were awake before sunrise, as usual, and ate breakfast, as usual, washing it down with cups of Arbuckle's. Then the punchers saddled their horses, as usual, and the cook loaded the chuck wagon, as usual, and they were ready to ride out when dawn breathed new life into creation.

Lon took point, as usual, and Slim and Cleveland took the flanks, as usual, while Owen and Pitney took their place between the longhorns and the chuck-wagon team. At a holler from the foreman, Lon touched his spurs to his mount, and Big Blue lumbered forward.

That was when the red cow moved ahead of him and assumed the lead.

"What in tarnation?" Slim blurted. "Look there! What does Emily think she's doin'?"

The cowboys had named the cows. Emily was the red, Mary the yellow. The cream cow earned the dubious distinction of being called Cleopatra. The black with white splotches was Lily. The brown with bay points became Brownie.

So far the cows had behaved. Not one had tried to turn back or scamper into the brush. Emily had been observed to be the feistiest, perhaps because she was the youngest, and she always insisted on walking ahead of the other cows. But now she had gone herself one better.

Big Blue appeared to be as surprised as the cowboys. He stopped and stared, and when he stopped, the other cows stopped, too. Not Emily. She continued on, halting only when Lon reined up and looked back to see what was going on.

The rest of the punchers also drew rein. Owen gnawed his lower lip and commented, "This could be serious."

"So what if she wants to lead the longhorns?" Pitney asked. "What possible difference can it make?"

"The difference between her livin' and dyin'," Owen revealed. "Bulls generally don't take kindly to bossy cows."

"What could he do to her?"

"Gore her to death, for one thing," Owen said. "On a trail drive there is always one bull or steer that takes the lead, and he will keep it even if he has to fight other bulls and steers to earn the right."

"Can't we separate them?" Pitney proposed. "Rope her so Big Blue can be in the lead again?"

"This is somethin' they have to work out between themselves. Otherwise we'll have the same situation tomorrow."

Big Blue snorted and moved toward Emily. She turned her head to watch him but did not move aside. She was the smallest of the cows, and he towered over her like a moose over a whitetail. Her horns seemed puny compared to his. In a clash, the outcome was foreordained.

"Females!" Slim growled. "Four legs or two legs, they are all the same."

Big Blue came to a stop a few feet from Emily. He snorted again, then lowered his head and swung his long horns from side to side.

"I don't like the looks of this," Owen said. "Cleveland, you're closest to the dunderhead. Rope her if he goes to pawin'."

"Will do." The cowboy from Ohio already had his rope in hand and was shaking out a loop.

A rumbling grunt from Big Blue hinted a crisis was imminent. Suddenly Emily turned and walked up to him. She touched her nose to his. For all of ten seconds they stood perfectly still, muzzles brushing. Then Emily wheeled and took the lead once again, and Big Blue docilely followed.

"I'll be switched!" Slim exclaimed. "She's done it. He's not goin' to put her in her place."

"Now I've seen everything," Owen said.

For the rest of the day Emily led. At noon they stopped and let the longhorns graze a while. Emily attached herself to the other cows and stayed with them until the punchers were once again ready to head out. As they formed up, Emily trotted past Big Blue. The giant bull did not contest her.

That evening Lon shot a doe with his Winchester. They were in need of fresh meat. Since there were no cows to spare, venison had become a steady part of their diet.

Benedito did the butchering. He cut out the heart and chopped it into pieces. He cut out the tongue. Part of the liver and the brains were broken apart and mixed with flour and salt and pepper, resulting in the venison equivalent of son-of-a-bitch stew.

"It ain't beef but it will do." Slim summed up the sentiments of his companions.

"So long as he goes on making those pies of his," Cleveland said, "he could cook skunk and I wouldn't care."

Another night under the stars. Another crisp dawn. Big Blue started to lead but Emily passed him. A new tradition had been established.

"He must secretly like her," Cleveland opined.

"She does have a saucy walk," Lon said.

They were far enough inland that the last thing Alfred Pitney expected to come across was swampland. It was more common along the Gulf coast. But come across it they did, a foreboding expanse of dark water broken by intermittent hummocks of lush vegetation.

"Do we go around?" the Britisher asked.

Owen did not want to. They would lose too many hours. But they had the chuck wagon to think of, so he had them bear to the west to skirt the wetland. A wise decision, everyone agreed.

It should have gone well.

But they did not count on the snakes.

11

Coyotes

Toothless was always one of the last to leave the Nose Paint Saloon. The married men were the first. They had to be home early or suffer the wrath of their wives. Next to go were the townsmen who had to open a business or be at work by six or seven a.m. the next day. Cowhands usually stayed late no matter how far they had to ride to reach their outfits, but then, cowboys generally had a carefree streak. Plus, they did so love their liquor.

So did old Toothless. Which was why he always hung around until closing, hoping to mooch one more drink. He did not care from whom. Married men, single men, townsmen, punchers, so long as they had money to spare.

Some were always kind to him and would buy a drink without much pleading on his part. Others could not be bothered. A few were outright mean, and if he dared ask, they would give him a severe tongue-lashing, or, worse, a poke in the ribs or maybe a cuff to the cheek. Only when his need was clawing at his insides like a grizzly gone amok did he ever approach the mean ones.

This particular night had been better than most.

Toothless had been treated to over ten drinks. He had that nice, warm, fuzzy feeling he enjoyed so much, and his mind drifted in liquid rapture. Only one other customer was still in the saloon, head slumped over a table, when Charley, the bartender, came down the bar.

"Two minutes, Toothless."

Toothless had been nursing his last drink for ten times that long. He was a master at nursing them. He would take the tiniest of sips, then savor the warmth as the whiskey burned a path to his stomach. "Can't you make it five? Have a drink with me and we'll jaw a spell."

"Two minutes," Charley repeated, and began wiping the counter. "It's been a long night and I'm bone tired. You wouldn't think serving drinks can do that, but it sure as hell can."

"You are a fine bartender, Charley. Why not treat yourself before you turn in? You deserve it."

"I thank you for the compliment but you can save your praise, you old goat." Charley grinned as he said it. "I'm wise to your wiles. They don't work on me anymore."

"Such a shame," Toothless said sadly. "There was a time when you were much more generous."

"So much for false praise." Charley stared at the figure slumped over the lone occupied table. "Who's that with his head in his arms yonder?"

Toothless did not have to look. He had gone over earlier to ask for a drink and been rebuffed. "Harold, the bank clerk. He drank himself into a stupor. Something to do with how much he misses poor Carmody."

"We all miss her," Charley lamented. "Damn all drummers to hell."

"It was a fine lynchin'," Toothless said. Especially since, afterward, most of the men had repaired to the Nose Paint to celebrate or drown their guilt, and he had been indulged for a total of nine drinks.

"A necktie social was too good for that bastard. They should have staked him out over an anthill, like the Indians do. Or tied him to a stake and set him on fire."

"Why, Charley. I never knew you have such a gruesome streak."

"Carmody was the best dove I ever worked with. She hardly ever got mad. And she wasn't as moody as most females."

"You don't need to tell me about their moods," Toothless said. "I was married twice."

"You were?" Charlie was surprised. "I never took you for the marrying kind. Fact is, though, I don't know a lot about you other than you used to punch cows for Goodnight years back, and then you went to work for the stage company for a while. Is that right?"

"Punchin' was hard work. Too hard for my likin'. So I gave it up to sit on a stool and sell tickets and help folks tote their bags out to the stage."

"When did you become a drunk?"

Toothless was about to take another sip. He had two or three good ones left in the glass. But he stopped with the glass almost to his lips, and said testily, "I'll thank you not to call me that. How many times have you ever seen me where I couldn't hold my booze?"

"Not many," Charley admitted. "You can drink most men under the table, but you seldom get to staggering or passing out. Must be you have built up a tolerance to the alcohol."

"Why, Charley," Toothless said, still irritated, "since when did you become an expert on drinkin' habits?"

"You old buzzard. That's enough. Clever of you to trick me into talking so you can stay longer, but I've caught on. Get done and get out or so help me, I'll boot you out on your backside."

"I would never try to trick you, Charley," Toothless lied. "You're the one man in town I can't afford to have mad at me."

"One minute, and that's all." Charley went around the end of the bar and over to the table and shook Harold by the shoulder. "I'm closing, Harry. Can you stand on your own or do you want help to the door?"

Harold slowly raised his head. He was thin as a rail and had a face that would have given his own mother the shudders. Blinking in confusion, he said, "Where am I? Oh. Still here?"

"Can you make it out on your own?"

"Sure." Harold swatted at the hand on his shoulder. "No need to treat me like I'm helpless. I'm a grown man. I can hold my liquor."

"Sure you can." Charley went to another table to collect glasses. "Prove it by leaving."

"You can be rude. Do you know that?" Harold stared to rise but his legs wobbled and he had to sit back down. "Whew. My head is spinning enough to make me sick."

"Not in here," Charley warned. "You do, and you clean it up, and I'll ban you for a week."

"Not only rude but mean." Harold braced his hands on the table and this time managed to stand erect but he swayed and did not let go of the table for fear of falling. "But don't you worry. They don't call me Iron Gut Harry for nothing."

"No one calls you that but you," Charley reminded him. "And your gut is made of paper, not iron. Two drinks and you slur your words. Four, and you can barely hold your head up. How many did you have tonight? Five?"

"I refuse to stay here and be insulted." Harold focused on the door, then launched himself toward it with a determined stride. Unfortunately, his body did not share his determination. He weaved like a sailor on a storm-tossed deck and had to stop and grip another table.

Toothless had finished his drink. Regretfully setting the empty glass on the bar, he straightened. "Want some help there, Harry?"

"How kind of you," the clerk said. "You would do that for me?"

"Why not?" Toothless would help anyone who bought him a drink now and again. He put an arm around Harold. "I ain't as strong as I used to be, so help out as best you can. You ready?"

"I am always ready," Harold boasted.

Together, they made it to the door, but had to cling there to catch their breath. Toothless remembered a time when he could have thrown Harold over a shoulder and strolled out as casual as you please. He hated growing old. Hated watching his limbs wither like dry corn on a stalk. Hated becoming weaker and weaker as the years went by. He hated it more than he'd ever hated anything.

"Do you know where my place is?"

"Sure. Don't you worry none. We'll have you there in thirty shakes of a lamb's tail."

"Isn't it supposed to be three shakes?"

"If we were sober, yes." Toothless firmed his hold

and marched out the door, refusing to say good night to Charley on general principle. Harold leaned so hard against him, Toothless nearly fell over. A post saved them. Then they gathered steam, moving faster, more confidently.

"I can't thank you enough. Remind me to buy you a drink tomorrow night, will you?"

"I'll remind you to buy me a whole bottle," Toothless said.

"Do you miss her as much as I do?"

"Carmody? Sure. She was a great gal."

"That she was." Tears filled Harold's eyes. "She was the salt of the earth. Always so kind, always smiling."

"Findin' a dove as wonderful to replace her won't be easy," Toothless said. "That fat one didn't impress me much."

"Who?"

"Some fat gal who wandered into town today. She came into the saloon and asked Charley if he was hirin'. I figured he'd be glad to find someone so soon, but he looked her up and down and said he wasn't in need of a girl."

"He had no call to do that. Was she nice?"

"I didn't get to talk to her," Toothless said. "She wasn't as easy on the eyes as Carmody, but there sure was a lot of her. Enough for half the men in town, I reckon, with some left over."

"I'd like to meet her. There aren't many single women hereabouts, and—hey!"

Harold yelped because two men had lunged out of a gap between the buildings and grabbed them. One of the men slammed Harold against a wall. The other threw Toothless to the dirt. They both had revolvers in their hands. The one man swung his. There was the *thuck* of metal on bone, and Harold folded onto his side, groaning, a nasty gash in his temple.

The other man raised his six-shooter to pistol-whip Toothless but a harsh voice out of the darkness growled, "Don't bother with that one. He's not worth our time."

Cringing in fear, Toothless saw Luke Deal step out of the shadows. The man standing over him was Bronk. It was Grutt who had nearly split Harold's skull. "What do you want?"

"Travelin' money," Luke Deal said. "We're tired of Whiskey Flats." He bent over Harold and rummaged in the clerk's pockets. A vest produced coins and a few bills. Luke counted them. "Twelve dollars. It's not much but it will tide us over."

"Hell," Grutt snapped, "I don't see why we don't just rob the stage office. They have a lot of cash sometimes."

"Oh, sure. We'll rob it first thing in the mornin'," Luke said sarcastically. "Then spend all of next week fightin' shy of a posse." He nudged Harold with the tip of a boot. "This idiot is safer. He didn't get a good look at us so he can't set the Rangers on our trail."

"How about you?" Grutt asked Bronk. "Whose notion do you like? Do we rob the stage company?"

"I'm with Luke," Bronk said.

"You always take his side of things." Grutt shoved his revolver in its holster. "Just once I'd like us to do what I want."

Luke Deal placed his right hand on his Remington. "Is that so? Does this mean you think you should be runnin' things?"

Grutt blanched and thrust his hands out from his

sides. "I never said any such thing! Don't be puttin' words in my mouth."

"And don't *you* be tellin' *me* what we should do," Luke warned. "Now I want to be clear. Are we still pards?"

"Always," Grutt said, glancing at Deal's gun hand. Evidently anxious to change the subject, he pointed at Toothless. "But what about this old coot? He's seen us. He can tell we took the money."

Luke Deal's slate gray eyes fixed on Toothless. "How about it, old-timer? Do you have a leaky mouth?"

"Not me, Mr. Deal. Never. No, sir. I know better than to cross someone like you."

"What does that mean, exactly? Someone like me?"

Toothless wished his head was clearer. The whiskey had him befuddled, and the three hard cases had him downright scared. "Someone who doesn't take any guff. Someone who stands up for himself."

"You're not as dumb as you look." Luke visibly relaxed and started to make for the street. "Let's ske-daddle. By sunrise we'll be long gone."

"What about Owen?" Grutt asked.

Deal stopped, then turned back, wearing the same cold smile. "How is that again?"

"I owe him for that shellackin' he gave me with his fists. How about if we go out to the Bar 40 and jump him when he least expects?"

It was always best when dealing with violent sorts, Toothless had learned long ago, to not say more than was necessary. He should have kept his mouth shut, but he heard himself say, "Owen ain't there."

"Then where is he?" Grutt demanded.

"I'm curious myself," Luke Deal said. "I heard he

went down to Mexico with his boss but they're supposed to have come back."

"Oh, they returned, all right," Toothless said. "But now Owen and three other hands have gone off north. They won't be back for months."

Suddenly Luke Deal was in front of Toothless, his expression smoldering with intensity. "Where did you hear this?"

"From a couple of Bar 40 hands who were in town yesterday," Toothless said. "Buck Tilman and Lute Bannister. You know them, don't you?"

"I've seen them around." Luke gazed northward. "Did they happen to say where Owen is bound? Or why?"

"The where is Wyoming Territory," Toothless informed him. "The why is he's takin' one of the Bar 40's best bulls to a ranch up that way. You ran into the buyer yourself. Don't you remember? That mail-order catalog? From England, I believe it is."

"He sure didn't look like no rancher I ever saw," Luke said. "And he bought a bull, you say?"

"Big Blue."

"Interestin'," Luke Deal said. "Mighty interestin'." He leaned down. "Tell me more, old man."

"That's about all they told me, except Buck Tilman is temporary foreman until Owen gets back."

"Tilman happen to mention the names of the punchers who went with him?"

"Let's see." Toothless had to concentrate. "It was Slim and that cowhand from Ohio. Oh, and Lon Chalmers."

"The gun hand," Bronk said.

"Just those four?"

Toothless did not understand Deal's sudden interest but he was not about to hold anything back. "The mail-order catalog went, too, I believe. Oh, and a cook, but I don't know much about him other than he's a Mex."

"I'm glad I didn't let Grutt split your noggin," Luke Deal said. Smiling, he squatted, his hands low on his legs. "If I had, you wouldn't have given me an idea how I can make a lot of money."

"Glad I could be of help," Toothless said.

"You can help me more by dyin'." Luke Deal's right hand came away from his right boot. A double-edged dagger glinted dully as he thrust the blade to the hilt into the old man's belly.

Shock glued Toothless in place. He glanced down at his stomach and bleated, "Dear God, no."

"Are those your last words?" Luke twisted his arm, slicing upward. "You can do better."

Agony such as Toothless had never known coursed through him. Throbbing, excruciating pain, and with it came a wet sensation that welled up in his throat and filled his mouth. "Please," he pleaded, feeling the wetness ooze over his lower lip and down his chin.

Grutt laughed mirthlessly.

Luke Deal bent and whispered in Toothless's ear, "Best make your peace with your Maker."

Toothless wet himself. He couldn't help it. "Why?" he mewed. A strange tingling spread outward from his gut.

"I always cover my tracks," Luke Deal said, "and you happen to be one of them." He drew out the blade and plunged it in again. "You can die anytime you want."

Belatedly, Toothless opened his mouth to scream. But all that came out was more sticky wetness. He tried to swallow and nearly choked.

"Tough old buzzard," Luke said. He smiled, then

merrily and methodically plunged the blade in over and over again. Ten times. Fifteen. Twenty. Finally he stopped and wiped the blade clean and slid the dagger into the sheath inside his boot.

Bronk snickered and nodded in appreciation. "When you kill 'em, you do it right. What about this other one? Want me to do him, too?"

"He never had a good look at us, remember?" Luke unfurled. "Hit him again, but not hard enough to break his skull. We just want to keep him here until mornin'." He walked out to the street and leaned against a post. He did not look around when his shadows joined him.

"Just when I think you're gettin' soft, you go and do somethin' like that." Grutt offered faint praise. "What made you turn that old buzzard into maggot bait, anyway? A couple of minutes ago you told us to leave him be."

"I didn't want him tellin' anyone he told us about Owen."

"What difference does it make?"

"A heap of difference when word gets out," Luke Deal said. "I don't want every lawman and Ranger in the state after us."

"Over that old drunk?" Bronk was skeptical.

"Try to pay attention. Not because of Toothless. Because Owen and his pards will be dead and we will have Big Blue." A cold smile curled Luke's cruel mouth. "That bull can bring us thousands if we play our cards right. Let's vamoose. We have a lot of ridin' to do."

They hurried down the street and were almost to the hitch rail where they had left their horses when their way was blocked by an apparition in a dress as huge as a tent. Cheap perfume filled the air like fog.

"Looking for a good time, boys?"

"You've got to be joshin'," Grutt told the woman. "I don't mate with buffaloes."

"Be nice," the apparition said. "Sure, there's a lot of me, but I come with a lot of experience."

"We're not interested, lady," Luke Deal said.

The woman pursed lips as thick as plums. "You won't say that once you've had a taste. One at a time or three at once, it's all the same to me."

"My kind of woman!" Bronk declared.

Luke glared at him. "We're sheddin' this two-bit town, remember? It will take us days to catch up as it is. Longer if we're shackled with a damn whore."

"I resent that," the woman said. "But what's this about you leaving? I've only been in Whiskey Flats one day and I can't wait to be somewhere else. Which direction are you boys heading?"

Luke started to brush past her. "In the opposite direction from you."

"Wait. Please." The woman gripped his sleeve. "Hear me out. I don't have the money for stage fare. I'm stuck here until I rustle it up, or until some friendly gents like you take pity on a poor workin' girl."

"I'm not in the pity business," Luke said.

"I can make it worth your while to take me." The woman bestowed a somewhat seductive look on Bronk and Grutt. "Free pokes every day until we get to wherever you're going."

Bronk lit up like a candle. "Free pokes?"

"For all of you as want them."

"And we can do it any way we want?" From Grutt.

"So long as you don't spill blood." The woman grinned. "What do you say? When was the last time you fondled treats like these?" She cupped her enormous breasts and jiggled them.

"I think I'm in love," Bronk said.

"It's fine by me," Grutt added, "but we ain't the ones you have to convince." He nodded at Luke. "We do whatever he wants."

"How about it, handsome?" The woman jiggled her breasts at him. "These can be yours to do with as you want."

"I'm not in the elephant business, neither."

The woman frowned and placed her thick fingers on her wide hips. "You're sure a mean one. Fine, then. Leave me stranded. I don't care. It's my own fault for followin' after that Bar 40 puncher."

Luke had taken several steps but he abruptly stopped and looked back. "Which puncher would that be?"

"He calls himself Slim. Him and a friend of his named Cleveland were told by the man they work for to see I got to Laredo. They gave me the money for a stage ticket, then had to skedaddle." The woman tittered. "I spent the money on booze. I passed out, I had so much. When I came to, the Bar 40 boys were gone."

"How would you like to see them again? Slim and his friends?"

"You're serious? You'll take me to the Bar 40?"

"They're not at the ranch but I know where we can find them," Luke Deal said, adding, "I know them real well. You could say I owe them, and what better way to repay them than to take you to your lover?"

"Slim never so much as laid a finger on me," the woman said, plainly disappointed. "But I could tell he was smitten. He might be the last chance I'll ever have of becomin' a decent woman." She softly sighed. "There was an English gent I was fond of but he was scared of me."

Luke smiled and came toward her, holding out his hand. "Then it's settled. We'll find you a horse." As they shook, he said, "I didn't catch your name, by the way."

"Most folks call me Sweet Sally."

First Blood

12

First Blood

Owen's outfit had been skirting the swampland for the better part of an hour. Behind him the chuck wagon rattled and creaked. Ahead, the longhorns moved with tireless effort. Lon was on point; Slim and Cleveland covered the flanks. Owen was satisfied that things were going well.

Then a wide, dark pool appeared on their right. No different from any of the other pools, the surface was as still as the hot air, broken only by a small island of vegetation at its center. The water looked inviting but Owen knew better than to drink it. To do so risked sickness and death.

Cleveland was between the longhorns and the swamp. They had passed other pools without incident so he had no cause to expect trouble. He was watching a large bird in the distance, trying to figure out what it was. He had about decided it must be a crane when he heard a flurry of hooves. Cleveland shifted toward the longhorns but the harm had been done.

The red cow was the culprit. Emily had darted for the pool, passing behind Cleveland's mount. She was at the water's edge before he could stop her. Since Big Blue and the rest of the cows followed her lead, they, too, made for the water. But where the cows moved briskly, eager to slake their thirst, Big Blue slowed and then stopped well short of the pool's edge.

Reining sharply around, Cleveland hollered and sought to cut the cows off. He partially succeeded. Two of the cows turned. But Emily was already in the pool, and the next moment so were Lily and Brownie. Cleveland immediately resorted to his rope. He had to get them out of there before they drank any of the water.

Owen spurred over to help. He, too, prepared to rope them, if need be, and haul them out. He saw Emily dip her muzzle and bellowed at her but he'd might as well have been shouting at a tree stump. The contrary cow paid no attention.

Lily dipped her mouth to drink. Brownie, though, kept on wading and passed the other two. She was eyeing the green island as if it were a smorgasbord and she was starved.

Lon and Slim galloped to help.

Alfred Pitney had never used a rope in his life— never, for that matter, herded any of the thousands of cattle on the BLC's vast range. It occurred to him it was an oversight he should remedy.

Benedito Chavez brought the chuck wagon to a halt. Since there was nothing he could do, he stayed where he was. He did utter a comment in Spanish that compared the intelligence of cows to the digested matter that came out their hind ends.

Suddenly Brownie stopped and snorted and looked down at the water, which had risen as high as her brisket.

Cleveland threw a loop over Emily, dallied the rope around his saddle horn, and wheeled his horse.

Lily stopped drinking and raised her head, which made Owen's task easier. Quick as thought, his rope flew toward her, the loop wide enough to settle over her long horns, and the deed was done. He, too, dallied his rope to his saddle horn and was about to turn his claybank when Lon and Slim reached them.

"What the hell?" Lon blurted. "Do you see what I see?"

The dark water around Brownie was roiling as if she had unwittingly disturbed a large school of fish. But the writhing bodies that broke the surface did not have fins. They were smooth and round and thick and scaly. There had to be scores of them, if not hundreds.

"Are they snakes?" Slim marveled.

As if in answer, a serpentine head rose out of the water next to Brownie's rear right leg. Its fangs glistened as it opened its jaws wide, exposing the whitish insides of its mouth, the light hue that had earned the viper its distinctive name.

"Cottonmouths!" Owen cried. "Get her out of there!"

The aquatic equivalent of rattlesnakes, only without the rattles, cottonmouths were widely feared. With good reason. Their bites could prove fatal. Aggressive natures compounded the danger they posed, for where most snakes, rattlers included, beat a hasty retreat when confronted by humans, or large animals such as cows, cottonmouths stood their ground, or their water, and greeted intruders with the fangs in their white mouths.

With a jab of his spurs, Lon plunged his mount into the pool. Slim was only seconds behind him. They stopped a safe distance from the roiling mass and swung their ropes over their heads.

The cottonmouth's fangs sank into Brownie's leg. She gave voice to a wail so humanlike it raised the hackles of the four cowhands. She tried to turn but the mass of writhing reptiles hindered her, entangling her legs. Frantic, she thrashed wildly, which only incited the snakes more.

"Dear God!" Slim breathed.

Cottonmouths were striking at Brownie from all sides, their fangs sinking deep into her thick hide. Bellowing in panic, she sliced at the mass with her horns. But she might as well have been slashing at phantoms. As near as the cowboys could tell, she did not impale a single snake, although a couple of times when her horns rose dripping from the water, cottonmouths were wrapped around them.

"Get her out of there!" Owen frantically repeated.

Slim's rope descended, and he had her. He turned his horse. The rope grew taut as he dallied it, then used his spurs.

Seeing that the skinny puncher had the situation in hand, Lon Chalmers did not throw his rope. Instead he let it drop and palmed his Colt. There was little he could do against so many but he did what he could. When a blunt head reared out of the water in front of Brownie, its fangs glistening, Lon banged off a shot. The cottonmouth's head dissolved in an explosion of gore. He fired again and a second snake sank, never to rise.

In the meantime Owen had hauled Lily out. She dug in her hooves but he would not be thwarted and did not rein up until she was safely beside Mary and Cleopatra. "Hold her!" he cried, thrusting the end of the rope at Pitney, and flew back to the pool.

By then Cleveland had Emily on dry ground. She

was shaking as if she were having a fit—or as if cottonmouth venom was coursing through her veins.

Slim spurred his horse in desperation but he could not get Brownie out of the water. She would take a few steps, and stop. Take a few more steps, and stop. Her movements were growing sluggish and she had stopped flailing at her tormentors with her horns.

Without warning a lone cottonmouth broke the surface close to Slim's horse. Owen stabbed for his holster, but someone else was faster. Lon's Colt spat and the cottonmouth was kicked into the air. Then it did the most remarkable thing: The snake bit itself, over and over, while slowly sinking.

Owen was beside himself. The longhorns were his responsibility. Bartholomew had entrusted them to his care. The cows were to be the nucleus of the herd the Brit wanted to build, and they could ill afford to lose one. Accordingly, he plunged his horse in and made for the roiling ball, determined to save Brownie if it was humanly possible.

"Pard, no!" Lon shouted.

Owen did not know what he would do when he reached her. Maybe plow into the snakes to scatter them. He might lose his horse, but in the greater balance of things, the cow counted for more.

Water splashed and sprayed, and Lon was alongside. He grabbed Owen's arm. "Be sensible! You'll only get yourself killed!"

Owen shrugged the hand off and would have rushed in among the snakes anyway. But Brownie abruptly bawled in agony and hurtled toward land. Like a ship cleaving the sea, she raised a wake, passing within a few arm's lengths of Slim, who glanced down to make sure the rope would not entangle his mount. What he saw turned him chalk white.

Wriggling furiously, cottonmouths clung to the cow's heaving sides and neck, their fangs embedded deep. One by one, though, they began dropping off, so that when Brownie clambered unsteadily out of the water and stood shaking violently from her horns to her tail, only one viper was still attached.

The cowboys rode out of the pool. Owen was first to alight. Removing his hat, he swatted at the cottonmouth but its fangs were hooked, somehow, and the snake could not let go.

Lon had dismounted. "Let me," he said. Gripping the cottonmouth by the tail, he yanked with all his strength. The fangs jerked free, and Lon instantly pivoted and swung the snake like a whip, smashing its head on the ground again and again and again until the serpent hung limp and lifeless. Then he threw it from him in disgust, declaring, "I hate the varmints."

Brownie took several shuffling steps toward the other longhorns. She lowed piteously and looked around her as if unsure of where she was. Drops of blood oozed from scores of holes, and her legs wobbled even when she stopped.

"What can we do?" Slim asked, choked with emotion.

No one answered. They all knew the answer. As cowmen, they made it a point not to become too attached to the cattle they tended. Why would they, when the cattle were destined for market, and slaughter? But they had grown to know these five cows well, and Slim had come to like them more than he should. But that was Slim; he had a weak spot for animals and women.

"There's no cure, no treatment." Owen gloomily voiced the truth they all knew. Angry at himself for not preventing the mishap, he smacked his chaps. "All we can do is wait for her to die."

Slim swung down, walked up to Brownie, and placed a hand on her head. "I'm sorry, girl," he said contritely. "You didn't deserve to end like this."

Lon spun toward the pool. His right hand fell to his Colt. He glared savagely at the now still water, and under his breath cursed every cottonmouth that had ever been born and ever would be.

Cleveland had removed his rope from the red cow and was coiling it. "It's all my fault," he lamented. "I should have stopped Emily before she reached the water."

"Cows can be tricky." Owen sought to soothe his guilt. "She waited until your back was to her so you couldn't stop her."

"It's my fault," Cleveland insisted.

"You managed to cut two of them off," Owen reminded him, "and the other two weren't bit."

"Are you sure?"

Owen ran to Emily and hunkered to examine her for drops of blood. To his great relief he did not find any.

Lon was carefully checking Lily, and he called out, "I think I found a bite." On one of the white splotches low on her left front leg were two pinpricks. They were not bleeding but they had clearly been made by fangs.

"Maybe the snake didn't bite deep enough," Cleveland said hopefully.

Owen gingerly touched the splotch and lightly pressed but all Lily did was turn her head and regard him inquisitively. He removed his hand and patted her ribs. "We can't lose two of you."

"I say!" Alfred Pitney called out. "The other cow is down!"

Brownie was on her front knees. As the punchers watched in silent sympathy, the longhorn lowered onto her belly. Her tongue lolled and she hung her head and made an assortment of sounds they'd rarely heard longhorns make, low moans and *chuffs* that were much like a human cough.

Lon asked, "Want me to put her out of her misery?"

"I should. It's my fault." Cleveland would not let it drop.

Owen shook his head. "No need. She won't last much longer. And I don't reckon she's in much pain, not with that much venom. More numb than anything else."

Brownie looked at them. Her nostrils flared with each labored breath and her eyes were drooping. Saliva ran down her tongue and dripped from the tip. Every so often she would tremble as if cold.

"Damn, I hate snakes," Lon growled. "When I was ten I lost an uncle to a rattler. He went into the root cellar and didn't see it in the shadows. When he reached for a basket of potatoes, the rattler bit him on the wrist. Got him right in the vein. My aunt sucked out as much of the poison as she could and sent for the doc but my uncle was dead inside an hour."

"I had a cousin who was bit by a black widow," Cleveland mentioned.

The other cowboys looked at him.

"Well, I did."

Brownie's breaths were like the blast of a blacksmith's bellows. Her head dipped almost to the ground but she snapped it up again and gazed wide-eyed at the other cows. She struggled to stand and join them but she was too weak. Lowing loudly, she shook her head, as if to stave off the inner night.

"From now on, every snake I see, I shoot," Lon vowed.

"Even garter snakes?" Slim asked.

"Every snake."

"But garters are plumb harmless. The same with king snakes and corn snakes and rat snakes. They eat all kinds of vermin. Then there are bull snakes and gopher snakes and those big indigo snakes that live down to the coast, and long-nosed snakes and striped snakes and those pretty little scarlet snakes they have over in the bayou country and—" Slim stopped.

Lon had held up a hand. "Mention one more goddamned snake and I'll shoot you."

"Now, now," Owen said.

Slim's feelings were hurt. "I was only pointin' out that some snakes don't do us any harm and don't deserve to be shot."

"Where did you learn about all those?" Cleveland asked.

"I've always liked snakes," Slim said. "When I was a boy, I'd collect all kinds. It got so I had me a snake zoo, with twenty or more. Folks would come from miles around to see it. There was this big old rattler I kept in a coal box. He was thicker than my arm and scared everyone half to death just to look at him. Why, I recollect—" Again he stopped.

Lon had made a sharp gesture. "So snakes are wonderful critters, are they?" He pointed. "Tell that to her."

Brownie was on her side. Her legs were stiff as sticks and she was shaking all over, her tongue half out of her mouth. As they watched, her eyes rolled up into their sockets and she uttered a last, final low.

"Damn," Owen said.

The cowboys gathered around the deceased and

Slim touched the tip of the horn that jutted into the air. "Do we bury her or leave her for the buzzards?"

Behind them came a soft cough, and Benedito was there, his sombrero in his hands. "Pardon me, señors. I have a suggestion."

The cowboys waited.

"The poison, it does not go deep into the meat. I can butcher her and we can have fresh beef for a few days. Sí?"

"That's harsh," Slim said.

"Well, she is a cow," Cleveland said. "Or was."

"I wouldn't mind some beef for a change," Lon remarked. "I'm sick to death of venison."

Owen was dubious. "Benedito, are you sure it will be safe? It won't make us sickly, or worse?"

"I am confident, señor. So long as I only take meat from certain parts, not the heart or the kidneys or where the snakes have bitten." Benedito brought his right hand out from under the sombrero. He was holding a long butcher knife. "Say the word, señor. I will be quick."

Owen glanced at Lon, who nodded, then at Slim, who shook his head. That left Cleveland, who was rubbing his hands together in anticipation. "Cut away."

Before Benedito could commence, Big Blue snorted and came toward them. This whole time, the giant bull had stood as still as Pikes Peak, seemingly undisturbed by Brownie's plight. But now Big Blue came over to the prone cow and sniffed noisily. A shudder ran through him, and throwing back his head, he uttered a peculiar series of bellows that fell to a low whine and then rose to what in human beings would be called a scream.

"The blood call!" Lon exclaimed.

Three of the four remaining cows immediately came over and milled about Brownie's body while adding cries of their own to those of Big Blue.

Alfred Pitney yelped in alarm. Straining at the rope, Lily was trying to reach the other longhorns.

"Slip the rope off her!" Owen hollered.

"How?"

"Danged foreigners," Slim said.

Owen ran over and hastily released Lily so she could join Emily, Mary, and Cleopatra in their display of grief.

"Good heavens!" Pitney exclaimed in amazement. "What in heaven's name are they doing? I've never witnessed such bizarre behavior in cattle."

"We call it the blood call," Owen said reverently. "When a longhorn dies, sometimes the others will gather around and set to caterwauling like riled cats. I once saw hundreds act up like this over a cow that was killed by a cougar. They bawled for hours."

"How do you quiet them?" The din was so loud, Pitney covered his ears with his hands.

"We don't," Owen said. "We let them bawl themselves out. Otherwise they become mean."

The blood call lasted a good half hour. Around and around Big Blue and the four cows walked, until they had satisfied the primal urge that compelled them to express their grief. Then, as abruptly as it started, the cries ended, and the longhorns stood as docile as lambs.

"If I had not seen it with my own eyes," Pitney said, "I would not believe it."

"Animals do lots of things we wouldn't think they do," the foreman commented. "Ever seen an earwig kill a spider? Or does fight by boxin' with their front hooves?"

"I admit I am not versed in wildlife or their habits," Pitney confessed. "The closest I came is the bird-watching I did as a youngster. I enjoyed sitting and listening to songbirds warble their delightful sounds."

"I like wrens," Owen said. "They're small but feisty."

"Just when I reckon I've heard everythin'. So you're a bird lover?" Lon had come up unnoticed, and was grinning like a cat that had just swallowed one of Owen's wrens. "And here we mistook you for a cowman. Wait until the boys at the Bar 40 hear this."

"You wouldn't," Owen said. "I'll be up to my neck in wren feathers."

"To say nothin' of all the naked wrens flyin' around," Lon said.

Slim and Cleveland were shooing the longhorns away from Brownie so Benedito could get to work. The butchering took another half hour. Benedito was a master. He knew exactly where to cut, knew which pieces to keep and which might be laced with venom. At one point he sliced off a square of raw meat and studied it quizzically. Then he stuck the end of the slice in his mouth, sucked a few times, spat in distaste, and threw the piece away.

"Be careful," Cleveland said. "If you die, we're liable to starve."

Eventually they were under way. The rest of the day was uneventful. The same with the day after, and the day after that. But on the following morning they came to the Nueces River and paralleled it to where the river changed course and bent its watery way to the southwest. They crossed at a ford used by nearly all the herds on the Western Trail.

Owen had been worried the longhorns would balk. Cattle often did when it came to moving water. They would refuse to enter or bolt like a pack of hounds were on their heels. But much to his amazement, the red cow, Emily, marched into the Nueces River as if it were her private bath and struck out for the other side. Not to be outdone by a cow, Big Blue forded, too, and since wherever he went, the rest of the cows went, in short order all the longhorns stood dripping wet on the other side.

"That was painless," Lon remarked.

"There are plenty more rivers," Owen reminded him.

Streams, too. The very next morning they struck a swiftly flowing narrow watercourse with high banks. Emily came to the top of the near bank and stopped. Whether it was the drop or the rush of water, she would not descend, even when Lon encouraged her with a whoop and his rope. "Danged stubborn lunkhead!" he fumed.

Owen rode up the bank to help but Emily would no more budge for the two of them than she had for just one. "Let's rope her and drag her across," he proposed.

"She's liable to kick," Lon warned.

"We have to show her who's boss."

Help came from an unforeseen quarter. Intent on Emily, neither noticed Big Blue until the bull strolled by as if he were on a Sunday jaunt. Lowering his haunches, Big Blue slid to the bottom as neatly as you please, then waded across.

If cows could look fit to be tied, Emily certainly did. She snorted and went down the bank much too fast, resulting in a giant splash that drenched her from nose to tail. Undaunted, she crossed with her head held high and, once out of the water, stopped next to Big Blue and shook herself, treating him to a shower.

Lon laughed and exclaimed, "Damn me if that cow doesn't make me think of the last gal I courted!"

With Emily across, Cleopatra, Lily, and Mary were anxious to catch up, and soon they were strung out in their usual formation. Owen and Pitney fell to discussing the state of the cattle industry.

A couple of miles from the stream, Lon Chalmers drew rein. Motioning, he shouted, "You best come see this. It could mean trouble."

Owen clucked to his mount and trotted to the spot. He leaned down. The short hairs at the nape of his neck prickled, and he remarked, "It was bound to happen sooner or later."

"I was hopin' for later," Lon said.

Clearly imprinted in the dirt where there could be no mistaking its maker was a human footprint. But not the print of a boot or a shoe.

The track had been made by a moccasin.

13
Chips

Sweet Sally could talk. She could talk from dawn until dusk, and talk twice as much from dusk until midnight. She talked every minute of the day, about everything under the sun. Her three traveling companions had never heard anyone talk so much. The first day out of Whiskey Flats they marveled at her ceaseless chatter. The second day out, they wished she would give their ears a rest. By the third day, two of them were ready to shoot her.

They had stolen a horse for Sweet Sally to ride. Not from anyone in town, but from a settler who lived half a mile out. Luke Deal knew the man kept several horses in a small corral. It was ridiculously easy for him to slip in and help himself, but there wasn't much to help himself to. Two were so old they were candidates for glue. Another was a swayback. Luke chose a big bay with white stockings and an oddly cropped tail.

Sweet Sally had assured them she could ride. She had not said anything about being able to climb on a horse unaided. She tried, but she was simply much too big to pull herself up. So Deal, Grutt, and Bronk gave her a boost.

As she dangled her huge legs down either side, the bay nickered and looked back at her. Somehow the animal did not seem pleased.

Since the settler kept his saddles inside, Sweet Sally had to go without. She told them she did not mind, that it was better for her to ride bareback. "Saddles chafe my soft skin something awful. They aren't made for beauties my size. It's tough being a giantess in a world of pygmies."

"If you ate less, maybe you wouldn't have so much trouble," Grutt could not resist commenting.

"You're one of those who figure I must stuff myself every waking second? Is that it?" Sweet Sally sniffed at the insult. "For your information, I have a delicate condition. A doctor said so. There's something wrong with me inside. Something I was born with. When you look at me, you see a cute little chipmunk trapped in the body of a buffalo."

"It's a good thing all chipmunks ain't like you, or there wouldn't be room for any other critters."

"That wasn't nice," Sweet Sally said stiffly. "If you expect me to travel with you, you must be gentlemen."

"We'll try, ma'am," Bronk said. "But we're a mite rusty at bein' nice."

"I'm patient. I have a lot of wonderful qualities. You can't judge someone by how they look. It's what's inside that counts."

"What you are inside is mostly fat," Luke Deal said.

Sweet Sally glared. "That is exactly the sort of rudeness I will not put up with. Make up your minds right this moment. Either you be nice or you won't have me for a traveling companion."

"Lady, I never wanted you for company in the first place," Luke declared.

"What can it hurt us to be nice to her?" Bronk asked.

"She promised us free pokes, remember?" Grutt brought up.

Luke Deal surprised them more than they had ever been surprised by smiling warmly and saying, "You're right, boys. What was I thinkin'?" He turned to Sally. "You have my word, ma'am, we will treat you as you deserve. Anyone who insults you must answer to me."

"That's better. Shows what a woman's influence can do. We could rule the world if we weren't always scratching each other's eyes out."

"Women rule the world?" Grutt laughed. "Where do you come up with these notions of yours?"

"Men rule it now. It's only fair us females have a turn."

"Some ruler I am," Grutt said. "A horse, a saddle, and ten dollars to my name."

"I didn't mean all men are Turkish sultans, with chests of gold and gems and harems of a thousand women or more," Sweet Sally said.

Bronk whistled softly. "I don't know as I could handle that many. Just one usually gives me more headaches than I can take."

"I wouldn't mind a hundred or so," Grutt said, "so long as they were all young and pretty and waited on me hand and foot. How about you, Luke?"

"Women are only good for one thing."

"That's where you're wrong, mister," Sweet Sally said. "Females have all kinds of uses. We tend you when you're sick, mend you when you're hurt. We keep you warm at night. We sew your clothes. We darn your damn socks. We do all that and more, and what do we get for it? Treated like dirt, mostly."

Now here it was, five days since they stole the horse, and they were riding north in single file, Luke Deal in the lead, then Grutt, Sweet Sally, and Bronk. It was the middle of a sunny morning. Birds were singing, and all was right with the world for Sally Fitzsimmons.

"Hear that robin? Isn't it beautiful? He's singing because he's in love and his sweetheart is sitting on the nest. Soon their little blue eggs will hatch and they will take their young ones under their wing and be one happy family until winter when they fly off to wherever robins go to, and next year the same pair will be back to build a new nest and start all over again."

"That's a thrush," Luke Deal said.

"Are you sure? Well, thrushes have nests, too, don't they? And sing when they're happy?"

"Birds do a lot of silly things."

Sweet Sally shifted her weight. The bay broke stride but recovered. "You're sure a surly cuss, you know that? How come? Were you born with so much acid in your system, the only way you can get it out is by spitting at folks?"

"When I spit at you, you'll know it," Luke informed her.

"Oh. You're one of those men who thinks he's better than everyone else. Who looks down his nose at the rest of the human race because they don't measure up to how he thinks they ought to be."

"I don't give a damn what others do. It's me I look after. I learned at an early age this world is dog eat dog, and I don't aim to be eaten."

"There are a lot of bad folks, sure," Sweet Sally said, "but there are a lot of good ones, too. Like those Bar 40 boys who saved me from that bunch of Mexican bandits."

"I've been meanin' to ask about that," Luke Deal said. "Tell me more."

Sweet Sally related how she ended up with Paco Ramirez. "Serves me right for not staying north of the border where I belong. I'm not much on Mexican lingo, and haggling over pokes was tiresome."

Grutt perked up his ears and said, "Speakin' of pokes, I recollect you mentionin' free ones if we brought you with us."

"That I did," Sweet Sally said.

"So when does the pokin' commence? It's been a while since I did any and I have a powerful itch."

Bronk said gruffly, "Don't rush her. It's enough she said she would. When she's ready, she's ready."

"Listen to you," Grutt retorted. "Since when did you become a saint? You want to poke her as much as me. You told me so."

"Enough about pokin'," Bronk said.

But Sweet Sally had not had enough. She jabbed her heels against the bay to bring it up near Luke Deal. "How about you? You never say a word about me spreading my legs."

"Spread them all you want. I won't graze."

"What's the matter? Don't you like girls? I admit I may not be the best-looking. But I keep myself fairly clean, and I can do things that will curl your toes."

Pulling his hat brim lower, Luke said, "There is another way to curl toes."

"I never heard of it," Sweet Sally responded. She regarded him thoughtfully for a while, the quietest she had been since the start, then said, "At last I think I have you figured out."

"That's important to you, is it, figurin' me out?"

"I'm female. Females like to know why things are

the way they are. That includes the mean people they meet. So, yeah, you have me curious."

Luke Deal chuckled. "Remember what curiosity did to that cat."

"Do you want to hear or not? If I'm wrong, tell me, and I won't ever bring it up again."

"Like hell you won't," Luke said. "As you keep remindin' us, you're female."

Now it was Sweet Sally who chortled. "See? You can be nice when you put your mind to it." She paused. "All right. Here goes. I think the reason you're such a surly cuss is because you have a chip on your shoulder. Not the everyday kind of chip most people have because they can't understand why we're born only to die, but a giant chip, a chip that eats at you every second of the day."

Luke deigned to look at her. "I'm impressed. You're not the stupid slug I took you for."

"There you go again, being mean for being mean's sake," Sweet Sally chided. "A fat body doesn't mean a fat mind."

"We'll carve that on your headstone."

"Quit acting so nasty. No one is as cold-blooded as you make yourself out to be. Hell, even Paco Ramirez had a streak of human deep down inside."

"I'm not some greaser," Luke Deal said. "But you're right about the chip. I admit it. I've had something eatin' at me since I was twelve. That was when my folks died."

"What killed them?"

"Not what. Who. We lived in east Texas on a farm. My pa broke his back day after day but we were always dirt poor. Barely had enough to eat. One shirt to wear, only on Sundays, and one pair of britches, patched so many places they looked like a quilt. Shoes were somethin' we dreamed about.''

"There are a lot of poor people in this world," Sweet Sally said. "Yet they don't carry the big chip you do."

"There's more to my story," Luke said, and under his hat brim his features had become severely hard, his lips pressed thin. His jaw muscles twitched. "My pa was a good man. As decent as they come. He took us all to church on Sunday and always gave of the little we had. He could read, and when he tucked us in at night, he would read from the Bible. My favorite was the part about Samson."

"Wasn't he the one with the long hair? Who poked a gal by the name of Delilah?"

"That's the one. But I liked him because he was the best killer in the whole Bible. Killed a thousand soldiers with the jawbone of an ass. Killed another six thousand when he brought a temple down on their heads."

"Of all the hombres in the Good Book, you liked him most? What about Adam and Moses and that Joseph character and all the rest whose names I can't remember?"

"They weren't killers."

"You were a boy. What did you know of killing? Sounds to me like you are making this up."

"You would think that," Luke said harshly. "But no, I'm bein' honest for once. I'm tellin' you things not even Grutt and Bronk know. As to why I liked him, maybe it was the seed of things to come."

"Now you've lost me."

"Seeds. Farmers plant them to grow crops. Might be you have heard of them."

Sweet Sally snickered. "So you're sayin' at the tender age of, what, ten years old, the seed to kill was planted in you?"

Luke Deal shrugged.

"Lordy, men do come up with the most ridiculous nonsense. But go on with your tale. I want to hear about the chip."

"When I was twelve, some men came to our farm. It was the year after the war. A lot of hate was left over. A lot of killin' was done. These men, they had fought for the South, and when they came back, their homes had been taken out from under them by Yankee land grabbers."

"It was a terrible time."

"My pa hadn't fought in the war. He refused to take sides. He always said as how we were one country and we should work out our squabbles without bloodshed."

"Your pa was wise," Sweet Sally said.

"My pa was a fool. He didn't know when to keep his mouth shut. He told those Rebs that the South should never have broke from the Union. That all the blood spilled was for nothin'." Luke Deal laughed bitterly. "Then he told them that they had brought the loss of their homesteads down on their own heads."

"Oh my."

"They didn't take kindly to the insult. One of them pulled his revolver and hit my pa across the head. Pa fell, and when Ma rushed to help him, another of those Johnny Rebs hit her with a jug. He only meant to knock her out, I reckon, but the jug broke and part of it stuck in her head, above her ear, and the next I knew, my ma was lyin' there in a puddle of her blood, as dead as dead can be."

Sweet Sally reached out an arm but could not quite touch him. "You poor baby. No wonder you carry a chip."

"I'm not done. There were four of us kids, all boys. I was the second oldest. We were scared, and we didn't know what to do. Then I heard one of the Rebs sayin' as how they couldn't leave witnesses, and another Reb with a red beard, he pulled out his hogleg and shot my pa in the head."

"Surely they didn't hurt you kids?"

"I'm gettin' to that. One of the Rebs wanted to let us live but the other three said it had to be done. My brother Zeb, who was barely a year younger than me, he ran to where my pa's rifle was leanin' in the corner, and a Reb shot him in the back. My oldest brother, Sam, he ran for the bedroom but they shot him down, too."

"If you'd rather not talk about it," Sweet Sally said, "I'll understand."

Luke Deal did not seem to hear her. "That left me and my last brother. We were scared to death. The Reb who didn't want us harmed ran between us and his friends, yellin' there had been enough killin'. It gave my brother and me time to get to the bedroom and the chest of drawers where my pa kept an old pistol loaded in case of an Indian attack. I took the pistol and I shot the first Reb who came in the door. It was the big one with the red beard. I blew off part of his face. I shot the second Reb in the chest and he howled like a painter so I shot him again and down he went on top of the one with the red beard."

"You killed two men and you were only twelve?"

"The old pistol jammed. I thumbed back the hammer and squeezed the trigger but it wouldn't shoot, and when I looked up, there was the third Reb, mad as hell and smilin' as he took aim. I thought I was a gone goslin', but there was a shot, and the third Reb had a new hole next to his nose. My younger brother had picked up a revolver one of the Rebs had dropped. He saved my life."

"Was that the end of it?"

"Not quite. The Reb who had wanted to spare us came into the bedroom, sayin' as how he was sorry about my folks, and was there anything he could do for us? And I picked up another revolver from the floor and shot him."

Sweet Sally's pudgy hand flew to the folds of her throat. "You didn't!"

"Three times. Then I went around to each of those Rebs and shot them in the head, to be sure." Luke looked at her. "Now you know about the chip," he said coldly.

"You've been soured on life ever since?"

"Not soured so much as mad. Mad at the Almighty for lettin' it happen. Mad at life for it bein' as cruel as it is. Mad at jackasses like you who think the world is a garden and we're all flowers."

"What happened to you was horrible. I won't deny that," Sweet Sally said. "But you're not the only one who has had something awful happen to them."

"Is that supposed to make me feel better?"

"No. I'm just saying that you can't go around with a chip on your shoulder forever," Sweet Sally said.

"You think you understand but you don't."

Suddenly Grutt let out a holler. "Riders comin'!"

They were threading through heavy brush country, bottomland thick with vegetation, insects, and wildlife. Ahead, winding toward them, appeared two men on horseback. Cowboys, by their attire, both of them young. They smiled and lifted their hands in greeting. One had enough freckles to fill a coffeepot, and the other had downy peach fuzz on his chin.

"Howdy," said the freckle-faced stripling as he drew rein on a buckskin. "We didn't expect to run into anyone out here in the middle of nowhere." He wore a wide-brimmed Stetson, a bright blue bandanna, and a new Smith and Wesson on his right hip.

"Sure didn't," said the other. Everything about him looked new—his clothes, his chaps, his gun belt, his saddle.

Grutt and Bronk reined up on either side of Luke Deal and Sweet Sally, and it was Grutt who smiled at the cowboys and asked, "You boys ridin' with an outfit, are you?"

"No, sir," said Freckle-face. "Me and my partner, here, are out to start us a ranch of our own."

"We're huntin' for longhorns," said Peach Fuzz. "You haven't happened to have seen any, have you?"

"Not since sunup," Grutt said. "We spotted a few a ways off but they skedaddled like their tails were on fire."

"The wild ones do that." The young man with the freckles touched his chest. "I'm Tommy Sanders and this is Cletus Jones. We came all the way from Dallas."

"We've heard tell this is the best country for longhorns," Cletus said.

"How many head have you gathered so far?" Grutt asked.

"Not a one," Tommy Sanders ruefully admitted. "They're harder to catch than fleas on a bluetick hound. Every time we get close, they run."

Sweet Sally flashed her most dazzling smile. "Maybe you boys would do better if you found someone who could teach you how to go about it."

"Our thinkin' exactly, ma'am," Cletus said. "Say, would any of you know the tricks of the trade?"

"The only tricks I know," Grutt said, "are with cards."

"I know a few," Luke Deal told them.

"You do?" Tommy Sanders straightened. "Can you show them to us, mister? We'd be obliged."

"Sure," Luke said, and just like that, his Remington was in his hand. He twirled it forward, he twirled it backward, he moved his arm high while twirling, then moved his arm low, still twirling. With the bright sun gleaming off the metal, the effect was dazzling. He gave a last twirl and the Remington neatly slid into its holster. "Those are some of the tricks I know."

"Oh. I thought you meant cows," Tommy said, disappointed.

"That was some show," Cletus admired. "You must be a gun hand."

"I have my moments," Luke replied, and leaned on his saddle horn. "There's another one I'll show you in a bit."

Something in the manner he said it caused Sweet Sally to worriedly say, "Don't you dare." To the cowboys she said, "Nice meetin' you. Good luck findin' cows." She raised the bay's reins to ride on but Luke Deal, Grutt, and Bronk made no move to go.

"I'd love to learn to do what you just did," Tommy Sanders said to Deal. "I'm not much good with a revolver."

"Me neither," Cletus Jones chimed in. "Oh, I've

shot a few snakes and such, but I can't hit much past ten feet."

"Me either," Bronk said, "which is why I like to get in close so I can't miss."

"You've killed before?"

"We all have," Grutt said. "More than once."

Tommy Sanders licked his lips and glanced at Cletus Jones. The two of them visibly tensed.

"Well, nice talkin' to you folks." Cletus was about to ride off.

"I have an idea," Luke Deal said mildly. "Why don't you let us help you round up some longhorns? Five riders can cover a lot more territory than two."

"You would do that for us?" Tommy brightened.

"How damn dumb are you?"

Confused, Tommy Sanders cocked his head. "But you just said you would lend us a hand."

"Boy, you couldn't pay me enough to cowboy." Luke radiated contempt. "It's miserable work, almost as miserable as farmin'. The hours are long and the pay is low. You spend all damn day in the saddle nursemaidin' a bunch of stupid smelly cattle. I'd rather do anything but punch cows."

"Well, we like the idea," Cletus said. "Five years from now we'll have a ranch of our own and be runnin' five hundred head or more."

"It's our dream," Tommy Sanders said.

"Not in five years," Luke said. "Not in ten. Not ever."

"How's that again, mister?" Tommy had gone pale.

So had Sweet Sally. "You wouldn't. You can't. They haven't done you any harm. Let them be."

"Stay out of this if you know what is good for you."

"Mister, we don't want no trouble," Cletus said.

Luke grinned at the two young cowboys. "Whenever you are ready to dance, light the wick."

"Mister, you're loco. We don't want no grief." Tommy nodded at Cletus and the two of them gigged their horses to go around.

"Be seein' you," Cletus said to Sweet Sally.

"In hell," Luke Deal responded, and his hand blurred. The Remington boomed twice. His first shot caught Tommy Sanders in the face and flipped him from the buckskin. His second shot struck Cletus Jones high in the chest, twisting him half around. Cletus's mount bolted, and after a dozen yards Cletus pitched to the earth.

Sweet Sally was thunderstruck. "You killed them! You just up and killed those sweet boys for no reason!"

Luke Deal slid a cartridge from a belt loop and began replacing the two he had spent. "You're forgettin' that chip on my shoulder."

14
Red Men

Few things spooked cowboys like Indians did. Word was spread to the others, and for the rest of the day they rode alertly, hands on their revolvers or with their rifles in their hands. Where there was one Indian there were bound to be more, and in their minds Indians spelled trouble with a large *T*.

Ever since the first whites arrived in the country that would later become Texas, there had been constant clashes between the white man and the red man. The red man had been there first, and many tribes did not take kindly to the brash, arrogant intruders who claimed the land for their own.

Bloodshed was inevitable. Race was not the catalyst, although there were many on both sides who hated the other merely because of the color of their skin. It was a clash of cultures, a difference so vast in the basic way the two sides regarded themselves and the world around them that the chasm could not be bridged short of eliminating those who were so different.

Other factors were involved. On the red side, warrior cultures dictated that they regard the whites as enemies. Raids and counting coup and stealing horses were ingrained in the fabric of their existence; they did it to other red men, they had done it to the Spanish, they saw no reason not to do it to the new invaders.

On the white side, there was the inexorable westward tide, the urge to expand, to keep pushing west until every square foot of the continent had been claimed and put under the plow or turned into a settlement or a town or a city.

To the Indians, the land was a nurturer. It gave them that which they needed to live, and in return they treated it with reverence.

To the whites, the land was property. Yet another commodity, to be bartered and bought and sold and claimed as private. The NO TRESPASSING signs the whites put up were not meant for Indians alone. White men regarded that which was theirs as their private domain, and woe to anyone who violated it.

It was inevitable that there were skirmishes between different tribes and the cowboys who made their living by herding cattle across the land the Indians once so freely roamed. The Comanches were the most feared, although in recent years their depredations had been largely contained. But they were not the only tribe. There were the Lipan Apaches, the Kitsai, the Tonkawas, the Quapaws, the Wichitas, the Osage, the Kiowa Apaches, the Kiowas, and more. Many more. Along the coast were tribes so small and so remote that the white man deemed them hardly worthy of notice.

As evening neared, the Bar 40 punchers became more anxious. They had good cause. They were worried about the longhorns more than their scalps. In recent years, Indians had taken to stealing cows.

That there was a correlation between the rise in missing cows and the slaughter of the buffaloes the Indians depended on for their very existence did not go unnoticed, but that did not mean cowboys condoned the taking of the animals they relied on for their own.

Owen chose a clearing beside a creek for their camp. The creek was to the east, to the west grew dense woods, to the north and south thick brush. He had Chavez park the chuck wagon on the creek bank so they had a clear view of the rest of the clearing. A rope was strung to keep Big Blue and the cows from straying. The horses were picketed. He gave instructions that the fire was to be kept small and that no one was to go off alone for any reason. Lastly, they would take turns keeping watch throughout the night in pairs, not singly.

Only when everything that could be done had been done did the foreman sit by the fire, propped on his saddle, and accept a piping-hot cup of black coffee from Benedito. Lon relaxed across from him. Slim and Cleveland were standing guard on either side of the clearing.

Alfred Pitney sipped tea while staring into the darkening depths of the woods. "I say, do you truly think hostiles will cause us trouble? We only saw the one footprint, after all."

"Better safe than dead, or our cows stolen," Owen said.

Lon patted his Colt. "I'd like to see them try. It's been a few years since I've killed a redskin."

"That's rather mean-spirited, wouldn't you agree?" Pitney asked.

"Mister, the Comanches killed six of my kin," Lon

said bitterly. "The Kiowas killed two more. Call it mean if you want, but I'd as soon there wasn't one Indian left in all of Texas."

"I take it you don't subscribe to the idea of the noble savage so prevalent in the newspapers?" Pitney said to make conversation.

"Noble, hell. There's not none that way. Indians are people, just like us. There are good ones and there are bad ones, and it's always the bad ones who spoil things for the rest."

"On which side do you place the blame for the spilling of blood?"

"Both sides have done their share," Lon said. "It's a waste of time to point fingers. All I care about is me and mine and those I ride with and work for. So long as the Indians leave us be, I'll leave them be."

"An aunt of mine was taken by the Comanches," Owen revealed. "It took my uncle three years to find the band that had her. He offered to buy her back and the Comanches were willin' but she refused to come home. She said she had grown used to Indian ways and she liked them better than white ways."

"I've heard of folks like that," Lon said. "Addlepated, if you ask me."

"In Wyoming some of the tribes have been tamed, as you Yanks call it," Pitney mentioned. "They wear white clothes and live as whites and send their children to white schools. But they are not happy about having a new way of life forced on them."

"Who would be?" Lon said. "But either they change or they die. That might sound too mean for you, comin' from a country where you don't have any Indians, but for those of us here, it helps us sleep better at night."

"Britain doesn't have Indians, no, but it has had its share of conflicts. The Celts, the Romans, the Picts, the Saxons, and many more, all have stained British soil with blood. You can count your wars on one hand. Ours have been without number." Pitney swallowed some more tea. "There are those who say warfare is our natural state. That so long as man exists, there will be wars and rumors of war. There will be the spilling of blood."

"A happy notion," Owen said dryly.

"Don't you ever give it any thought?"

"No. I'm too busy livin' to fret over what might be. There are always those who think the sky is fallin' but it's still up there."

"Would that more souls had your attitude," Alfred Pitney said. "The world would be a friendlier place."

Lon snorted. "Friendly has nothin' to do with life. Friendly is for Bible-thumpers and those who wear blinders. Out here"—Lon gestured at the benighted wilderness—"bein' too friendly can get a man killed."

Suddenly Slim was by the fire, nervously fingering his Winchester and saying, "Owen! I think I heard somethin'. Someone is movin' about in those trees yonder."

They rose and ran to the edge of the woods and listened, but all they heard was the sigh of the wind and the rustle of leaves. In the far distance coyotes yipped, and once a bird screeched.

"Whatever it was, it must be gone," Slim offered.

"Or lyin' low, waitin' for us to turn in," Owen said. "From now on stay ten feet back so they can't jump you."

A mouthwatering aroma filled the clearing, rising from the stove Benedito Chavez was industriously bent over. He would not let the threat of an Indian attack interfere with his duties. Come rain or shine, storm or calm, Indians or outlaws, he would perform his duties.

Tonight the fare was fit for a prince: juicy slabs of Brownie, smothered in wild onions; potatoes, skinned and sliced, served in a sauce with a cornmeal base and heavy with butter; the inevitable fresh, hot sourdough; and a rich berry pudding that everyone had two helpings of. All washed down with delicious coffee, except in Pitney's case. He much preferred his treasured tea.

They ate in shifts. Owen and Lon partook, then they stood guard while Slim and Cleveland ate. Pitney, pricked by guilt, offered to stand guard, too, but Owen would not hear of it. "You're not one of the hands."

"But I'm a member of this party. I should do my fair share of the work. Wouldn't your employer help if he were here?"

"Yes, he would," Owen conceded, "but you are Mr. Bartholomew's guest, and he gave me special instructions on how you are to be treated."

"I resent the special treatment," Pitney complained.

"Then look at it another way," Owen suggested. "If anything were to happen to you, would the BLC still buy Big Blue?"

Pitney had to think about that. "Perhaps not. I conceived the idea, I came to Texas on my own initiative to buy him."

"There you have it. We can't expose you to extra risk or all we've done will be for nothin'."

Benedito was exempted from standing guard by virtue of being the cook. As he explained it to Pitney when the Brit asked why he never did any of the work the cowboys did, "Because, señor, I am the one who feeds their bellies that they may do the work they do. I am of more value to them than everything in their lives but their horses. I am a step below God, and do you see God punching cows?"

Pitney laughed and said, "You are exaggerating."

"Ask them, señor. They will tell you. The cook never does the work they do. Not at the Bar 40, not anywhere. Cooks are kings, as the gringos say. It is enough that I work hard to feed them."

"You don't appear to be especially exhausted."

"Was that humor, señor? You are poking fun at poor Benedito, no? Or have you not noticed I am always up before the cowboys so I can heat the stove and have their coffee ready and start breakfast? Have you not noticed how many hours I spend cooking? How I am always looking for things I can cook? How I make of each meal what you would say is a"— Benedito paused, searching for the right word—"what you call a masterpiece? Have you noticed none of these things?"

"Now that you mention them, I have," Pitney said. "I also noticed that you do not wear a revolver or have a rifle. What if we are attacked? How will you defend yourself? Or don't gods bother?"

"You poke more fun, señor. But I would not give my life up without a fight. And I have something better than a gun." From under his serape Benedito slid a long-bladed weapon. He tapped the blade with a fingernail and it rang softly like the chime of a bell. "My machete."

"Good Lord! You could cleave someone in half," Pitney exclaimed.

"That is one use, señor." Benedito smiled. "But a neck is much easier to cut, and when an enemy loses an arm or leg, much of the fight goes out of them."

"I didn't even know you carried that thing."

"This, and a shotgun in the wagon. It would be a big surprise to a Comanche, sí?" Benedito gazed toward the woods. "Or whoever is out there now."

Owen gave orders that the fire be maintained all night. He sent Lon and Slim out to gather fuel to last them.

The woods were deathly still. The wind had died, the coyotes were quiet. The two cowboys left their rifles behind so their arms were free to carry limbs. Hands on their revolvers, they roved about under the trees. Now and again their spurs would jingle lightly, and about the fourth or fifth time Slim glanced down in irritation and said, "I wish we had thought to take them off."

"If they're spyin' on us, they know where we are anyway," Lon said. "I half hope they jump us. It will be their last time."

"Easy for you to say," Slim replied. "You can unlimber that smoke wagon and put three holes into a man before he so much as blinks. I'm lucky if I can hit the broad side of a barn."

"All it takes is practice."

"Horse feathers. I could practice from now until doomsday and not be half as good as you. It takes a knack and I don't have it." Slim glanced at Chalmers. "I heard about what you did down in Mexico with Mr. Bartholomew. Four bandits, they say, done so quick, they were dead before they touched their hardware."

"One did," Lon said.

"See? Damnation. If you hadn't become a cowboy, I bet you'd be as famous as John Wesley Hardin or Ben Thompson."

"Or dead."

Slim began gathering wood. Lon stood watchful as a hawk, his lightning right hand always on his Colt. When Slim had an armful, he clasped the dead branches firmly with his left arm and drew his revolver with his right. Then it was Lon's turn to collect fuel. When he had as much as he could carry, they backed toward the clearing.

They were almost to it when something moved deep in the trees. Instantly, Lon's Colt was out and pointed and the hammer gave a distinct *click*.

"What is it?" Slim whispered in dread.

"Hush, you infant," Lon scolded. They waited in breathless anticipation of a war whoop or the twang of a bowstring or the blast of a shot, but silence continued to lay over the woods like a mantle. After a few minutes Lon nodded at Slim. "Keep goin'. I'll cover you."

Slim didn't argue. He was no gun hand. His whole life was cows, and if it were up to him, he would never be put in a situation where he had to take a human life, white or red. Some of the other hands liked to joke that he was too tenderhearted for his own good because he was fond of calves and puppies and always treated women with the utmost respect, but he let their jests go in one ear and bounce out again. He could not change who he was.

Owen saw them backing toward the fire and darted to their side, his rifle to his shoulder. "Did you see something?"

"Something," Lon said.

"It could have been a deer," Slim speculated.

Lon shot the lanky puncher a hard look. "Or a Comanche."

They settled in for the night. Owen and Lon lay on

their backs with their rifles at their sides. Slim and
Cleveland would wake them at one a.m. Pitney spread
his blankets close to the fire and was about to lie down
when Lon asked him what he was doing.

"Turning in. What does it look like?"

"Sleep in the flames, why don't you."

Perplexed, Pitney sat up. "I like to be warm."

"Do you like bein' dead? Because if there are red-
skins skulkin' about, and they take it into their heads
to exterminate us, the first one they shoot will be the
British dandy lyin' near to the fire where they can see
him as plain as day."

"Oh," Pitney said. "I hadn't thought of that."

"It's the little things that can get us bucked out
in gore," Lon warned. "Try to put yourself in their
moccasins and not do anything that makes it easy for
them to slit your throat."

Pitney moved his blankets out of the ring of
firelight.

Over under the wagon, where he always slept,
Benedito was already snoring. He was always the
first to turn in so he could always be the first to
awake in the morning. His sombrero was pulled low
over his face, and fluttered with each loud breath
he took.

Big Blue and the cows were dozing. The bull
seemed to fill half the clearing, he was so huge. His
horns shone like twin swords.

As had become her habit, Emily lay close to him,
their backs nearly brushing. Lily, Cleopatra, and Mary
lay in a cluster of their own.

The camp quieted. More snores broke the stillness,
mixed with the occasional jangle of Slim's and Cleveland's spurs.

About one a.m., Slim woke Owen and Lon. Arching his skinny back, he yawned and said sleepily, "All yours. Things have been quiet."

"Not a sign of Indians or anything else," Cleveland added. "Other than a hoot owl."

"Could be we're worried over nothin'," Owen said. "Could be the owner of that moccasin and his friends if he has any are miles away."

Lon cradled his Winchester in the crook of his left elbow. "Could be cows can fly."

"If they are out there, why haven't they done anything yet?" Cleveland asked him.

"Indians aren't stupid. They don't want to die any more than you do. They won't light the wick until they're damn sure they can kill us without us killin' them."

"Maybe they are waitin' until mornin'," Cleveland said. "Some tribes don't like to fight at night, I hear. It's supposed to be bad medicine or some such silliness."

Owen was wiping dust from the barrel of his rifle. "Their medicine is no sillier than a white man carryin' a rabbit's foot."

"It's more like a religion, isn't it?" Cleveland said. "Something to do with their Great Spirit or Great Mystery or whatever they call it."

"Hokum," Slim said. "Red bunk. I don't set store by any of it."

"They do," Lon said, "and that's what counts." He strode toward the perimeter.

Slim turned to Owen. "What has him as techy as a teased snake?"

"He gets like this when he's on edge. Bein' shot and nearly dyin' will do that," Owen said. "He's on the prod, all horns and rattles, and I wouldn't want to be those Indians if they try to rub us out."

But the rest of the night was uneventful. The cows and the horses rested undisturbed. Owen stood watch over the north half of the clearing, Lon prowled like a restless panther about the south half.

The sky was still dark when Benedito stirred. His sombrero had slid off and the first thing he did was put it back on. He crawled on hands and knees out from under the wagon and slowly uncurled. He shook himself a few times against the morning chill, then went to the Dutch stove. For breakfast it would be eggs, bacon, and toast. The eggs were in a flour sack. Before leaving the Bar 40 Benedito had poured the flour into a pot, then carefully refilled the sack, adding as many eggs as was safe. Eggs were easily broken, and the flour served as a cushion.

Soon the stove was hot. Benedito cut strips from the heavily salted slab of bacon and placed them flat in a buttered pan. Only when one side of the bacon was nicely brown did he break eggs open over another pan and place buttered bread in a third. He already knew how the punchers liked theirs done: Owen always wanted his eggs scrambled, Lon and Slim liked theirs over easy, Cleveland liked his yokes hard and the whites well done. The Englishman did not like eggs. He usually ate only a couple of biscuits for breakfast. Benedito would never say so to Pitney's face, but the man from the other side of the world had the appetite of a bird.

Slim, surprisingly enough, was the biggest eater of them all. His stomach was a bottomless well. Benedito continually marveled at how much the cowboy could eat, yet Slim never gained a pound. Which irked

Benedito. He had to watch how much he ate or his large belly would be even larger.

The cowboys always took a few minutes after breakfast to relax, to sip coffee and let their food digest. But today the four had rifles at their sides, and while they gave the impression they were relaxed and at ease, a closer scrutiny revealed the tenseness in their postures and the wary darting of their eyes.

Dawn broke. A golden crescent framed the tangle of brush bordering the far side of the creek. The longhorns were all standing except Big Blue, who was usually the last to rise.

"Do you still expect trouble?" Alfred Pitney inquired.

"Any minute now," Owen answered. "If it's Indians, they'll move on us before we ride out."

"It's Indians," Cleveland said.

"You're startin' to sound like Lon." Owen grinned. "Always lookin' for storm clouds when it might not even rain."

"There's a storm cloud now," Cleveland said softly, and pointed.

Owen, Lon, and Slim whirled, Lon's Colt flashing in the morning light. Alfred Pitney nearly dropped his cup. Benedito dived his hand under his serape but did not draw the machete.

There were five of them. Two were an old man and woman, wrinkled and stoop-shouldered, an ancient warrior and his wife. The other three looked enough like the old pair to be their children or their grandchildren. All were bones and sagging skin. Their eyes were dark sockets, their cheeks hollow. The old man smiled, showing mostly gums where a full mouth of teeth had once been. They wore worn, frayed buckskins, and moccasins that had been stitched and re-stitched to mend holes. Only one was armed, a young one with a bone-handled knife at his waist. The bone handle was cracked.

"Good Lord!" Alfred Pitney declared. "They're scarecrows!"

"They look sickly to me," Slim said. "You don't reckon it's catchin', do you?"

Owen walked toward them. He held his right hand in front of him with the first two fingers pointed at the sky and moved his hand as high as his head. "We are friendly," he said. "Do you speak English?"

Their blank looks demonstrated they did not.

"What can we do for you?" Owen inquired, and gestured to get his point across. "What is it you want?"

The old warrior pointed a bony finger toward the Dutch stove. He placed his hand on his stomach and rubbed it in a circle while moving his mouth as if he were eating.

"They're hungry," Cleveland said.

"They're starved," Lon amended. "They can't hunt much with just a knife."

Owen said over his shoulder, "Benedito, rustle up a sack we can spare. Fill it with whatever is left of the sourdough and our breakfast leavin's and anything else you can think of."

"Sí, señor. Pronto."

The Indians watched hungrily as the cook scurried to comply. Drool dribbled over the old man's lower lip when Benedito brought the sack over. He accepted it gratefully, his eyes misting, then raised an arm in gratitude or salute, said a word to the others, and the five of them trudged off into the woods as silently as the wraiths they resembled.

For a while no one spoke. Then a horse whinnied, breaking the spell.

"All that worryin' we did," Owen said.

Lon Chalmers shook his head and sighed. "Does anyone else feel as ridiculous as me?"

"What will happen to them?" Pitney asked.

"The same thing that happens to all of us," Lon said, "only odds are they'll die sooner than we do."

15

Tail Wags Dog

A miracle occurred. Something so extraordinary, Luke Deal, Grutt, and Bronk were stunned: Sweet Sally did not say a word for two days after the deaths of the cowboys. Not a single, solitary word. When Luke or Grutt or Bronk spoke to her, she ignored them. She treated them as if they did not exist.

A great sadness had come over her. A sadness that shielded her from their taunts and crude jokes and insults. She did not care what they said. She did not care what they did.

Sweet Sally's sadness was tinged with fear. She had not considered herself in any danger until Deal proved otherwise by coldly, brutally shooting the two young men. Her glib tongue had put her in peril. Now she regretted persuading Deal to bring her along.

By nature, Sally was one of those who always looked for the best in people and tended to overlook the bad. She liked people, truly liked them. From her fondness stemmed her belief that deep down inside of every human being, no matter how evil they might appear to be, was a shred of goodness. Paco Ramirez had been a prime example. To the world at large he was a bandit, a murderer, a thief, and a rustler. But he had treated her with kindness, and never once hurt her out of spite or just to hurt her for hurting's sake.

Sally recollected someone telling her once that there was an exception to every rule. Luke Deal was the exception to hers. The more she came to know him, the more they talked and the more she saw of him, the more convinced she became that he was the first and only truly evil person she had ever met.

He did not care about anyone or anything. Not so much as a drop of the milk of human kindness was to be found anywhere in him. He was empty inside. Where most people had a heart and a soul, he had emptiness. It was as if he were hollow, as if all kindness and consideration had been drained out of him, or eaten out, devoured by whatever inner demons had caused him to become as he was.

He would kill anyone or anything without being provoked. He killed just to kill. When the deed was done he showed no regret or sadistic joy, no emotion of any kind. To him, killing people was no different than killing bugs or birds or anything else. Killing was killing, and he did it as casually as most folks put on clothes, or breathed.

Sweet Sally was sure it had to do with the brutal deaths of his parents. That day, something in Luke Deal had forever changed. All trace of human feeling had been erased and replaced by something so hideous, so vile, it changed a small boy into a monster.

The second day of her silent treatment they were winding along a track between two settlements when they stopped at midday to briefly rest their horses. Sweet Sally found a convenient log and wearily sat down. She was tired of riding. She was not built for it. Her legs were sore. Her backside was tender. She wanted to stop at the next settlement and get a room for a few days and do nothing but eat and sleep and take long hot baths and eat some more.

A shadow fell across her and Sweet Sally glanced up. She nearly gave a start. But she had learned long ago to master her expression so it did not give away her true thoughts and feelings. A woman had to be adept at hiding her true self when dealing with men.

Luke Deal had his thumbs hooked in his belt. Those gray eyes of his were as icy as a mountain glacier and as empty of emotion as a tomb. "Enough is enough."

Sweet Sally did not say anything.

"Grutt and Bronk are upset that you won't talk to them, and I don't aim to listen to them bellyache about it the rest of the day. So start talkin', and start talkin' now."

Sally smiled. The silent treatment always had an effect. It was one of the most powerful weapons in her personal arsenal.

"I reckon you didn't hear me." Luke Deal drew his Remington and touched the muzzle to her forehead. "Start talkin' or have your brains splattered all over creation. Your choice."

"What do you want me to say?"

Deal smirked and replaced the revolver with a flourish. "That's better. I don't care what you say so long as Grutt and Bronk stop gripin'. I didn't bring you along to make my life miserable."

Sweet Sally took advantage of the opening. "Why did you agree to bring me along? Sure, I begged you, but it certainly wasn't out of the goodness of your heart."

"I have plans for you, cow."

"Please spare me the insults." Sally fought down

a rising surge of fear. "What sort of plans? I'd like to hear."

"I bet you would." Luke's contempt was transparent. "But I'll keep them a secret a while yet. I wouldn't want you to get any ideas."

"Ideas about what?" Sweet Sally pressed him. "Come on. Be reasonable. Haven't I treated all of you nicely? Haven't I given Bronk and Grutt their pokes without complaining about how they could both use a bath and a clean set of clothes? Have I ever once said anything mean to you?"

"Is all that supposed to impress me?" Luke retorted. "Is it supposed to make me think you're special? You're a whore. A common, good-for-nothin' piece of trash. You give your body to anyone who wants a nibble." Luke spat at her feet. "You're a worthless wretch. The hombre who puts windows in your skull will be doin' the rest of the world a favor."

Sweet Sally felt a cold wind blow over her. Yet, oddly, the trees were still. "You can't go on as you are."

"You're still tryin' to figure me out, aren't you? Fair enough. I'm the curious one now. What have you learned?"

"You need a woman, Luke."

Laughter burst from Luke Deal like water over a falls. He laughed and laughed and then laughed some more, and when he stopped, he looked at her in disbelief. "You're loco. Do you know that?"

"I mean it. You need someone good in your life. You need someone to teach you how to live again."

Again Deal laughed, then put a hand to his side and choked back more. "I had no idea you could be so comical. You're worth your weight in gold."

"What's so funny about what I just said?" Sweet Sally refused to be intimidated. "I'm right and you know it."

"Of course you are. You're a woman. Women are always right." Deal snorted and smacked his leg.

"Spare me your disrespect, if you don't mind." Sally had opened a crack in him and she was going to keep prying at his shell. She patted the log. "Sit down. Talk a spell. It can't hurt you any."

Luke glanced toward where Grutt and Bronk were seated in the shade near the horses. "For a minute or two," he said, and deposited himself on the log just beyond her reach. He folded his hands on his knees and looked at her expectantly. "Well? Let's hear the rest of your silliness."

"Is it silly to be kind to people? To care enough about them that you want to help them?"

"You don't care about me. You don't care about any man. To you, men are like toothpicks. They have their use, then you throw them aside."

"What a strange thing to say. I've given every man I've ever been with his money's worth. And I've never pushed any out of my bed." Sweet Sally paused. "Except that prospector who hadn't taken a bath in a year and a half, and whose teeth smelled like rotten meat."

"We were talkin' about me."

Sweet Sally looked quickly away so he would not see her sudden smile. Composing herself, she faced him and said earnestly, "You claim that I don't care about anyone. When was the last time you did?"

"What?"

"You heard me. Quit stalling. When was the last time you cared about anyone other than yourself?"

"I don't care if I live or die," Luke said.

"That's not what I asked. When was the last time you cared about another person? Was it your parents? Your brothers?"

Luke averted his face. His hands, where they rested on his legs, became hooked claws. "What if it was?"

"Don't you see? You let what happened to them change you. You let it twist you and break you. But you can change back. You don't need to go on doing as you are. You can be nice."

"There's that word again. 'Nice.'" Luke swiveled and his gray eyes peered intently at her from under his hat brim. "Is that what you think you are? Nice?" He said the last "nice" slowly, hissing it between his lips.

Sweet Sally did not take the bait. "I like to think I am, yes. I admit I haven't made much of my life. A whore is a whore is a whore. But I have always been nice to everyone I meet. I make it a point to be."

"That's your purpose in life, is it?"

"There you go again, being mean. I don't know as I have a purpose. A preacher once told me we all do, but for the life of me, I can't figure out mine."

"Maybe pokes are your purpose." Luke's grin was devious. "Maybe God put you on earth so every man you meet can poke you and go away happy at how nice you are about it."

"Go to hell. Poking isn't a purpose. It's what I do for a living. Nothing more." Sally quelled her anger. She reminded herself that he had a knack for getting her riled and she must not let him.

"I have a purpose," Luke surprised her by saying.

"Really? Care to share what it is?"

"My purpose in life is to have no purpose. It is to go wherever I want to go, to do whatever I want to do. My purpose is to live as I please. To kill as I please. To beat and break as I please."

"That's not a purpose," Sweet Sally said. "You're just saying that to get my goat. If you tried, if you honestly and truly tried, you could find a better purpose."

Luke returned her thrust. "That works both ways. What about you? Maybe you have a higher purpose than givin' men pokes. But I don't see you makin' any effort to change."

"Shows how little you know. If a decent man were to ask me to be his, I would give up this life in a heartbeat."

"So that's your purpose? To marry and have a passel of brats and live happily ever after?" Luke's bark was brittle.

Forgetting herself, Sweet Sally countered by saying, "It was good enough for your parents, wasn't it?"

"Quit bringin' them up." Luke fidgeted on the log, and scowled. "I don't like to think about them."

"Hurts you deep down inside, does it?" Sweet Sally said. "That shows there is hope for you. That you're not as completely evil as I thought."

Luke's head jerked up. "Did you really? Think me evil, that is?"

Sweet Sally wanted to kick herself for her lapse in judgment. "Somewhat," she hedged. "After what you did to those cowboys, what else was I to think?" She added meaningfully, "But I was mistaken. You're not evil. You're hurt and confused, a little lamb who has gone astray."

Luke Deal clapped his hands and roared with robust mirth. He laughed longer and louder than he had before. He laughed so long and so hard, when he finally subsided, he had tears trickling from the corners of his eyes. "Oh my, oh my, oh my, oh my," he exhaled. "You tickle my funny bone more than anyone I have ever met."

"Why, thank you," Sweet Sally said, sincerely flattered.

"I would never have thought it." Luke put a hand on her knee. "I'm glad I didn't shoot you back in Whiskey Flats."

Sweet Sally's felt her cheeks grow red and her body tingle with unexpected warmth. "What a nice thing to say. See? You can do it when you try."

Luke rose, his gray eyes twinkling. "Yes. This promises to be great fun. We're bound to have a chance or two to test your notion."

"How do you mean?"

"You'll see," Luke said enigmatically, then hollered to his companions, "Mount up! We're headin' out."

Over the course of the next hour, Luke Deal gave voice to short bouts of laughter and slapped his thigh. The first time it happened, Grutt and Bronk looked at one another in bewilderment, and Grutt shifted in his saddle to say to Sally, "What in hell did you say to him back there?"

"We talked about being nice," Sweet Sally revealed, "and he said he is going to give it a try."

"You stupid cow," Grutt said.

"What did I do?" Sweet Sally bristled. "If you're going to talk to me like that, don't talk to me at all."

Bronk and Grutt slowed to put more distance between them and Luke Deal, and Bronk said quietly so Deal would not hear, "Damn her. This is goin' to be El Paso all over again."

"Ain't it, though," Grutt agreed.

A seed of doubt sprouted in Sweet Sally. She asked them to tell her about El Paso but neither would give her the courtesy. There was a new tenseness and unease in their posture and their manner. It took her a while to figure out that they were afraid, which made her afraid. For if Luke's own friends were suddenly so scared of him, what would happen if they ran into someone else?

As if in answer, shortly thereafter a small cloud of dust appeared to the north.

"Riders, you reckon?" Grutt called out.

Luke Deal shrugged. "We'll find out soon enough."

It was a buggy, a black buggy with a two-horse team and a middle-aged man dressed all in black, with a black jacket and black pants and a small, round black hat. Only his collar was white. His face bore the weathered stamp of someone who was outdoors a lot. As he brought his buggy to a stop, he smiled warmly. "Greetings, brothers and sister."

Reining up alongside, Luke asked, "Who have we here?"

"Reverend Tomlin, at your service, young man," the minister said. He patted a Bible on the seat beside him. "I'm making my monthly rounds."

Luke glanced up at the bright sky, and laughed. Then he smiled at the reverend and said, "Ask and ye shall receive. Isn't that how it goes?"

"Why, yes, that is an exact quote," Tomlin said. "Are you a student of the Lord's Word, young man?"

"Only if that word is 'nice,' " Luke replied.

"I'm afraid I don't understand." Reverend Tomlin nodded at Bronk and Grutt, then his kindly gaze alighted on Sweet Sally. "I never expected to come across a woman way out here. You must be very brave, sister. Put your faith and trust in our Lord and He will see you safely through."

Luke said, "She puts her faith and trust in 'nice.' "

"I still don't understand." Reverend Tomlin glanced from him to Sally and back again. "Perhaps you would care to explain?"

"Oh, she and I had a talk earlier about how we should all be 'nice,' " Luke said. He continued to accent the word, and to smirk when he said it.

"Nice is fine but it is not enough," Reverend Tomlin stated. "We must be spiritual. We must be loving. We must take the teachings of our Lord to heart, and live them."

"Is that what you do?"

"Why, of course. I am a man of the cloth, am I not?" Reverend Tomlin smiled. "I live by the Word."

"You've taken all the teachin's in the Bible to heart, have you?" Luke asked him good-naturedly.

"I like to think I have, yes," the minister said.

"Does that include the one about turnin' the other cheek?"

Sweet Sally's insides churned. "Luke, please," she said, but her appeal fell on stone ears.

"That one most of all," Reverend Tomlin said. "It is one of the cornerstones of my faith."

"You don't say." Suddenly Luke bent and grabbed the minister by the arm and flung him from the seat.

Taken utterly unawares, Reverend Tomlin tumbled into the grass. Rolling onto his back, he rose on his elbows, his black jacket and pants sprinkled with dust. He was not hurt, only shocked. "Hold on! What is the meaning of this?"

"We're findin' out if you practice what you preach."

"But to do what you just did!" Reverend Tomlin

sat up and brushed at his sleeves. "Really, young man. I must protest such cavalier treatment. You have proven nothing by your roughhouse."

"I'm just gettin' started." Luke slowly drew his Remington. The nickel-plating gleamed in the sunlight.

"No!" Sweet Sally slapped her legs against the bay but Bronk caught hold of the bridle.

Grutt seized her wrist. "If you like breathin'," he whispered, "stay right where you are and keep your big mouth shut."

Reverend Tomlin was frozen in disbelief. "Surely you don't intend to shoot me, young man?"

"Surely I do," Luke Deal mimicked him.

"But—but—" the minister stammered, and looked around in incredulity. "This can't be happening."

"It is."

Tomlin asked the question that would be uppermost on anyone's mind. "Why, in heaven's name? What have I ever done to you that you should abuse me like this?"

"Not a thing," Luke admitted.

"Please. I want to comprehend. Enlighten me. What is going through your head? What purpose does shooting me serve?"

Sweet Sally realized the man of the cloth was desperately stalling. She also knew it would do him no good. Frantic, she tugged at the bay's reins but Bronk and Grutt would not let go.

"You haven't been payin' attention, Word-man," Luke Deal said. "You claim to always turn the other cheek. Let's find out if you do." He slowly thumbed back the Remington's hammer.

"Please!" Reverend Tomlin said.

Luke squinted up at the sky. "Strange. There aren't any bolts comin' out of the blue to stop me, so I reckon the Almighty must approve of what I'm about to do." Quick as a striking sidewinder, he leveled his right hand and shot the minister in the leg.

Bucking upward, Tomlin cried out in agony and clasped his hands to his calf. He thrashed wildly from side to side, his teeth clenched. Blood seeped between his fingers. It was several minutes before he stopped and lay limp on his side. Then, weakly lifting his head, he said, "I forgive you your trespass."

Luke cackled. "If that's not turnin' the other cheek, I don't know what is. But what's one little bit of lead in the leg?" He took deliberate aim and shot Reverend Tomlin in the right shoulder.

The minister could not help himself; he screamed and thrashed more wildly than before, one hand to the new wound, the other over the hole in his leg.

As nonchalantly as if he were target shooting, Luke began replacing the spent cartridges. "Are you mad as hell yet? Do you want to bring the wrath of the Lord down on my head?"

Reverend Tomlin could not have replied if he'd wanted to. His face contorted from the torment, he quaked and groaned. But not for long. He abruptly clasped his hands and raised his eyes in appeal to the heavens for succor. Then he fainted.

"I'll be jiggered," Luke said. "He doesn't have enough sand to fill a thimble. "Should we leave him here for the buzzards, Sally, or test his cheek turnin' a few more times?"

Sweet Sally unleashed a torrent of obscenities. Burning with fury, she used every cuss word she knew. She blistered Luke Deal's ears as they had never, ever been blistered, and when she was done, she glared and held her head high as if defying him to punish her.

Instead, he laughed.

It triggered another outburst. Sweet Sally tried to get close to him but Grutt and Bronk still would not let go of her horse's bridle. With supreme effort she regained her self-control and said, "Leave that poor man alone. You have done enough. It's me you're mad at, not him."

Luke turned to her in surprise. "Why, Sal, that's not true. I'm not mad at either of you."

"Then why are you doing this?" Sweet Sally wailed. "What does it prove? He's unarmed, defenseless. A preacher, for God's sake!"

"That he is." Luke nodded. "Ever notice how his kind always think they are better than us lowly sinners?"

"You don't know him! You don't know he's like that!" Sally was nearly beside herself again. "He could be the gentlest, kindest person who ever lived!"

"Then you don't want me to shoot him again?"

"No! Please, no!"

"You would be upset if I shot him in the knees, say, or the elbows? Or between his legs?"

"I'm begging you! Think of how much pain you've caused him! Don't make him suffer any more!"

Luke Deal scratched his chin with the tip of the Remington's barrel. "I suppose you're right. He shouldn't suffer." Extending his arm, he shot the minister in the head. Once, twice, three times, the Remington cracked, then he turned to Sally and said with the most charming air, "There. I put him out of his misery like you wanted. Are you happy with me now?"

Tears streamed down Sally's cheeks. Her whole body slumped and her arms sagged and she cried and cried until someone nudged her, and she looked up into twin fiery pits of molten gray.

"You haven't answered me. Was I nice enough for you?"

16

Cutters

The Atascosa. Indian Lakes. The Concho River. The course of a trail was dictated by its waterways. Cattle could not go long without water. So herds that followed the Western Trail went from one river or stream or lake or water hole to the next, always by the shortest route. There were a few stretches where geography dictated the cattle had to go without water for two or three days, and those were the stretches punchers dreaded because those were the stretches where cattle became irritable and uncooperative. Those were the stretches where stampedes were likely to occur.

Owen and the hands with him were lucky in that regard. Instead of a herd of three thousand head, they had one bull and four cows. A stampede was the one problem they need not fear.

Big Blue and his harem could still bolt if sufficiently startled: a flash of lightning, the boom of thunder, any other sudden loud noise, a scent they did not like. So the Bar 40 boys treated the five longhorns as they would three thousand head, and took all the ordinary precautions. They sang to the longhorns at night. They avoided firing a gun close to them, or doing anything else that might startle them. They let the longhorns think they were choosing the direction of travel by merely nudging them north each morning and then watching that the longhorns did not stray.

The four hands had it easy, and they knew it. There was a lot less work, a lot fewer worries. After the incident with the Indians, or, as Lon came to call it, "our red silliness," they had one uneventful and pleasant day after another. Which was exactly how they liked it. No problems, no calamities, nothing to concern themselves about except ensuring that Big Blue and the cows were hale and happy.

By now they were nearly through the Concho River country. Water was plentiful, grass was abundant. The longhorns grazed to their bovine hearts' content and had not lost any weight. In fact, the opposite had happened: Big Blue and the cows had gained pounds.

To Alfred Pitney, everything seemed to be as ideal as they could ask. So he was considerably puzzled when he noticed the cowboys were riding in that extra-vigilant manner they sometimes adopted, their eyes always scanning the countryside, their hands on their revolvers. He let three days go by before his inquisitive nature compelled him to turn to Owen and ask why.

"Trail cutters," the foreman said.

"I beg your pardon?"

Owen nodded at the lush hills they were wending through. "This is rustler country. A lot of outfits have lost a lot of cattle hereabouts to hombres who pretend to be cuttin' cows for other outfits."

Pitney breathed deep of the sweet, humid air. "What makes this country more prone than other parts we have been through?"

Owen had a litany. "It's as far as anywhere can be from a town. If they have to throw lead, and kill someone, it can take weeks for Rangers or a federal marshal to get after them, and by then they are long gone. With all the grass and water, they can keep the cows they steal fit. There are a lot of places to hide out."

"I get the idea," Pitney said. "But we are well armed. I wouldn't think these cutters you speak of would dare confront us."

"They travel in packs, like wolves. Upwards of ten to twenty at a time. They won't think twice about attackin' a small outfit like ours."

Now Pitney was on edge, too, and that evening, along a narrow creek, as they were bedding down the longhorns and Benedito was preparing supper, Cleveland came over to where Owen and Lon were stripping their horses.

"Better have a look at what I found."

Cleveland went across the creek at a point where cattle normally crossed. The earth had been churned by the passage of countless heavy hooves, leaving dirt where grass had once grown, and there, clear in the fading light of the setting sun, were the fresh prints of shod horses.

"I make it as a couple of hours ago," Cleveland said, "but you gents are savvier at reading sign so I leave the exact time to you."

Owen went to one knee and ran his finger over several of the tracks. "Not half an hour," he corrected the puncher from Ohio.

"Do you reckon they know about us?" Lon wondered.

"Could be," Owen said. "Or it could be they are

huntin' other herds and don't know we are behind them."

"Want me to ride on ahead and discourage them from tanglin' with us?"

"By 'discourage' you mean shoot a few?" Owen asked. "For someone who swore off bein' a quick-trigger artist, you sure aren't shy about showin' off your talents."

"A man has to keep his hand in." Lon grinned.

"I'd rather you stay with us. If they jump us, we can use that gun hand of yours to even the odds." Owen rose. "I reckon we're not in any danger tonight, but come tomorrow, every one of us better grow eyes in the back of his head."

"It's as serious as all that?" Pitney inquired.

"Serious enough," Owen answered. "If havin' Big Blue and the cows stolen and all of us turned into coyote bait counts."

That night Lon and Cleveland stood watch first. Owen, Slim, and Pitney sat around the fire, sipping coffee, while Benedito busied himself cleaning up. Chavez prided himself on keeping a clean chuck wagon, and always attended to the pots and pans and utensils as soon as their meals were over. Often he enlisted the aid of one of the cowboys, but tonight he spared them.

Slim took a long swallow, stretched out his long legs, and let out a sigh. "This sure is the life. I hope I can cowboy until I'm eighty."

Owen winked at Pitney, then said, "What about your notion to take a wife and raise a family?"

"There's always that," Slim said, "if I ever come across a female who takes a shine to me."

"That heavyset gal we found south of the border

sure did," Owen remarked. "Why, the way she batted her eyelashes, a body would think the sun rose and set just for you."

"Pick on someone else," Slim said, but he was grinning.

"Yes, sir," Owen said soberly to Pitney. "That gal was smitten, or I'm a jackrabbit. All the men Sweet Sally bragged about bein' with, and she set her sights on our Slim." Owen turned an innocent face on the rangy puncher. "What's so special about you, anyhow? There must be somethin' we've missed."

"If you were to fall off your horse and break your neck, I would whoop for joy," Slim taunted.

"Now is that any way to talk to a man who is payin' you compliments?" Owen countered.

"My ma didn't give birth to me yesterday." Slim held his own. "What you are payin' me is brown and comes out the hind end of horses."

"You have to admit she cottoned to you."

"I admit she was friendly," Slim allowed, "but not a lick more. Besides, bein' friendly to men is what she does for a livin'."

"I say," Pitney interjected, "you wouldn't really marry a woman like her, would you? A prostitute?"

"A used saddle can be more comfortable than a new one," Slim observed. "Less breakin' in to do."

"But all the men she has been with. Wouldn't that bother you? It would bother me," Pitney said.

"Well, you're a gentleman, and gents like you have high standards," Slim said. "The rest of us can't afford to be fussy."

"I would never wed a prostitute. The scandal would ruin me. Every time I touched her, I would think of all the others, and it would make me physically ill."

Slim shrugged his slender shoulders. "I can't hardly throw stones. I'm not exactly a virgin. Not respectable at all by your standards."

"I never implied any such thing," Pitney said. "I'm not judging you."

"Good. 'Cause it seems to me the only one who can do that is the Almighty. The rest of us all fall short in some way or another."

"Why, that is quite profound." Pitney smiled. "I never took you for a philosopher, Mr. Vrains."

"Just because I punch cows doesn't mean I can't think."

Owen returned to the subject of Sweet Sally. "Maybe you'll run into that big gal again. Toward the end there she was hangin' on you like her leg was broke and you were a crutch. That's always a sign a woman is about to throw her loop."

"She can make it as wide as she pleases," Slim said. "I'm not ready yet to put down roots."

"Give her ten minutes alone with you and you will be."

Slim and Owen laughed but their laughter died when Lon strolled out of the dark, hunkered by the fire, and poured himself a cup of coffee.

"Aren't you supposed to be on guard?" Owen mildly asked.

"I wouldn't want the hombre watchin' us to guess I'm on to him," Lon said. "Only one, on horseback."

"Where?"

"Across the creek on the first hill. He made the mistake of showin' himself against the stars."

"There are bound to be more," Owen said.

"If there are I couldn't spot them, and I've been around our camp twice." Lon drank some coffee.

"You warned Cleveland?"

"No. I'm an idiot."

Slim choked back a snort.

"Cleveland is keepin' an eye on the rider," Lon said. "Want me to circle around and invite him to join us?"

Owen was thoughtful a bit. "As much as I would like to question him, it's best they don't know we know."

"Whatever you want." Lon set down the cup and stood. "I'll back your play, just like always."

Spurs jingled, and Cleveland rushed into the firelight. "He's coming! That rider on the hill is heading this way."

Owen shot erect. "Is he alone?"

"As near as I can tell."

"Go on back. Let him in but stay there and watch like a hawk for any friends he might have. He could be a decoy, sent to distract us," Owen said. "Stay where it's darkest, down low. You'll hear them before you see them. Don't be shy about discouragin' them with lead."

Cleveland nodded and ran off.

Owen turned to Slim. "You take the south side. Do the same as I told Cleveland. Don't let the firelight reflect off your rifle."

"Will do." Slim snatched up his Winchester and hastened past the chuck wagon, whispering, "We have company!" to their cook as he went by.

Benedito stopped putting his utensils away and climbed up on the wagon. He slid the scattergun from under the seat, broke it open to verify that both barrels were loaded, then snapped it shut and placed it across his lap.

"Where do you want me?" Lon asked.

"Right here. Sit down. Relax. Pretend you're that idiot you claimed to be." Owen smiled and suited his own actions to his instructions. He refilled his tin cup and leaned on an elbow, giving the impression he did not have a care in the world. "You, too, Mr. Pitney. You look like you're sittin' on a cactus."

"What can this man want?"

"Cutters are careful critters. They usually send one or two men in to get the lay of the land, you might say."

"He's taking our measure? Is that it?"

"He thinks he is."

A high, friendly voice came out of the night. "Hello the camp? Mind if I share your fire a spell?"

"Are you by your lonesome?" Cleveland responded.

"Just me and my horse."

"Come right ahead!"

Hooves clomped, and they heard splashing as the horse crossed the creek. Then a sorrel and the man on it loomed out of the dark. The man touched his hat brim and said amiably, "Howdy, gents. I'm friendly if you are."

"None friendlier," Owen said. "Light and sit a spell, mister. We have coffee to spare if you're thirsty."

"I'm obliged." The man's saddle creaked. He opened a saddlebag and brought out a tin cup. Smiling broadly, he squatted and helped himself. "Cozy camp you have here, friend."

The reputed rustler was not much over five feet tall. Short-cropped brown hair framed a pear-shaped face. Dark, glittering eyes darted from Owen to Lon to Alfred Pitney, where they lingered, then to the chuck wagon, and Benedito. He had a long, bony nose, pinched cheeks, and the makings of a brown beard from not having shaved recently. His clothes were no different from those of the punchers, except he wore his pants inside his boots and his boots came almost to his knees. A Colt was at his left hip, a knife at his right. A red bandanna in need of a wash hung loosely around his neck.

"Come far?" Owen asked.

"I'm on my way from Dodge to El Paso," the man said. "How about you?"

"From down near the Gulf." Owen did not divulge more than that. "On our way to Dodge," he lied. "Since you've just been there, you can tell us how the market is for beef these days."

"Oh, it's good. Mighty good. Cows bring near thirty, a three-year-old steer will fetch close to sixty, and a bull will bring you anywhere from eighty to a hundred dollars." The man's dark eyes fixed with ill-concealed covetous desire on Big Blue. "Speakin' of bulls, that there is the grandest I've ever seen. A longhorn, unless I'm mistaken."

"There are no rocks between your ears," Lon Chalmers said.

The man cast a glance of annoyance at him but let the remark pass. "Not much of a herd if you're fixin' to sell at Dodge."

"Who knows where we'll sell." Owen evaded the question.

"Yes, sir. That bull"—the man was once again admiring Big Blue—"is one handsome animal. Look at those horns! And how high he stands. Compared to him, buffalo are puny."

"He is a big one."

"I don't suppose—" The man stopped, as if embarrassed. "I don't suppose you would consider sellin' him before you get to Dodge? I'd be willin' to go as high as two hundred dollars."

"Well, now," Owen said, "that's a generous offer. But no thanks. He's already spoken for."

"That's a shame," the man said, sounding genuinely sad. Tearing his gaze from Big Blue, he glanced toward their horses. His forefinger tapped his cup, once for each animal. Then he looked at Pitney and said, "What's this apparition, by the way?"

"He's British," Lon said. "An English lord takin' a tour of our country. They dress like that over there to scare off the French."

"A lord? You don't say? That makes you royalty, doesn't it? And royalty is always rich."

Lon replied before Pitney could. "He's a personal friend of the queen's. Right when you showed up, he was tellin' us how he once sparked the maid who cleans her chamber pots."

"What is she like? The queen, I mean?" the man asked. "Is it true she wears a crown covered with diamonds?"

"That she does." Pitney went along with Lon's fibs. "It is encrusted with sapphires and rubies and emeralds, too. Her robe is made of spun gold and she always carries her scepter of office, which is a solid gold staff with a diamond as large as that coffeepot."

The man's mouth hung open in rapt greed. "What I wouldn't give to see a rig like that."

Pitney was enjoying himself. "Not only that, her throne is gold. Precious gems are embedded in the arms. Her footstool is sterling silver. I have never been into the queen's private chambers, naturally, but the, er, maid I courted told me they are filled with chests of jewelry and money, wealth gathered from around the empire."

"She should be careful someone doesn't steal it," the man said.

"Oh, that would be quite impossible. The palace guards protect her day and night. No one can get anywhere near her inner sanctum. A lout tried once and was beheaded for his effrontery."

"Beheaded? You're tellin' me they lopped off his head for a little thing like that?"

"Oh yes. The guillotine is still very much in vogue in England. So are the rack and the corkscrew. Why, last year alone, two thousand people were tortured and executed by the queen's orders."

The man believed the drivel was true. "No insult intended, mister, but it beats me how you people over there put up with her shenanigans."

"The secret is in how we are raised," Pitney said, embellishing his story even more. "Every household is required to have a copy of the crown over their hearth. As soon as children learn to walk, they are required to bow to the crown three times a day as a sign of loyalty."

"You would never catch me bendin' my knee to anyone or anything," their visitor declared.

"You wouldn't have much choice," Pitney took delight in assuring him. "Anyone who speaks ill of the crown is banished to the coal mines. They toil twelve hours a day deep in the earth, and are only fed gruel and water."

"Thank God for George Washington." Lon entered into the spirit of things.

"And here I thought I might like to visit England

one day," the man said. "I've always hankered to see other countries but it wasn't meant to be."

"A man is never too old to change his ways," Lon remarked.

Owen cleared his throat. "Might I ask your name, friend? If you won't take it as pryin', that is."

There was hesitation, then, "Givens. Bill Givens. I used to ride for the Q L Connected, down to the Pecos country."

"I've heard of them." Lon was sitting cross-legged, and now he set his coffee cup to one side and folded his hands in front of him. "They had quite a reputation, as I recollect."

Bill Givens smiled.

"As brand blotters," Lon continued, smiling as he dished out the insult. "Real careless with their brandin' irons. They never kept their twine on the tree, and all their cows always had twins."

A flush crept up Bill Givens's face. "That, sir, is a damned lie. The Q L Connected was as honest as the year is long."

"Then our years must be down to twelve days, one for each month," Lon said. "Next time be more careful who you admit your long rope to. You probably figured none of us ever visited that neck of the woods."

Givens appealed to Owen. "You're in charge here, I take it? Are you goin' to lie there and let your man make rank accusations?"

"He's grown up," Owen said. "He can do as he pleases."

"I don't like it, I tell you. What ever happened to common courtesy? I wouldn't insult you if you paid our camp a visit."

"Then there is more than one of you?"

Bill Givens was a terrible liar. "No. Did I say 'our'? I meant 'my.' I'm all alone, remember?"

"So you claimed," Owen said. "But let's stop blowin' smoke and talk about how many of you there are, and when you plan to hit us."

Givens stood up. "You, too? I don't have to stand for this. I'm leavin', and I hope to God I never set eyes on any of you again."

Lon stood, too. "You're not goin' anywhere, mister, until you answer my pard's questions."

Bill Givens switched his cup from his left hand to his right and lowered his right hand almost to his revolver. "Is that a fact? I've got news for you. There hasn't been a puncher born who can stop me from doin' what I've made up my mind to do, and I've made up my mind to go."

"By all means," Lon said. "Try."

Givens's hand moved the barest fraction and then stopped, for he found himself staring down the barrel of Lon Chalmers's Colt. "Jesus!" he blurted.

Owen gave his cup to Pitney and slowly rose. "Now then. Let's try again. Before you answer, keep a few things in mind. My pard, here, doesn't take kindly to rustlers. I don't either, but he likes to have a rustler for breakfast and every other meal besides."

"I've heard such brag before."

"I wouldn't doubt it," Owen said with civil courtesy. "But my pard doesn't wear his six-shooter for bluff or ballast."

"Care for a sample?" Lon asked. Taking a step, he smashed the Colt against the rustler's knee.

Bill Givens shrieked and dropped, clutching his legs to his chest. He cursed luridly, and went to shout.

"No you don't." Lon shoved the barrel into Givens's wide-open mouth and thumbed back the hammer. "One peep out of you and you will have to make do with only half your face."

Owen smiled down at the brand artist. "Let's try this again." He nodded at Lon and Lon took a step back, his Colt low at his side. "How many are we up against?"

Givens glowered in pure hate, then spat in the grass. "Eight besides me."

"They sent you to look us over. So you can report back on whether it will be easy or hard."

"It will be hard," Lon said.

"Don't flatter yourselves," Bill Givens said. "We've trimmed bigger outfits than yours. Before tomorrow is out, I will piss on your graves."

17

Tears of a Dove

Sweet Sally was scared, more scared than she had ever been, more scared than she had ever thought she could be. The fright that sprouted since she left Whiskey Flats had grown into an all-pervading fear. Now she understood why Grutt and Bronk trod on eggshells when Luke Deal was in one of his moods.

The murder of the parson and the two young cowboys had shown her that Luke Deal might take it into his head at any moment of the day or night to end her life. He was as unpredictable as a tornado, and many times as deadly.

Sweet Sally had met rough characters before. In her profession it was inevitable. Footpads, confidence men, thieves, cardsharps, self-styled pistoleros, badmen of every stripe had poked her at one time or another. Often, in the quiet hours of the night, they confided some of their vilest deeds, as if by allowing them the poke, she had earned the right to know the darkest secrets of their soul.

But never, in all her wide travels and in all her many pokes, had Sweet Sally met anyone as undeniably dangerous, as ruthlessly violent, as coldly callous, as Luke Deal.

The most amazing aspect to her was that Luke Deal had no regard for human life. None whatsoever. Nowhere in his being was there the slightest flicker of compassion for his fellow human beings.

Sweet Sally had always believed she could handle any situation, any man. She knew her limitations, and her strengths. She was not, by far, the prettiest dove ever born, but she was friendlier and cheerier than most of her sisters, and her easygoing, open nature made up for her lack of looks. Many times she had been in tense situations—drunks who turned vicious, fights that broke out, jealousy that erupted in bloodshed. Always, each and every time, she would smile and be friendly and talk to those who had lost their self-control, and always she was able to smother the flames of violence with her kindness and sincerity.

But there was no talking her way out of this predicament. There was no persuading Luke Deal not to kill her if he decided to. He would laugh in her face, as he had laughed in the face of the poor parson, and murder her without a qualm.

What scared Sweet Sally more than anything, the essence of her fear, was her realization that Luke Deal intended to turn her into buzzard bait. That, in fact, he had intended to kill her from the beginning.

She could not say exactly why she was so sure. He had not lifted a finger against her. He had not even threatened her. But her womanly intuition told her that he was only biding his time, that she was as good as dead if she stayed with Deal and his two friends.

Sally made up her mind to flee. She must get away and she must do it at the first opportunity. The problem was, she never had the chance. They were with her every minute of the day and night except when she went into the bushes to heed nature's call, and then one or another always held her horse for her until she was finished. Until the minister came along, she had thought they were doing it out of simple courtesy. But now she suspected they stuck close to her so she could not elude them.

She had been foolish. She had not regarded the three men any differently than all the others she had been with. They had not seemed to be any worse than Paco Ramirez. Certainly Grutt and Bronk were no different. And since Luke Deal had left her pretty much alone, she had had no cause to suspect she was in dire peril.

Now she knew better.

But how to get away? That was the question. She racked her brain but could not come up with a plan.

Then, about a week and a half after the parson's death, Sweet Sally thought fate smiled on her.

They had left the settlements far behind and were following a broad trail pockmarked by the prints of the countless cows that had preceded them. When Sweet Sally asked Grutt, he told her it was a route many cattle drives took to Dodge City. She was not all that familiar with the cattle business. Few things bored her more than cows. But from snippets of talk she'd had with the many cowboys who had poked her, she knew that at that time of year a lot of herds were driven north. And since cattle moved a lot slower than men on horseback, she could realistically expect for them to come on a trail herd before too long.

Four days later Sally was proven right.

Tendrils of dust appeared far ahead, rising in a thick column, and it was not long before Sweet Sally heard

the lowing of cows and the whistles and yells of cowboys. Soon she saw some of the latter, the dust-caked
drag riders who goaded the rear elements of the
herd along.

Luke Deal reined to the left to swing wide. Almost
immediately a cowhand spotted them, and gave a
whoop, and presently two other cowboys came gallop-
ing back from up near the front of the herd.

One was tall and rangy and had the stamp of au-
thority about him. The other was middling-sized and
wary, and held a rifle across his saddle.

Acting as friendly as could be, Luke Deal came to
halt and raised a hand in greeting. "That's some herd
you have there."

"We think so," said the tall man. "I'm Gus Shantry,
trail boss of this outfit." He looked at Sweet Sally and
touched his hat brim. "Ma'am. It isn't often we see a
female in these parts."

"Females are always trouble," said the trail hand
with the rifle. "I can do without them."

"Hush, Buck," said Gus Shantry. "Pay him no
mind, ma'am. He never learned any manners." Shantry smiled at her, then turned to Luke Deal and the
smile died. "Suppose you tell me what you're doin'
here, friend. And in case you decide not to, all I have
to do is give a holler and I'll have twenty men by my
side to help persuade you."

"No need for threats, mister," Luke said, still playing at being friendly. "Why, you'd think we were
rustlers."

"You could be," Shantry said. "They try all kinds
of tricks to catch us off our guard."

"Or you could be sellin' the woman," Buck declared, "which is as bad as bein' a rustler, if not
worse."

"Consarn you," the trail boss growled.

"Sorry, Gus. But all it takes is one look at her to know she's a whore."

Shantry leaned on his saddle horn. "Again, my apologies, ma'am." To Deal he said, "My men need to keep their minds on their work. If you're lookin' to sell her services, you can forget it and be on your way."

"Why, I'm scandalized," Luke Deal said. "We're not after your cows, and we're sure as hell not in the painted cat business. Fact is, we're lookin' for friends of ours from the Bar 40. Maybe you've seen them? A few cowboys takin' a big bull up to Wyoming? The top man is called Owen?"

"I've heard of the Bar 40," Gus Shantry said, "but I can't say as we've seen any sign of a small outfit like you describe."

"Friends of yours, you say?" Buck probed.

"Known them for years. One of the cowboys, Slim Vrains, is real partial to the lady here."

"Is that so, ma'am?"

Sweet Sally noticed Luke's right hand was on his hip, close to his Colt. "Yes, that's so," she admitted. "He's plumb sweet on me."

Shantry seemed to relax a bit, but not Buck.

"Strange this Slim doesn't care enough to tell you a cow trail is no place for a female. You should be on a stage."

"Slim doesn't know she's comin'," Luke Deal said. "It's a surprise. She decided to accept his proposal after he'd left." He lowered his voice and leaned toward them as if to impart private information, even though Sweet Sally was right there and could hear every word. "You know how women can be. She told him no, then changed her mind."

"Still not too smart to bring a woman out here," Buck said.

Gus Shantry, though, had a romantic nature. "I wish a woman would think that highly of me. Ma'am, you're welcome to ride with us a while if you'd like. Our cook won't mind feedin' a few extra mouths tonight. He's married."

Sweet Sally opened her mouth to accept. She saw it all in her mind's-eye: how she would contrive to whisper to the trail boss about the parson and about how Luke Deal and the others were after the Bar 40 punchers for some other and no doubt sinister reason, and how Shantry would rally his hands and they would draw their guns and tie up Deal and Grutt and Bronk and turn them over to the law at the first town they came to. She had it all worked out, and she tingled with excitement at being shed of them.

Then Luke said, "That's generous of you, friend, but she's in a powerful hurry to find her Slim. We need to be pushin' on."

"Fine by me," Buck said.

Gus Shantry touched his hat brim again. "I understand, ma'am, and I wish you and your cowboy all the best."

Luke clucked to his mount. "Let's mosey."

Her chance slipping away, Sweet Sally almost shrieked in dismay and begged the cowboys for help. But as she was about to, she envisioned the outcome, envisioned Shantry and Buck dead on the ground, no match for the quick hands of Luke Deal. She could not bear to be responsible for their deaths. So she smiled and said thank you to the trail boss and rode on after the demon in mortal guise.

When they were well beyond the herd, Grutt

snickered and said, "You sure handled them slick, Luke."

"The Bar 40 boys must be a ways ahead yet," Bronk commented.

"Doesn't matter," Luke said confidently. "We'll catch up to them sooner or later."

Sweet Sally fought to keep her voice calm. "What happens when you do? Why are you so interested in them?"

"That's right. I haven't told you yet." Luke turned in his saddle. "The bull they're takin' north is a breedin' bull, missy. That makes him special. A man could get rich ownin' an animal like that."

"Somehow I don't see you becoming a rancher," Sweet Sally ventured. "Or are you going to turn over a new leaf and work for a living?"

Luke bestowed a thin smile on her. "I never said I would breed the bull myself. I don't need to. There are plenty of ranchers who would pay through the nose for the privilege."

"You hope."

"Are you tryin' to rile me?" Luke asked. "Because if you are, I can make do without the bait."

"Is that what I am to you?" Sweet Sally had thought it might be something like that. "How does it work, exactly?"

"Simple. We wait for them to make camp for the night, and you go ridin' in. They'll gather around, maybe pester you with questions, and be dead before they know it."

"You'll shoot them all in the back, I suppose?" Horror seared Sweet Sally like a red-hot poker.

"After what I did to that Bible pusher, you have to ask?"

No, Sally did not. It was a vile plan, well worthy of the walking embodiment of evil who went by the name of Luke Deal. They rode on a while, with her pondering fiercely how she might forewarn Owen and the others, when two things occurred to her simultaneously: One was the welcome thought that Deal intended to keep her alive until they caught up; the other was that when Deal and Grutt and Bronk started blasting, she would be caught in the crossfire. Luke aimed to rub her out with the cowboys.

Sweet Sally's fear eased a smidgen. She had a while to live yet. She would use the time to think, to plot how to turn the tables on the killers she had unwittingly thrown in with. There had to be a way. There just had to.

But as the hours went by and turned into days and the days turned into another week, Sweet Sally began to despair. Deal and his friends never let her out of their sight. There was always one or another close by.

Sally considered sneaking off on foot in the middle of the night and decided against it. She could not move fast, given her size, and anyway, her ankles had always been weak. They would catch her before she went a hundred yards. Even if by some extraordinary miracle she succeeded in escaping, she was left with the daunting challenge of surviving alone and without food or water or weapons. She wouldn't kid herself. She would be lucky if she lasted three or four days.

Sally's only recourse was to stay and hope and pray something happened.

Twice they came upon trail herds. Luke always asked about the Bar 40 punchers and their bull, but no one had seen them.

"Maybe they took another trail," Grutt suggested.

"Not if they're bound for Wyoming Territory," Luke said.

Then came the worst moment in Sweet Sally's life.

It was the middle of a hot morning. Dust devils were being stirred by a vagrant breeze. Luke Deal was in the lead, as always, riding slouched over, his hat low against the sun, when he abruptly straightened and glanced down. "What's this?"

"I'll be," Bronk said. "How long ago, do you reckon?"

"Not more than an hour, if that," Grutt guessed.

Sally did not understand why they sounded so excited. They were staring at wagon tracks, at ruts that crossed the trail from side to side. She could not tell if the wagon had gone east or west but apparently Luke could. He reined his horse west and then sat with a peculiar little smirk on his face.

"Do we or don't we?" Grutt asked.

Sally's curiosity got the better of her. "Do you or don't you what?"

"It's only one wagon," Bronk said. "Should be easy."

Comprehension washed over Sally like freezing rain. "You can't. Whoever they are, they don't deserve it."

"None of us deserve to die but we all do," Luke Deal said. "And if us dyin' is good enough for the Almighty, it's good enough for me."

"Please," Sweet Sally said.

As if to spite her, Luke gigged his chestnut, saying, "Come on, boys. We're goin' to have us a look-see."

Grutt snickered wickedly and followed. Sweet Sally hesitated, desperately wishing she could forestall them somehow.

"After you," Bronk said.

"How can you?" Sally asked him. "How can you stay with him and stand idly by while he commits the atrocious deeds he does?"

"I've done the same many a time," Bronk told her.

"He'll kill you one day. You know that, don't you? You and Grutt, both. He doesn't care about either of you. I'm surprised you have lasted as long as you have."

"Nice try, lady. But Luke and us go back a long ways. We're the only pards he has. He's not about to buck us out in gore."

Sweet Sally's temper flared. "You're a fool. It's right in front of you and you refuse to see."

"After you," Bronk repeated sourly. "And keep your mouth shut, if you know what's good for you."

"I hate you," Sweet Sally said. "I hate all three of you."

"Want me to tell Luke that?" Bronk asked, and laughed.

The wagon tracks bore to the southwest. Luke was in no great hurry, and hummed to himself. Presently dust rose in the distance. Then a canvas hump became visible. Made of hemp and waterproofed with linseed oil, it resembled an oversized turtle shell.

"A prairie schooner," Grutt said gleefully. "Some pilgrims have gone and lost their way."

"Could be rich pickin's," Bronk remarked.

Luke Deal gestured. "Who cares about that?"

The wagon was one of the larger Conestogas more common east of the Mississippi. Judging by the depth of its tracks, it was much too heavily loaded, a typical mistake made by those who valued their possessions more than common sense. Two children were perched on the rear gate, girls in cute bonnets, bright cherubs who saw them and smiled and waved and called out to let their parents know.

The team consisted of six oxen. Some emigrants preferred mules. Oxen were slower but a lot stronger.

A large, brawny, bearded man was walking beside the left rear animal when the girls yelled. He glanced back, then brought the oxen to a stop and handed his whip to his wife. She handed down a rifle.

"Get up here with me," Luke Deal commanded Sally out of a corner of his mouth, "and be quick about it."

Reluctantly, Sweet Sally flicked her reins. The man and the woman were watching uneasily. The woman said something and the girls scooted forward and sat on the seat beside her.

Sally could not take her eyes off the girls. They were so adorable. They made her think of the children she had always wanted and could never have. New fear spiked through her, fear so potent she nearly swooned.

Luke drew rein a dozen yards out. He flashed his most disarming smile. "Didn't mean to frighten you folks. Saw your tracks and figured you might be in some kind of trouble."

"No trouble," the man replied. "We are on our way to Santa Fe."

"All by yourselves?" Luke clucked in disapproval. "It's not my business to tell you how to do things, mister, but you're takin' an awful chance. This country is crawlin' with hostiles and outlaws. If I had a wife and kids, I'd hook up with a wagon train."

The wife glanced at the husband. "See? But you wouldn't listen to me."

"Don't start in on me again, woman," the man re-

buffed her. "By doing it on our own we save the fee."
His chest swelled. "I can protect you just fine my
own self."

"You must have been in the army," Luke Deal said.

"Not ever. Wearing a uniform and having to march
all day isn't for me." The man lowered his rifle a trifle.
"I'm a farmer. I like being able to do what I want
when I want, and not take orders from anyone."

"Why, I feel the same way," Luke cheerfully
declared.

The older girl, who was not much over twelve, whispered to her mother and the woman smiled at Sweet
Sally. "Rebecca says she thinks you have pretty hair,
miss."

"How kind of her," Sweet Sally said. "But I'm
afraid it's a mess from the wind and the dust." She
had a sudden idea and added, "You wouldn't happen
to have a brush, would you?" She was sure they
would. "Would you mind if I climbed down and bor-
rowed it for a minute?" They were bound to say yes,
and she could secretly warn them about her
companions.

"Better save your brushin' for when we stop for the
night," Luke Deal quickly said. "Your hair will only
be a mess again by then."

"We have a brush if you want to use it," the
woman said.

Sweet Sally was torn. Should she or shouldn't she?
With the farmer standing there holding a rifle, she
doubted Luke would start anything. "I would love to
use it. Thank you very much." She shifted her sweaty
legs to climb down.

Luke Deal drew his Colt and shot the farmer in the
right shoulder. The *crack* of the shot was like the crack

of a whip. The impact spun the farmer half around and crumpled him to his knees. His wife and daughters screamed, and the wife swung down from the seat to leap to his aid. But Bronk was quicker. Spurring his horse in close, he wrapped an arm around her waist and lifted her into the air.

"Let go of me!" The woman struggled and reached back to claw at his face but could not reach him.

"Mama!" The older daughter launched herself at Bronk. She landed squarely on his back. Her small fists pounded his head and neck in an vain bid to force him to drop her mother.

The smaller girl was not to be left out. She scrambled over the edge, dropped lightly to the ground, and was turning toward her father when Luke Deal shot her through the head.

Everyone froze—Bronk, Grutt, the mother, the oldest daughter. Even the father looked up in shock, his shattered collarbone forgotten.

Then the mother let out a wail worthy of a panther and twisted sharply to rake her fingernails across Bronk's face. The ferocity of her attack caught him unawares, and she ripped him open from above his eyebrow to his chin. Enraged, he hurled her to the earth. The older daughter screeched and hooked a thumb in his eye. Seizing her wrist, Bronk bellowed like a mad bull and hurled her to the earth, too. But where the mother had landed on her shoulder and was only stunned, the older daughter hit on the crown of her head. The *crunch* of her vertebrae breaking explained why she did not move after she hit.

"Damn you," Luke Deal said. "I wanted to do her."

"Sorry," Bronk said.

Sweet Sally had been paralyzed by the savagery of

it all. But now, her blood boiling hot in her veins, she reined the bay between Luke and the mother and father. "No more!" she wailed. "For God's sake, no more!"

Luke motioned brusquely with his Colt. "Move."

"No," Sweet Sally cried. "I won't let you!"

Luke pointed the Colt and cored the bay through the eyes. The horse shook violently, nearly pitching Sally off, then fell where it stood. Sally tried to roll clear but she was much too big and much too slow. Her right leg was pinned from the knee down. She threw up her hands, expecting the next slug to do to her what the last one had done to the bay. But Luke was not looking at her. He was looking at the mother.

A sculpture of pure horror, the woman glanced from one dead daughter to the others, tears streaming from her eyes.

The father lunged for his rifle. His fingers were wrapping around it when Luke's shot ripped through his torso from back to front. He flopped up and down a few times, and was gone.

Luke gigged his horse over to the mother. She looked up, the embodiment of misery.

"Why?"

"Why not?" Luke shot her through the heart, then immediately began reloading. "Grutt, help the cow out from under the horse and put her on one of the oxen."

"People can ride an ox?"

"She rides an ox or she rides your horse until we find another for her. Take your pick."

Grutt hurriedly dismounted and scooted to the team.

Choking back great sobs, Sweet Sally sprawled on her back. Tiny mews issued from her throat.

Luke Deal finished reloading, slid the Colt into its holster, and grinned down at her. "Am I nice enough for you yet?"

18

Hot Lead

"It's been two days," Slim said. "Why haven't they lit into us yet? What are they waitin' for?"

Owen glanced at the chuck wagon, where Bill Givens, bound at the wrists and ankles, sat slouched on the seat beside Benedito. Behind the wagon, added to their string, was Givens's mount. "Our friend there is more important than he's let on," Owen guessed. "It could be he's their leader."

"And they haven't attacked because they don't want anything to happen to him?" Slim surveyed the rolling sea of hills and more hills. "Could be. But how long will that hold them back?"

"Not forever." Owen wished it were otherwise. He had no hankering to spill blood. "Only until they think up a way to get at him without losin' any of their men."

"Here's hopin' they're all as dumb as rocks," Slim said, and reined to the left to take up his normal position flanking the longhorns.

Alfred Pitney had been a keenly interested listener. "What's to stop them from picking us off from a hilltop with rifles?"

"If they don't drop all of us right away, Givens is as good as dead and they know it."

"You would shoot an unarmed man who can't possibly defend himself?"

"I wouldn't like it but I would do it, yes," Owen said. "If it was Lon, he would do it and like it."

They both looked to where Lon Chalmers was riding point. Owen had instructed him to ride closer to the cows than he normally did, and to be ready for anything. Not that Lon needed the warning.

"I don't quite know what to make of him," Pitney admitted. "He can be quite vicious."

"Only when he has to," Owen said. "But he's a good man. He's walked both sides of the tracks and picked the side of decent livin'. A lot of wild ones never change their ways until they are six feet under."

"You like him a lot, don't you?"

"He's my best friend," Owen said. "I would do anything for him and he would do anything for me."

Pitney's mouth curled in a rueful grin. "I wouldn't mind having a friend like that. Most of my business associates are just that. I've been so busy making money for the BLC, I haven't had the time to really make friends."

"You have now."

Pitney blinked, then smiled self-consciously. "I must say. You cowboy types have the disconcerting habit of always being forthright. It's enough to make a grown man blush."

Just then Owen rose in the stirrups and stared at a hilltop to the northeast. Frowning, he sank back down.

"Something?"

"Maybe. Thought I saw a flash. Could be they have a lookout with a spyglass keepin' an eye on us. Or it could have been the sun on a rifle."

Alfred Pitney studied the same hill but did not see

anything. "I feel like one of those targets at an amusement arcade."

"We all do." Owen slowed and reined aside so the chuck wagon caught up with him and he could ride beside it. "How's our guest?"

"He is poor company, señor," Benedito said. "Me, I like to talk, but he will not say a word except to insult me and my mother."

"It must be his upbringin'," Owen said. "His folks never taught him how to be polite."

Bill Givens swore. "You think you're so damn funny? You'll all be laughin' out new holes in your faces by the time we're done with you."

"If big talk was gold, you would be rich," Owen said.

"Yes, sir." Givens went on as if he had not heard. "We're goin' to blow out all your wicks. I want to do that smart-mouth one myself." He fixed his glare on Lon Chalmers. "I want to stick the barrel of my revolver in his mouth like he did his in mine, and keep squeezin' the trigger until the cylinder is empty."

"You're welcome to try," Owen said, "but I doubt you would clear leather."

Givens swiveled toward him. "Cowboys! I hate every stinkin' one of you. Acting' like you own the world, and all you do is smell the hind end of cows for a livin'." He spiced his comments with a string of profanity, ending with, "The only thing I hate more than cowboys are stupid, good-for-nothin' greasers."

"That is most strange, senor," Benedito said, "since you, yourself, are a stupid, good-for-nothing gringo."

More profanity ended with, "It won't be long! You'll see! My boys will make coyote bait of the whole bunch of you!"

"Thank you," Owen said.

Givens tilted his head. "For what?"

"For admittin' what I've suspected all along, that you're the head polecat. So long as we have you, those boys of yours will be gun-shy."

"You think you have it all worked out but you don't. One of my men is Ben Sloane. Maybe you've heard of him?"

"I seem to recollect hearin' the name," Owen said. "Isn't he the one who killed an Indian gal and made a poke out of her skin?"

"The very same," Givens crowed. "He's my second in command, you might say, and compared to him, your Lon Chalmers is a Sunday school teacher."

Owen remembered more. "Ben Sloane was the varmint who robbed that stage a while back and killed all the passengers, includin' a couple of women."

"That was him," Givens confirmed. "Ben likes killin' women, likes it more than anything. He's a woman hater through and through. I hate them, too. But not as much as I hate cowboys and stupid greasers."

"What about blacks?" Benedito interjected.

"I hate niggers as much as greasers."

"And Indians?" Benedito said. "Do you love them or are they on your list as well?"

"Injuns and niggers and greasers and women," Givens hissed. "Every stinkin' one of you."

"What about chickens?"

"What?"

"Or ducks. I should think you must hate how they walk."

"What the hell are you talkin' about?"

"Hummingbirds? Do you hate hummingbirds? They fly so fast you cannot see them. That is a nuisance."

"You're loco, greaser."

"Pigs?" Benedito went on. "Now there is an animal worth hating."

"Injuns and niggers and greasers and women," Givens repeated. "Pigs I like. They have those funny snouts and curly tails."

"You have looked in the mirror, then?" Benedito said. "That is good. A man should always know what he looks like."

Owen laughed, and they were treated to more livid swearing. He rode briskly on around Mary, Lily, and Cleopatra, past Big Blue and then on ahead of Emily. "Nice day if it doesn't rain."

Lon Chalmers grinned. "We'll be out of these hills by early afternoon. My money says they'll jump us before then."

Owen agreed. Once they were out on the prairie, it would be that much harder for anyone to sneak up on them unnoticed. "I just heard something you might like to know."

When the foreman did not go on, Lon said, "Do I pay you or beg or tickle your feet until you 'fess up?"

"Ben Sloane is with them."

"I've heard of him," Lon said. "Small things with a six-shooter."

"Maybe not so small. They say his tally is a dozen or more."

"Most couldn't shoot back. Show me a coyote who likes them unarmed and I'll show you a weak-kneed coward." Lon placed his hand on his Colt. "I hope these boys don't get cold feet. I'm lookin' forward to swappin' hot lead. With Ben Sloane most of all."

"There are eight of them, remember," Owen said.

"They may not amount to much, but they're bound to hit something."

"Maybe we shouldn't wait for them to make the first move," Lon proposed. "Maybe I should go poke around and if I find them, whittle the odds some."

"They might get lucky and whittle you and we can't afford to lose you."

"You're worse than a mother hen."

Another grassy hill reared ahead. They wound to the right around it. Beyond, to the northwest, a belt of vegetation hinted at a creek. It had been a day and a half since they struck water and the longhorns perked up at the scent. Big Blue tried to pass Emily but she would not have it and walked faster.

Lon smirked. "Females are all the same whether they have two legs or four."

"You talk mighty big when there are none of the two-legged variety around," Owen observed.

"I like breathin'."

Their banter came to an end when a rider appeared out of the trees, a rifle held vertical in front of him, the stock on his knee, a dirty white cloth tied to the barrel below the front sight.

Owen raised a hand and drew rein. Lon wheeled his mount to halt the longhorns, and Slim and Cleveland closed up on either side.

The man holding the improvised truce flag rode slowly toward them. He had broad shoulders and a broad chest, and a face the ladies would like a lot. Strapped to his waist was a Colt with ivory grips. He grinned smugly. When ten feet separated them, he came to a stop. "We need to parley."

"You must be Sloane," Owen said.

The big man's grin widened. His face was as flat as

a plank except for a bump of a nose, his upper lip perpetually curled upward. "Heard of me, have you?" he asked, his pride flattered.

"We hear you're partial to gunnin' down women," Lon said. "It's too bad we didn't bring one with us so you could show us how tough an hombre you are."

Ben Sloane was not amused. "I'll show you soon enough. In the meantime, we want him." Sloane pointed at Bill Givens. "Hand him over and none of you will be harmed."

"You're a god-awful liar," Lon said.

Forgetting himself, Sloane started to level his rifle. He stopped, though, and said testily, "Keep on flappin' your gums, mister. I haven't killed anyone in a couple of weeks and I have the itch."

"We're not handin' Givens over," Owen said. "He stays with us until we're in the clear."

"When will that be? When you strike Dodge?" Ben Sloan shook his head. "You'll free him now. There are seven rifles trained on you and your friends. All I have to do is whistle and you die."

Owen calmly twisted and gestured toward the chuck wagon.

Nodding, Benedito reached behind him and produced the scattergun. He thumbed back both barrels and pressed the twin muzzles against Bill Givens's ribs.

"Go ahead and whistle," Owen said to Sloane.

For a few moments the outcome might have gone either way. Ben Sloane clearly wanted to give the signal.

A yell from Givens decided the issue. "Bide your time, Ben! They're bound to make a mistake! You and the boys be ready!"

"Don't listen to him," Lon said. "Fill your hand with that equalizer of yours and prove how equal you are."

"For that," Ben Sloane snarled, "I will deal with you myself."

"Do I soil my britches now or later?"

Ben Sloane's mouth worked but he did not reply.

Owen bobbed his chin at the trees. "You and your friends make yourselves scarce or I will let my pard do what he wants with your pard."

"You know what I want," Lon said. "The only good rustler is a dead rustler."

"You would, wouldn't you?" Ben Sloane said to him.

"Just like this," Lon said, and grinning, he snapped his fingers.

Sloane raised his reins. "We'll go. But this doesn't end it. Not by a long shot." With a quick glance and a nod at Givens, Sloane reined his horse around and made for the vegetation.

"I should shoot him in the back," Lon proposed.

"That would make you no better than he is," Owen said. "The gun smoke will be on our terms, not theirs."

Sloane and his mount melted into the greenery. They heard him yell but could not quite make out the words. Other figures briefly appeared, flitting rapidly away.

"I only counted five," Lon said.

"They won't tempt the shotgun," Owen said with confidence. Still, he placed his right hand on his six-shooter. "Take it slow. We'll let the cattle drink but only a little."

Quiet had fallen among the cottonwoods and oaks.

A meandering blue ribbon wound among them, its surface sparkling where the sun filtered through. Under other circumstances it would have been enjoyable to rest in the shade a while.

Emily and Big Blue dipped their mouths to the water and seconds later so did the other three longhorns.

Lon crossed the creek and drew rein. He studied the shadows, the thicket growth, the crotches of trees, but if the rustlers had laid an ambush, they had laid it well.

Alfred Pitney sensed the cowboys were as taut as wire. But he was sure the rustlers would not try anything so long as Givens was their prisoner. He had no qualms about dismounting and sinking to one knee. Taking a monogrammed handkerchief from a pocket, he held it in the creek to soak it. The water was wonderfully cool. Partially wringing the handkerchief out, he wiped it across his brow and cheeks and neck. "Sweet relief," he said to himself.

Big Blue stopped drinking and lifted his huge head, his great horns glistening. He sniffed a few times, then stamped a front hoof.

Owen whipped around. Big Blue was staring at a thicket. No shadowy shapes lurked in its depths, and Owen had about dismissed the bull's warning when something at the base of the thicket pricked his interest. There was a hump where there should not be one. Leaves and downed branches covered it. The rest of the ground was flat.

Belatedly, Owen realized the thicket was nowhere near a tree. "It's an ambush!" he shouted, bringing his rifle up. But he was a few shades too slow.

The hump was rising from a shallow hole scooped out of the earth. A buck-toothed rustler cackled and fired, but not at Owen. He fired at the nearest cowboy, who happened to be Cleveland, and who also happened to have his back to the thicket.

The slug caught the Bar 40 puncher low in the back. Arching his spine, Cleveland threw both arms out, then slumped forward.

Owen sent a round into the buck teeth, and all hell erupted.

Rustlers rose from concealment on all sides. One rushed from behind an oak, only to be stopped in his tracks by a blast from Lon Chalmers's Colt. Lon turned and snapped a shot at another who had popped out of a patch of weeds. Pivoting at the hips, he fired at a ragged stripling with a Sharps.

Benedito Chavez had his scattergun pressed to Givens's side. He would hold it there until Owen told him otherwise. But when a rustler hurtled out of the greenery and blistered the canopy above Benedito's head, Benedito let the rustler have a barrel in the chest.

Slim was shooting his rifle as rapidly as he could work the lever. He had seen Cleveland hit, and he was filled with a terrible rage. He aimed at a running shape. His rifle belched lead and smoke and the shape toppled.

Up on the chuck wagon, Bill Givens had flattened on his side. He rolled to the end of the seat, glanced at the cook to be sure the Mexican was not looking at him, and rolled off the wagon. He contrived to land on his shoulders, his teeth clenched against the pain. Coiling his legs under him, he rose and hopped into the undergrowth. Triumph lit his features but only for a few seconds, until he tripped over a rock no bigger than an apple and pitched onto his stomach.

A shadow fell across him.

Out of nowhere towered Ben Sloane. "I'll have you free in two shakes of a mare's tail." His left hand swooped to his boot and out came a knife. A single stroke severed the rope around Givens's ankles, and Sloane bent to cut the rope around his wrists.

"I'd rather you didn't, woman-killer."

Sloane spun. Givens twisted to see the speaker. Both imitated statues, and Ben Sloane blurted, "You!"

"Me," Lon Chalmers said. In his right hand was his smoking Colt, level and steady.

Starting to straighten, Ben Sloane reconsidered. "My pistol is in my holster. It wouldn't be fair."

"How about those ladies on that stage you robbed?" Lon rejoined. "Was it fair of you to shoot them?"

"I was at the other end of Texas when that stage was stopped. The law pinned it on me because they had no else to pin it on."

"The driver lived. He recognized you."

Sloane glanced at the knife he held and then at Lon as if debating whether to use it. Instead, he spread his fingers and let the knife drop. "You wouldn't shoot an unarmed man, would you?" He smirked.

"You still have your six-gun," Lon said, and shot him in the breastbone.

"No!" Ben Sloane exclaimed, his last mortal comment, and then his big frame crumpled in on itself until his forehead touched the ground and his big arms splayed outward.

"You killed him!" Bill Givens shrieked, accenting his outrage with curses.

"That was the general idea." Lon jerked Givens to his feet and shoved him toward the wagon. "Get a move on."

The shooting had stopped.

In the ear-ringing silence that marked the aftermath of every gun battle, the groan of a dying rustler was unnaturally loud. Benedito was still on the wagon seat. Owen was by the longhorns, a dead rustler at his feet.

Slim was hunched over Cleveland. Whining pitiably, he raised tear-dampened eyes and declared, "He's dead! My best pard in all the world, and he's gone."

"Two got away," Owen said. "I heard them ride off."

"We still have this one." Lon Chalmers gripped Givens by the scruff of the neck and slammed him to the earth. Then Lon began reloading, replacing each cartridge with slow deliberation.

"Retie his ankles so he can't run off," Owen directed.

"No need."

"We'll turn him over to the law."

"Only a federal marshal has jurisdiction," Lon said without looking up from the cartridge he was inserting, "and it could take a month of Sundays to find one. My way is better."

Ben Givens began to crawl backward, pumping his elbows and his heels. "Now hold on, mister! You can't do this!"

"Your men killed our friend." Lon inserted yet another cartridge, winked at Givens, and said, "Two to go."

Givens appealed to Owen. "You're the reasonable one. Talk to him. I'd rather take my chances in court."

"I bet you would," Lon Chalmers said, and shot the rustler in the throat. He watched Givens thrash and shriek, then stood over him and emptied the Colt, shot by shot by shot, until the hammer clicked on a spent cartridge.

Owen walked over and somberly regarded the rid-
dled remains. "Sometimes you worry me, pard. You
truly do."

"I should have done it when he first showed his
face," Lon said. "Cleveland might be alive."

"You don't know that. None of us can read crys-
tal balls."

Slim had picked up Cleveland and was carrying him
into the trees. His spindly legs shook under the weight,
and his cheeks were damp.

"Wait for us," Owen said. "We'll help you."

"*No!*" It was practically a scream. "Thanks, but it's
mine to do."

Benedito called out, "Someone to watch your back
then, señor? Perhaps the two who left will return."

"I wish to God they would," Slim said.

An expression of puzzlement came over Owen and
he looked around in concern. "Say, where did that
Brit get to? He was here when the lead started flyin'."

"I haven't seen him in a while," Lon said, rotating
right and left. "If anything has happened to him, Mr.
Bartholomew will have us staked out over an anthill."

Benedito rose and from his elevated position
scoured their vicinity. "There!" he suddenly cried,
pointing. "Are those not his?"

A pair of black shoes was all that was visible, jutting
from high grass on the bank. Owen and Lon raced to
the spot. Owen got there first and stopped so abruptly
that Lon nearly ran into him.

"Lord, no."

Pitney lay on his stomach, one arm outstretched,
the other under him. His hat was missing, and a scarlet
furrow ran from above his right ear to his right eye.
Blood matted his hair and was drying on his neck.

"Help me," Owen said. He slid an arm under Pitney and carefully sat him up, Lon doing the same on the other side.

"Is he—?"

"We need water." Owen was rising when Alfred Pitney's eyelids fluttered and opened.

"I say. I'm still alive?"

"From the neck down," Lon said.

"The last thing I remember is a blow to my head and staggering about. I was terribly fortunate, what?"

Lon Chalmers gazed toward where scraping and digging sounds came from among the trees. "You could say that."

19

Big Sieves and Little Sieves

The day finally came when Luke Deal asked the question he had asked of every trail boss and received the answer he had been waiting for.

"A small outfit with a big bull? Sure, saw them, oh, about ten days ago," said the rugged trail boss for the Slash H, who were pushing two thousand head toward Dodge. "We had to stop early and they went past us about four in the afternoon. I rode over and talked with a ranny named Owen. Would he be the friend you're tryin' to find?"

"One of them," Luke Deal said with a smile.

"That was some bull they had," the Slash H boss declared. "Big Blue, they called him. I'd give all I own and then some to have an animal that fine."

"How many others were with Owen?" Luke inquired.

"Let me see. I recollect two other trail herders and a foreigner. An Englishman, he was. He had a peculiar name. Pick-something. Pickles, maybe. Plus their cook."

"Only two other herders? Are you sure? I thought there were supposed to be three."

"They lost one. Owen told me they swapped lead

with some mangy rustlers and one of his men was killed. He was real upset about it. Speaks well of a foreman when he cares that much."

"That's Owen for you," Luke said. "He wouldn't stomp a snake if the snake wasn't doin' him any harm."

"Well, neither would I," the Slash H trail boss said. He touched his hat brim to Sweet Sally. "Nice meetin' you folks, ma'am. Hope you catch up to your friend soon."

"We all do," Luke answered for her.

The trail boss wheeled his mount and left them. Bronk waited until he was out of earshot to ask, "Which one do you figure is feedin' the worms?"

"What difference does it make?" Luke rejoined. "The important thing is that there is one less, which makes it easier for us."

From that moment on, Sweet Sally's fear was compounded by her worry for Slim and the other Bar 40 punchers. Any day now Luke would overtake them, and she had no illusions about what would happen. Luke's past performance allowed for no doubt. He would kill them, and her, and take the bull and the other longhorns and sell them for a lot of money. The money was all he talked about of late around the campfire at night. He was thinking about heading for San Francisco. He had heard a lot of grand things about the city on the west coast, about the gambling and the nightlife. How it was a den of iniquity the likes of which to rival New Orleans. The perfect haunt for a man like him.

Sweet Sally could not let Slim and the others come to harm. She must stop Luke somehow. But *how* when she was only one woman and there were three of them? Three of the vilest human beings it had ever been her misfortune to know. Compared to Luke Deal, Paco Ramirez had been a saint.

She was no match for them physically. She was stronger than most females but she was terribly slow. Even Grutt could whip her.

The logical course, Sally decided, was to get her hands on a weapon. A gun, a gun of any kind—pistol or rifle, it didn't matter, so long as it was loaded. She had not done a lot of shooting and was not familiar with a lot of firearms, but how hard could it be? Revolvers were simple enough to use. You pulled back the hammer and squeezed the trigger. Rifles took a little more work. You had to move the lever to feed a new cartridge into the chamber. And even though she was probably one of the worst shots on the planet, it didn't matter if she was close enough when she pulled the trigger. At arm's length everyone was a marksman.

Sweet Sally devoted every waking moment to conspiring to get her hands on a firearm but it proved more difficult than she'd counted on.

Neither Luke, Grutt, nor Bronk ever let his rifle out of his sight. The rifles were in their saddle scabbards when the men were riding and in their hands or close to them when they weren't. At night they slept with their rifles at their sides. Their rifles were a part of them, like their arms and legs.

As for their revolvers, the only way she would get one would be to pry it from their lifeless fingers. Their six-shooters never left their waists except when they used them or cleaned them. They even slept with the damn things on, or, in Grutt's case, tucked under his belt with his hand on it.

Five days went by. Sally was always vigilant, always on the lookout for a chance, but none presented itself. By the evening of the fifth day she was so worried she barely touched the rabbit stew Bronk made. She sat staring glumly into the flames, depressed to her marrow.

"What's the matter with you?" Grutt unexpectedly demanded. "You've been sulkin' all damn day, woman."

"I'm fine," Sweet Sally said.

"You're a liar."

Bronk chuckled and nudged him. "What woman ain't? They never give a man a straight answer."

"I'm fine, I tell you," Sweet Sally insisted. It might have been wiser to keep her mouth shut but she was tired of their teasing and sick of their contempt and mad as hell over the murders she had been forced to witness and those she saw no means of preventing, including her own.

Luke Deal was on his back, his head propped on his saddle, his hat brim low. Now he pushed it up and studied her with that cold, calculating way he had. "It's not hard to figure her, boys. She's frettin' over her friends. She doesn't want them hurt."

"Well, they will be," Grutt said, and snickered. "Me, I want to put a few into that Lon Chalmers. I bumped into him once in the saloon and spilled some of my whiskey on his shirt and the bastard made me apologize."

"Chalmers is hell with the hide off," Bronk said. "He's all yours. I don't want no part of him."

Luke Deal made a sound of disgust. "Listen to you yellow-backs. He pulls his pants on one leg at a time like the rest of us, doesn't he?"

"He also whips out that hogleg of his faster than just about anybody I ever saw," Bronk said. "Remember the social the church put on? And the shootin' match? Chalmers won."

"I missed out on that," Luke said. "I was down in Mexico."

"Well, I saw him," Bronk said. "They stuck playin' cards on a board with pins, six for each shooter. The idea was to hit all six dead center but no one came close. Owen hit two in the middle and nicked the rest, which I thought was good shootin', but then Chalmers walked up to the line and as slick as you please he drew and emptied his Colt and damn me if he didn't hit all six cards, four of them smack in the center." Bronk shook his head. "I never saw such shootin' in all my born days."

"They say Hickok could shoot like that," Grutt mentioned. "Now there was one tough hombre."

"Wyatt Earp is supposed to be a gun shark," Bronk commented.

Luke Deal swore. "Wyatt Earp is a windbag. The same as most of that gun-wise crowd who crow about their shootin' affrays."

Despite herself, Sweet Sally's interest perked. "I met a man once," she said softly. "About the nicest gentleman you ever saw. He always treated the ladies with respect. He could shoot, let me tell you. I saw him practice many a time from the shack where I was livin'. He would go out every mornin' and line up whiskey bottles and the like, and back off twenty steps with a revolver in each hand."

"He broke bottles?" Grutt said. "Hell, I can break bottles."

"No, he shot the necks off the bottles," Sweet Sally

said. "He never missed either. He would flip up those revolvers and bam, bam, it was done."

"This prodigy have a handle?" Luke Deal idly asked.

"Ringo. Some folks called him Ringgold for some reason but his real name was John Ringo."

"I've heard of him," Bronk said.

Luke snorted again. "The fuss people make over leather-slappers makes me sick. Half the stories about them are tall tales and the rest are outright lies."

"You sound jealous," Sweet Sally said with sham politeness.

"What would I have to be jealous about?" Luke contemptuously responded.

"That windbag, as you called him, doesn't go around murdering parsons and shooting women and children."

"Your point?"

Sweet Sally heard the threat in his tone but she answered him anyway. "That Earp and those like him are better men than you'll ever be. You talk about your friends here being yellow when you're the most yellow son of a bitch I've ever met."

Grutt, about to refill his tin cup, turned to marble. Bronk let out a long breath, his eyes growing to the size of walnuts.

Luke Deal did not say a word. He lay there as still as a log, the firelight dancing on his hard features, and stared at Sally with those icy, flat eyes of his for what seemed an eternity. Then he folded his hands on his chest and said, "Well."

"Well what?" Sally baited him. "What do you have to say for yourself? You know I'm right."

"What I know is that there are big sieves and little

sieves," Luke said, "and some plans don't always work out. I also know you still reckon you have me figured out but you don't."

"You're not yellow?" Sweet Sally did not hide her disdain.

"Do you think it's easy to kill? To shoot a parson like I did? Or that family? It's not. It takes more grit than you'll ever have."

Sally indulged in a bitter laugh. "Shooting defenseless little girls? Face it. You only kill those who can't fight back."

Deal did not rise to the insult. "I've never backed down from a scrape in my life."

"I've read about Wyatt Earp in the newspapers," Sweet Sally mentioned. "I've never read about you."

"That's because I'm smarter than he is," Luke said. "I don't want the law comin' after me so I keep quiet about my doin's. Braggarts like Earp crow just to see their names in print."

"I'd like to see you call him that to his face," Sweet Sally sneered. "Just so I could gloat over your grave."

"You'll never understand," Luke said. "You can't help it, bein' a woman and all."

"I understand more than you give me credit for," Sweet Sally jousted. "I understand you've probably killed more people than Wyatt Earp and John Ringo combined, but that doesn't make you better than they are. Maybe Wyatt is a windbag, but he's a windbag on the side of law and order. You're a snake in the grass who only cares about himself."

"Call me all the names you want," Luke said. "It won't ruffle my feathers any."

"All right," Sweet Sally said. "You're a bastard. You're scum. You are slime. You are as low as a human being can go. You don't care about anyone but yourself. You are dead inside, so you make everyone else as dead as you are. Something happened to you that night your parents were killed. Or maybe it was always there, inside of you, and didn't come out until you were on your own." Sally paused to take a breath.

"Are you through?"

"Not by a long shot." Sally had been holding her emotions in check for so long that her pent-up feelings spilled from her like water over a burst dam. "You deserve to die, Luke Deal. You deserve to die the most horrible death any man has died since the dawn of time. Hanging is too good for you. Too quick. Too painless. You deserve to suffer. Not a little but a lot. You deserve to die kicking and screaming and in the most god-awful agony ever inflicted."

Sally stopped. She had said too much. Way too much. But she was glad she'd done it, glad she'd stopped hiding behind the wall of fear that had paralyzed her, glad she had told him how despicable he was.

"I gather we're not friends anymore."

"I've never hated anyone so much in my life." Sweet Sally leaned back, pleased with herself until she saw Luke's eyes. Regret spiked through her. She had made a mistake, gone too far.

Sally glanced toward the string. They had traded the ox for a horse the second day after Luke exterminated the family in the prairie schooner. A trail boss named Weaver had lost a lot of head in a stampede and did not want to lose any more to fill the bellies of his men, so he made the swap.

"Ox isn't beef but it's not shoe leather," was Weaver's assessment.

Now, pushing to her feet, Sally walked toward some bushes barely visible in the dark.

"Where do you think you're goin'?" Grutt snapped.

"That coffee went right through me." But what Sally really needed was some moments alone to think. She went past the bushes and sat down, her elbows on her knees, her chin in her hands. Since she had not been able to get her hands on a weapon, she had to do something else, and she had to do it quick. In a couple of days they would overtake the Bar 40 bunch.

If she was going to slip away in the dead of night, Sweet Sally reflected, she must do it that very night. She would take a horse, and lead it by the reins until she was far enough away to climb on and ride without being heard. She must not stop until she caught up to Slim and the rest. Once they were warned, they could give the high and mighty Luke Deal a taste of his own medicine.

Sweet Sally longed to see that. She longed to see Luke Deal die. She had never been a vengeful or hateful person but she craved his death more than she had ever craved anything in her life.

There was a hitch to her plan, though. The three hard cases took turns keeping watch. Luke always took the early watch, Grutt the middle, and Bronk sat up from about three a.m. until daylight. To steal a horse from under their noses might be impossible. If she was caught, they would punish her. Luke would punish her. She shuddered at the thought.

Boots crunched, and Bronk gruffly asked from the other side of the bushes, "What's takin' you so long back there? Luke wants you at the fire."

"I'll only be another minute," Sally said. "It's not as if I'll run off in the dark." She gazed longingly into the night, wishing she were younger, wishing she were thinner, wishing she could flee with the speed of a bounding antelope.

With a sigh, Sweet Sally heaved upright. Bronk was waiting for her. She walked past him without saying anything, and he reached out and snagged her wrist.

"Hold up."

"Let go of me."

"How about a poke? It's been a while. The first couple of weeks you gave Grutt and me all the pokes we wanted but now you won't let us touch you."

"I liked you then. I don't now." Sally tried to pull free but he would not let go. "Damn you, unhand me."

"What if I were to pay you?" Bronk proposed. "I have four dollars to my name. Is that enough?"

"I wouldn't let you poke me now for four hundred," Sweet Sally had the pleasure of telling him. "You or your smelly friend."

"Don't hold it against us because you're mad at Luke," Bronk said. "Grutt and me have no say in what Luke does. You've seen for yourself how he is."

"You ride with him." Sweet Sally stated her indictment.

Bronk glanced toward the fire. Luke was moodily staring into the crackling flames. Grutt was picking his teeth with a twig. "There was another of us once," he whispered. "We called him Prairie Dog on account of he looked like one. He rode with us for over a year. Then one day he allowed as how he missed his family back in Maryland, and how he had put off goin' back long enough. He said he would leave in the mornin', if that was all right with Luke, and Luke said it was."

Sweet Sally waited. She knew what was coming.

"So that night Prairie Dog turned in, all smiles. I fell asleep later and woke up when someone screamed. It was Prairie Dog. Luke was doin' things to him."

"What sort of things?"

"You don't want to know," Bronk said. "I have nightmares when I think of it." He glanced at the fire again to be sure the other two were still there. "Sure, I ride with Luke, and I'll go on ridin' with him because I don't want to end my days like Prairie Dog did."

"You still don't get a poke."

"Fine. Be tight-legged. Once you've served his purpose, Luke is fixin' to kill you anyway." Bronk angrily tromped back.

Ignoring them, Sweet Sally spread her blankets a little farther from the fire than she normally would. She did not have a saddle. She used her arm for a pillow. She closed her eyes but not all the way. She would stay awake and await the best opportunity that came along.

Grutt and Bronk jabbered about what they aimed to do with their share of the money. Grutt said he wanted a week of "wild women, whiskey, and cards." Bronk wanted a new pair of boots, ones that did not crimp his toes and chafe his ankles. Apparently the pair he had on he had taken from a man Luke Deal shot. He took them because they were newer than his own. They were also smaller by a full size, which explained his daily morning ritual of tugging into them while huffing and puffing like a steam engine.

Usually Bronk turned in first. Tonight was no different. He simply plopped down, his shoulders and head on his saddle, pulled a blanket up, and within minutes was snoring noisily.

Grutt took a pair of dice from his pocket and practiced rolling them. He would say things like, "Seven! Give me a seven!" or "Come on, come on, be sweet to me!" He rolled them for a quarter of an hour. Then he placed them in his pocket, stretched out on his blanket, and said to Luke Deal, "It won't be long now, will it?"

"No, it won't."

"What about Owen?"

"What about him?"

"I couldn't do it. I've done a lot of terrible things but never that. I guess there's a line I won't cross."

"Lines are like superstitions," Luke said. "They only affect you if you believe in them, and I stopped believin' it was bad luck to walk under ladders long ago. Now shut the hell up and get to sleep."

"Sure thing, Luke."

Sweet Sally wondered what that had been about. She had come to sense that of all the people in the world, Luke Deal hated Owen the most. Or if it wasn't hate, it was something close to it. Whenever Owen was mentioned, Luke always got a certain look about him, as if someone had stabbed him in the gut and was twisting the knife.

Soon Grutt snored, too. He did not snore as loud as Bronk. His snores were like those of a dog Sally had once had, short ones, like Grutt himself. She focused on Luke Deal, careful to keep her eyes slitted so he would not suspect she was still awake.

For a long while Luke stared into the fire. What he saw reflected in the flames only he could say. His arms were folded across his chest and his brow was puckered, lending the notion he was pondering a problem of some size.

Sweet Sally remembered the little girls, and inwardly

shivered. What kind of man could do that? To say he was vile was not enough. To call him wicked did not do his nature justice. Branding him evil was not an explanation. Deep down inside he was twisted. He was not entirely human. Outwardly he seemed normal enough, but he was filled with a darkness darker than the night.

Her musings were brought to an end when Luke eased onto his side and pulled his hat brim down. That was usually the sign he was going to sleep. She waited, scarcely breathing, for some sign that he had.

Minutes dragged past. Sweet Sally tingled with excitement. She was sure her time had come. She did not feel the least bit tired. Once she was on the bay, she would not stop until she overtook the Bar 40 boys.

Sally's excitement climbed. Luke Deal's chest and shoulders were moving in the rhythmic embrace of heavy sleep. She waited a bit longer to be sure, then slowly sat up.

Now came the dangerous part. Sweet Sally pushed up off the ground. She inadvertently grunted as she rose, then bit her lower lip and glanced fearfully at the sleeping forms. None stirred.

Straightening and steadying herself, Sweet Sally picked up the bridle she had been using and edged around the fire. The horses were used to her and did not whinny or stamp. She had to pull out a picket pin but it was not as difficult as she had fretted it might be. She slid the bridle on and adjusted it. Then she turned to lead the bay off into the night, and safety.

Climbing on later posed a problem. Sally could not do it on her own. But she had a solution. She would find a handy log or boulder, climb on that, and from there onto the animal's back. She prayed she wouldn't slip, and the horse wouldn't move when she was half-way on.

Sweet Sally took a step and tugged on the reins.

"Goin' somewhere?"

Sally spun. She almost tripped over her own feet and had to lean against the horse to keep from falling. "Luke!" she blurted. "I thought I heard something and came to check on the horses."

"I've changed my mind," Luke said.

"About what?"

"Needin' you to distract Owen and the others. I can take them without you."

"Don't," Sweet Sally pleaded.

Luke Deal slowly drew his Colt. He slowly pointed it at her and slowly thumbed back the hammer. Their eyes met, and Sweet Sally opened her mouth to scream. Luke shot her in the right knee. The horse squealed and shied, and Sally landed hard on her back, flooded with torment.

"No, Luke! Please!"

Luke Deal shot her in the left knee. Sweet Sally screamed. He shot her in the belly and her scream became a shriek. He shot her in the throat and the shriek faded to a gurgle. He shot her between the eyes and the gurgling stopped.

Grutt and Bronk came running, their revolvers out, and Bronk asked, "What in blazes happened?"

"It's like I told her," Luke Deal said.

"What?" Grutt asked.

"There are big sieves and little sieves."

20
Showdown

By Owen's reckoning they were ten days out of Dodge City. Dodge was the midway point, or thereabouts, and they still had a long way to go. But beyond Dodge the perils lessened. They had little to dread from rustlers or hostiles until they neared Wyoming Territory, and then their main worry would be roving bands of warlike Sioux. Dodge was cause to celebrate, to relax, to rest a few days, to rent rooms and sleep in comfortable beds with a roof over their heads for the first time in months.

"I can hardly wait," Alfred Pitney happily declared. "To set eyes on civilization again will be a delight."

"Don't get your hopes too high," Owen advised. "Dodge isn't New York City."

"It has people and buildings and streets, doesn't it?" Pitney lightheartedly replied. "It has dining establishments and hotels and a theater, I do believe."

"It has all that," Owen conceded. "It also has hombres who will steal you blind or buck you out in gore and ladies who will fleece you out of every dollar you have as slick as grease."

"It's as bad as all that?" Pitney grinned. "Sodom and Gomorrah rolled into one?"

"Once it was," Owen said. "Dodge was the wildest, wooliest town this side of anywhere. There was drinkin' and gamblin' and carryin' on every hour of the day and night."

"You have been there before, I take it? During those wild days?"

"A few times. On trail drives. In the old days the town council welcomed cowboys with open arms. Beeves were money on the hoof, and they let all us Texas wolves howl as we pleased. But we howled a mite too loud and were much too rough, and the respectable folks complained." Owen paused. "Can't say as I blame them. A man with a wife and children doesn't want a drunken cowboy outside his window at midnight shootin' at the moon."

Pitney chuckled. "So it's not that wild anymore?"

"Not nearly. There were killin's and stabbin's and the like all the time until the town council set down new laws and hired peace officers to enforce them. Men with the bark on. Bat Masterson, Wyatt Earp, Mysterious Dave Mather—"

"I say," Pitney interrupted. "He really calls himself that? 'Mysterious'? Rather juvenile, what?"

"Mather doesn't ever say much of anything. He's the quiet type. His past is pretty much a mystery. So somewhere he picked up the nickname and it stuck. The one thing everyone does know is that he's mighty quick with his pistol, and he will shoot a lawbreaker as dead as Moses and not bat an eye."

"I've heard of those other chaps you mentioned, Masterson and Earp. The newspapers write about them from time to time."

"It shows the caliber of Dodge peace officers, and why it wasn't long before Dodge went from bein' wild

and wooly to fairly respectable. These days it's no
nearly as rough. There's even been talk that the town
council is tired of the beef trade. They say it's more
trouble than it's worth, and I've heard rumors they're
thinkin' about postin' Dodge off limits to any critter
with horns and hooves and anyone wearin' a six-
shooter."

"They would do that?" Pitney marveled. "With al
the money they are making?" His businessman's sensi-
bilities were shocked.

"It's only a rumor. But Dodge does have the railroad now. It makes money from other things besides
cows. If they lose the Texas trade, they reckon they'l
survive."

Pitney gazed eagerly northward. Ahead stretched a
seemingly endless vista of prairie, as it had day after
day after day. He had never seen so much flat land in
his life. "So long as they don't impose the ban before
we get there, and they have hot baths available, I wil
be happy. I would give my right arm for an hour of
luxuriating in hot water."

"We do tend to get whiffy on the trail," Owen said

"If by 'whiffy' you mean we are caked with dust
and dirt, our hair and clothes are filthy, and we smell
abominably, then yes, we certainly are."

The afternoon passed at its customary snail's pace.

Owen rode on the right flank, as he had every day
since they lost Cleveland. The dead hand's effects
were in the chuck wagon. The money in Cleveland's
war bag would be sent to his sister in Ohio, along with
a couple of photographs and his dofunnies.

Slim had taken the death hard. For over a week he
barely uttered a word to anyone. Then one evening a
moth flew into the pot of beans Benedito was stirring
and the cook gave vent to a barrage of obscenities that

would have blistered the ear of an army drill sergeant. Benedito had cursed that moth in every cussword in two languages. He disliked bugs, especially flying bugs, and for one to get into his food was the ultimate outrage.

Slim had started laughing and couldn't stop. He laughed until his cheeks glistened with tears and he was holding his sides in pain, and after that he was his old self again.

Pitney had been glad to see him restored. He would not admit as much, but he had grown quite fond of the Bar 40 cowboys. As much as he longed to reach the BLC and begin his program of infusing new blood into the BLC's herd, he would regret their journey's end. It had been an experience unlike any other, a once-in-a-lifetime adventure, and despite the many hardships, despite the blistering sun and the dust and the rustlers, he had enjoyed himself immensely.

The sun hung low in the vault of blue when Lon Chalmers came riding back from point. He swung his mount in alongside Owen's and Alfred Pitney's and pushed his hat back on his sandy mop. "We won't strike water again until tomorrow about noon. Do you want to push on or bed them dry for the night?"

"They've behaved this far."

"Easiest trail drive I've ever been on." Lon grinned. "We should spread the word. From now on, all trail herds should be ten cows or less."

"They wouldn't make much money," Pitney observed, "and making money is the whole point in bringing cattle to market, is it not?"

Lon found the comment amusing. "As a cowboy you would make a fine banker. There's more to life than ledger books."

Stars were blossoming when they made camp. The

horses were tethered, the longhorns were bedded down, and Benedito fired up the Dutch stove to prepare supper. The cowboys and the Brit sat around the fire, waiting for the coffee to come to a boil. The wind was still and the prairie was quiet save for the rattle and clank of pots and pans.

"Peaceful, ain't it?" Slim said contentedly. "And my ma used to wonder why I joined the cow crowd."

"I'd rather be married to a cow than a woman," Lon said. "Cows don't sass a man to death."

Slim arched a thin eyebrow. "You shouldn't be let loose without a handler. I'll take a two-legged female over a four-legged any day."

Lon winked at Owen and Pitney, then said, "I reckon Sweet Sally will be happy to hear that. You should write her when we get to Dodge, and propose."

"Cut that out. We were friendly, nothin' more."

"She sure took a shine to you," Lon teased. "Must be that beak of yours. They say women like men with big noses."

The talk turned to women they had known, and then women in general, and then the differences between women and men. At this point Slim commented, "Women sure are peculiar critters. You have to wonder what the Almighty was thinkin' when he took that rib from Adam."

Benedito mentioned to Owen that he was running low on supplies. He had to stock up in Dodge. But he had enough left to make them delicious frijoles and rice laced with strips of succulent meat from a plump grouse Lon had shot. To mop up the juice they had hot bread steeped in the inevitable butter. For dessert there was apple pie made with the last of their dried green apples. A gallon of coffee washed everything down.

By then night had descended. A cool breeze out of the northwest was more than welcome. To the west a coyote yipped. Another yipped to the east. A shooting star blazed a bright trail below the Big Dipper.

Slim breathed deep and said, "I don't care what my ma thinks. This will always be the life for me."

"You and me, both," Owen said. "Cows are all I know. Cows are all I ever want to know."

Lon leaned toward Pitney and put a finger to his lips. "Don't tell Cynthia Langstrom. The schoolmarm thinks she's his true love."

"Go to hell," Owen said.

Slim rummaged in his saddlebags and brought out a worn pack of cards. Since they were close to Dodge, Owen allowed an exception to the no-gambling rule so they could practice. They played poker with blades of grass for chips. Benedito finished putting his utensils away and joined them.

The scene would forever be etched in Pitney's mind: the crackle of the warm flames, the cozy companionship of men who had shared trials and tribulations, the giant longhorn bull lying a dozen feet away, watching them inscrutably, and the eyes of the cows aglow in the wash of firelight. For a while all was right with the world, and he was as happy as he could ever remember being.

Then Lon said to Slim, "I see your five blades of grass and raise you ten more, and if that's not enough, I'll pluck extra."

"I'll just call your raise," Slim declared. "It's my lucky night. I can feel it in my bones."

A gun blasted, booming like thunder, unnaturally loud because it was unexpected. They all heard the fleshy thwack of the slug that slammed into Slim's bony chest. The impact knocked him flat on his back.

He didn't cry out, he didn't move. He was dead before he struck the ground.

Frozen in astonishment, they gaped at the body. They were barely aware that the longhorns, including Big Blue, had heaved up off the ground, or that several of the horses whinnied and pranced.

Lon Chalmers was the first to awaken from his daze, the first to twist and start to rise as he flung his cards down and stabbed for the Colt at his waist. But even he was too slow.

"I wouldn't, were I you," said a voice that dripped death like a caress, and out of the darkness from three points of the compass materialized Luke Deal, Grutt, and Bronk. Thin wisps of gun smoke curled from Luke's Remington.

"You!" Owen exclaimed.

"Me," Luke Deal said, imbuing that simple word with supreme malice and contempt, and something more.

Grutt and Bronk held rifles. Grutt pointed his at Lon Chalmers and taunted, "Go ahead. Unlimber your hardware. I dare you."

Alfred Pitney tore his horrified gaze from the scarlet mist pumping from Slim's smashed sternum. "Are you men insane? What's the meaning of this outrage?"

"What do you think it is?" Luke rejoined, and nodded at Big Blue. "That there is my ticket to California."

Bronk wagged his Winchester. "Let's get it over with. Someone might have heard the shot."

"Don't wet yourself. People shoot all the time," Luke said. "The nearest trail herd is five miles back, remember? We have these gents all to ourselves, and I aim to do it nice and slow." He smirked at Owen.

"I've been waitin' for such a long time, I can't deprive myself, now can I?"

"So it's come to this," Owen said.

"Admit it. You always knew it would." Luke Deal grinned and gave a little shiver. "Damn, this feels good! Almost as good as sleepin' with Carmody."

Owen began to rise but stopped when Bronk swung a rifle toward him. "Don't mention her again. You only dallied with her to spite me."

"True," Luke admitted, and laughed. "She was so mad at you takin' up with the schoolmarm, she was easy to fool."

Instead of Owen growing madder, his features softened. "I'll never understand where you went wrong. When you were younger you were the best of us. I always looked up to you."

Luke Deal stepped back as if he had been punched. "Don't you dare play that card!" he spat. "It's a little late to be bringin' up the good old days."

"Ride out," Owen said. "Leave now and we'll give you an hour's start. You have my word."

"You'll give *us*—?" Luke stopped and snorted and shook his head. "You amaze me sometimes. We're holdin' guns on you and you act as if it's the other way around."

Bronk nervously shifted his weight from one foot to the other. "What is the point of all this jabberin'? We should get it over with."

"Are you cross at me?" Luke Deal asked.

"No. Never. Of course not," Bronk timidly answered. "I'm sorry. If you want to jabber, you go right ahead."

"I'm glad I have your permission." Luke moved to the left and a step nearer to the fire but still stayed well out of reach. "I suppose you have a point, though. We shouldn't take all night." He trained his Remington on Benedito Chavez. "You there. The Mex. On your feet."

"Sí, señor." His hands in the air, Benedito slowly stood. "I am unarmed, señor, so I hope you will not shoot me."

"You're a liar, Mex," Luke Deal said. "I saw the machete under your serape when we were lyin' out in the grass spyin' on you. You used it to chop the head off the grouse."

Grutt sneered savagely and sighted down his rifle. "Let me do him, Luke. You know how I hate greasers."

"Be my guest."

The rifle cracked and Benedito was whipped partway around. He crumpled without a sound, lying so close to the fire that the flames threatened to engulf his clothes.

Cackling gleefully, Grutt worked the Winchester's lever, ejecting the spent cartridge. "One less chili pepper!" he crowed.

Lon Chalmers was quaking with fury. He did not appear to care that the muzzle of Grutt's rifle had now swung toward him. Glancing at Owen, he rasped, "It ends here, it ends now."

"That it does," Luke Deal said, and pointed his Remington at Alfred Pitney. "Shuck your hardware, gents, or the foreigner is next."

"He's under our care," Owen said.

"I figured," Luke said. "And I know how your mind works. You won't let anything happen to him if you can help it. So if you want him to go on breathin' a while yet, you best do as I say." His tone hardened.

"Shed the six-shooters. Use two fingers, and pretend you're molasses."

"No!" Pitney cried. "Don't disarm on my account! They plan to kill us anyway, don't they?"

Owen lowered two fingers toward his Colt but suddenly stopped and turned toward Lon Chalmers, who was coiled like a rattler. "Lon?"

"No."

"They'll shoot him."

"No."

"We gave our word to Mr. Bartholomew. The Englishman's welfare above our own, remember?"

"If I'm to go down, I go down shootin'," Lon Chalmers vowed, and locked eyes with Grutt. "Start the ball, you son of a bitch, and let's dance."

Grutt's pockmarked cheek was pressed to his rifle's stock and his dark eyes glittered with bloodlust. "It will be a pleasure to put windows in your skull."

Tension crackled like invisible lightning. The two cowboys did not stand a prayer. They knew it, and Alfred Pitney knew it, and so did Luke Deal and his two curly wolves. In another moment Lon would flash for his Colt and rifles would crash and revolvers would crack and it would be over.

But in the few heartbeats before that crucial moment, Big Blue sniffed and rumbled deep in his barrel chest and moved toward the prone form of Slim and the pool of blood forming around Slim's body. In doing so, the tip of the bull's horn brushed Bronk, who yelped and sprang aside, afraid the longhorn was about to gore him.

For a fleeting instant, Luke Deal and Grutt took their eyes off Lon Chalmers and Owen. It was just the distraction the cowboys needed. In that instant,

Lon Chalmers streaked his right hand to his Colt. Owen, slower but just as quick-witted, went for his own.

To Alfred Pitney everything that happened next was a blur of thunder and blood. He saw Lon's Colt flash into Lon's hand, saw the top of Grutt's head explode in a rain of hair and brains. Bronk, rushing his shot, fired and missed. Lon Chalmers whirled. Bronk's rifle and Lon's Colt cracked simultaneously. Bronk staggered. Swift as thought, Lon fired again, and Bronk's legs started to go.

"Luke! Help me!"

Lon let his Colt answer the strangled bellow, not once but twice. No more were needed.

Half of Bronk's face was blown away.

At the very split second that Lon shot Grutt, Luke Deal had snapped a shot at Owen, and backpedaled. Owen jerked, tucked his elbow to his side, and fired back. It was Luke's turn to jerk; he fired once more, spun, and ran.

Owen ran after him.

So did Pitney, much to Pitney's surprise. He was up off the grass and racing in their wake before his mind realized what his legs were doing. He could just make out Owen. Luke Deal had been swallowed by the darkness.

The night spat flame and Owen responded in kind.

It dawned on Pitney that he might be hit by a stray bullet. He slowed, and almost immediately lost of sight of Owen. He slowed even more, his eyes straining. Another shot rolled off across the prairie. Once more Owen answered.

A curse rent the air.

Not wanting to miss the outcome, Pitney discarded caution and sped toward the voice. Then he saw them.

Luke Deal was on his back in the grass, an inky stain spreading across his shirt. Owen stood over him, his Colt angled down.

"Do it, damn you!"

Owen did not respond.

"What are you waitin' for?" Luke Deal spat. "If you expect me to beg, I won't. If you expect me to cry and whine, I won't. I don't regret a single thing I've done. Do you hear me? Not a single thing."

"You strayed too far," Owen said.

Alfred Pitney stopped well back. He did not understand the cowboy's hesitation. Were it him, he would shoot Deal dead and be done with it.

"Listen to you," Luke snarled. "Always on the straight and narrow. Always his favorite."

"That's not true. He was as fond of you as he was of me. Why do you think he said it was all right for those men to stay for supper? He didn't trust them. I could see it in his eyes. But you were so excited."

In a small voice, a tiny voice, the voice of a little boy, Luke Deal said, "I liked their uniforms. I always liked soldiers. I wanted to be one when I grew up."

"And you've been blamin' yourself ever since."

Luke Deal's voice grew husky with emotion. "I can't stand it, anymore, Owen. I can't stand me. Just squeeze, will you?"

Owen extended the Colt and curled his thumb around the hammer. "It didn't have to come to this."

"Yes it did. Don't you remember? The night we shot those Rebs? You bawled and said as how you never wanted to kill another person as long as you lived."

"So?"

"I liked it, Owen. God help me, but I liked blowin' those bastards to hell and back. I liked the *killin'*. I've liked it ever since."

"That's loco. No one can enjoy something like that."

Luke Deal coughed and dark flecks appeared at both corners of his mouth. "I don't want another of your lectures. Get it over with."

Owen thumbed back the hammer and took precise aim. Seconds went by. Then a whole minute. Owen slowly lowered the Colt and slid it into his holster. "I can't. I'm sorry. I just can't."

Something brushed Alfred Pitney's sleeve.

Lon Chalmers strode past. Without saying a word, he walked up to Luke Deal and shot him four times in the chest, one shot right after the other, *crack, crack, crack, crack*. Without looking at Owen, he said gently, "Benedito needs you, pard. They only winged him."

The Bar 40 foreman numbly nodded and moved woodenly toward their camp.

Lon finished reloading and twirled the Colt into his holster. He raised his boot as if to stomp it down on Luke Deal's face, then slowly lowered it, and sighed, and glanced at Alfred Pitney. "It had to be me."

"I know."

"No one should have to kill their own brother."